Time Sailors
of
Pizzolungo

Scott Abrams & Adam Blockton

First published in the United States in 2015.

ISBN 978-0-9905278-0-0

Cover design by Jill Rucizka.

Visit http://www.timesailors.com for more information about the authors and the book. (Beware of potential spoilers.)

For all the adventurous kids who, like the Time Sailors of Pizzolungo, yearn to explore the world.

Time Sailors
of
Pizzolungo

—Chapter 1—

A Father, a Son and an Adventure Begun

There are seafaring men. And there are glorious seafaring men. Men who have sailed the seven seas; men who have clipped through hazardous arctic passageways and treacherous tropical straits; men who have ridden waves as high as the heavens and battled all the elements Mother Nature could throw at them, and lived to tell the tale. To the people of the poor Sicilian village of Pizzolungo, Captain Guillermo Infante was a seafaring man. But to his son, Guillermo Jr., he was the most glorious sailor who ever lived.

Guillermo Jr. always kept count of the days until his father's famed cargo ship, the *Coraggio*, would arrive home from exotic places like the Gulf of Taranto and the Bay of Naples. Each summer young Guillermo would ask his father if he could accompany him on one of his voyages, assuring him he'd make a helpful deck hand. But each summer he received the same response: "You have the heart of a captain, but for now you're still too little. Maybe next summer."

Guillermo hoped above all hopes that this summer would be different. And as he would soon find out, this summer would be very different indeed.

There are seafarers like Captain Infante. And then there are seafarers like Captain Rumrino. Alfonso Rumrino was drunk at dinner and sometimes even more drunk at breakfast. Not long ago, just after his morning pastry and rum, he crashed right into the *Coraggio* while trying to dock his tugboat. When Captain Infante went down to the port later that day all he could see of his ship was the top of its mainmast and exhaust stack. He climbed aboard the sinking vessel just in time to salvage a framed picture of his family and his treasured admiral's compass which his father had given him. Moments later the ship slid fully beneath the harbor's surface, taking half the wooden dock with it. The *Coraggio* was no more.

Left with no other choice, the Captain was forced to fly to Rome, hat in hand, to plead with the men who held the *Coraggio*'s insurance papers. The days passed as everyone back home anxiously awaited his news. And then finally one night, as the arms of his household clock stood upright, a noise stirred young Guillermo awake. At first he thought it was laughter. He wondered whether his father had returned home with a new ship. He slipped silently onto the floor so as not to awaken his little sister, Piccola, who slept in the next bed. If his father really had arrived, Piccola would surely siphon off the lion's share of his attention.

But as Guillermo tiptoed closer to his parents' bedroom he realized it wasn't laughter he was hearing. It was weeping. He poked his head into the room and saw his mother on her cell phone talking to his father, using a handkerchief to catch her tears. Down in the shadow of the corridor, he was just able to make out his father's faint words on the other end of the line. Although too young to understand terms like 'insurance lapse' and 'missed premium payments,' he could grasp the pain in his father's voice as he spoke about how his days ahead would be spent on land rather than at sea. Young Guillermo knew that for a seafaring man a future on land would be a tragedy of immense proportions.

Just then Piccola crawled over to eavesdrop beside her brother, arriving in time to overhear the worst part of the story. With his business in ruins, their father would have no choice but to sell the family home and move everyone in with their cousins in Siracusa, all the way on the other side of Sicily.

Guillermo and Piccola crept back to their room, fighting back tears. It took until nearly dawn for their heartbeats to return to normal. But from that point on very little else would be normal.

Guillermo stared out of his bedroom window toward the dark sea below. His chest was tight as he struggled to swallow. He was tormented by the thought of leaving Pizzolungo. And while he loved the house in which he was born and the town where he grew up, they didn't compare to the anguish of having to leave behind the most valuable thing of all—his friends.

—Chapter 2—

A Captain and his Crew

The yard at Pizzolungo Elementary School brimmed with excitement. Balls were flying, ropes were swinging, and children were running about as if being chased by *L'Uomo Nero,* the Boogeyman himself. Normally at this time of day the students would have been immersed in multiplication tables and grammar exercises, but the teachers conceded it was too hot to be indoors and besides, the bell was about to announce the beginning of summer break. As any student—or teacher for that matter—will tell you, the formidable scent of an impending summer vacation interferes with the absorption of subjects like math and grammar.

Enzo Bonaventura and Luca Brizzi stuck their heads over the side of the tree house in the schoolyard. The three dilapidated boards were nailed between the lower branches of the courtyard's only tree. 'Tree shack' would have been a more fitting description, but that mattered not, since those finely assembled planks doubled as the 6th graders' sailing vessel.

Enzo scanned the horizon from the second plank. His long jaw protruded even more than usual. "*Attenzione!* We've got company," he shouted with alarm. "Pirates, and plenty of them!"

Luca maneuvered up to the third plank, his swift movements belying his stocky frame. He peered down into the sandbox where Tony Benetto's chopstick arms were sending shovel after shovel of sand onto the nearby grass. "Leave the treasure Tony, grab the guns. They're coming up on our starboard side. If we flank them from the rear and fire the cannons when their backs are turned, we might be able to hit both ships with one shot." He leaned back against the branch, proud of the military stratagem he'd just laid out.

"But I haven't found the gold yet. According to my map," Tony glanced down at the map on his iPad screen, "it should be right beneath us."

"Then keep digging sailor, but hasten your search. The captain wants all hands on deck." Luca then turned to Mario Bintelli, who was milling about under the tree feasting on a box of butter cookies. "Get the weapons Mario! Be useful for once!"

Mario reluctantly scrambled off into the bushes, crumbs spit firing out of his mouth like a Tommy gun as he huffed and puffed in search of some long sticks for the crew to use as guns. His belly held enough reserve space for a pound or two of linguini per day, and he made sure to always keep it fueled—even if its size interfered with his ability to effectively combat pirates. He bundled up a handful of 'stick guns' and headed back to the tree house just as Guillermo, the ship's captain, returned to duty from the school bathroom. Taking his place at the helm, Guillermo had all the presence and fortitude one would expect from the son of a real captain. His wise brown eyes, moppy hair and thoughtful expression conferred on him an air of gravitas far beyond his twelve years.

As Mario began distributing the sticks, a tiny yellow buttercup growing at his feet beckoned and distracted him from his duties. He picked the delicate flower and nudged it behind his ear for safe keeping. Guillermo rolled his eyes, knowing exactly where the flower was heading.

Guillermo climbed to the top of the tree house and projected his voice, "Sailors, the pirates are closing in on us. Hoist the Genoa sail and start the bombardment."

Enzo and Luca began launching the mud cannonballs they'd prepared, flinging them off the tree house in all directions. Meanwhile Tony continued to dig furiously in the sand, which ultimately generated a stern warning from Signore Malesco, Pizzolungo's most feared (and only) gym teacher.

As the boys battled their pirate adversaries Mario furtively crossed the yard to where the 5th graders were playing. Piccola stood off to the side of the others filling out the answers to the Pizzolungo Post's daily word jumble and observing the pirate game from the corner of her eye. Mario handed her the flower, "I picked this for you." He tried to get as close to her as possible, hoping to touch her lacy brown hair and smell her soft skin, but his belly kept him at a generous distance.

"And why should I care?" she asked, her thin rosy cheeks getting a shade rosier.

"Well, I thought that maybe tomorrow you could come over and I could cook you my famous spaghetti carbonara."

"Maybe. I might burn ants with a magnifying glass tomorrow." She tossed her hair over her shoulder and went back to her word puzzle. Her mood had been sour all day, due to her midnight eavesdropping.

"I want all hands on deck!" the captain shouted from afar.

"Get a move on, Six-to-Four," Luca shouted to Mario, who winced at the nickname and grabbed Piccola's hand.

"Come with us, you can help us outwit these pirates, and the sooner the better, I'm starving."

Piccola sensed an opportunity to get in on the game. The two ran full tilt toward the tree house. Mario lumbered up the lower branch with Piccola in tow. But Luca put his hand out to block her, "Sorry, captain's orders."

"Then I demand to speak to the captain."

"Can't you see he's busy fighting pirates right now? We're at war!"

Piccola pushed past Luca to get next to her brother as gravity worked its magic on Mario and returned him to the ground with a thump.

"Guillermo!" Piccola shrieked.

The captain turned around after having given the order to fire the cannons. "Hey, you can't be up here. You're too little."

"You always say that. I can help you beat these pirates. I've been contriving a five-pronged strategy to mitigate the pirates' firepower and capitalize on your ship's agility in shallow waters."

"We're doing just fine on our own," Guillermo scowled, pretending he knew what the words 'contriving', 'mitigate', and 'agility' meant.

The captain turned to Tony—who had finally located the coins he'd buried before school—and motioned for him to get back to navigation, his preferred trade. "How are the maps coming along?"

Tony wiped off his sandy hands and zoomed in on their current location. "I have them here." He placed the tablet beneath the tree as the crew descended from the branches and gathered around. "Judging from the coordinates I'd say the current carried us north, so we should head—"

"If you don't let me play I shall tell mama," Piccola interrupted.

"Urgh! Mama can't do anything. In a few minutes that school bell is going to ring and we are going to be 7th graders. Adults. And you will only be a 6th grader. Now leave us be, we are in the middle of a battle!"

"Maybe we can let her play just this once?" Mario cautiously suggested.

"Fine, then I'll tell papa when he gets home," Piccola threatened.

This stopped Guillermo cold. In all the commotion of the pirate game he had forgotten about his father's plight and what now lay ahead for his family. But this was the last day of school, normally the best day of the year, so he tried not to burden anyone—especially himself—with the grim news.

Just then the school bell echoed across the yard, followed by an eruption of jubilant cheers from the children.

"Until the next adventure," Luca proclaimed.

"Until the next adventure," Guillermo agreed as the playground emptied.

"Hey, can anyone help me get all this sand back in the box?" Tony pleaded.

Nobody paid attention.

"Guess that's a 'no' then," he continued as he started shoveling the sand back in.

"Who wants to stay over at my house tonight?" Guillermo asked. "My mother will cook us dinner."

Enzo flashed a thumbs-up sign, "That's a big affirmative, captain."

"Sounds like a plan. I've been meaning to give her a few pointers on her *Rollatini di Melanzane*," Mario said, referring to her signature dish.

"We can camp out at Mariner's Fort, one last time..." Guillermo let slip, biting his tongue.

"Why? What's happening to the island?" Luca asked.

"Nothing, I meant one last time while we're… still 6th graders."

The sailors made their way toward the school exit and three months of summer freedom. It took them five minutes—ten in the case of Mario—to pedal down the path leading toward the harbor and the Infante household, where they let their bikes fall into a heap in the middle of the driveway.

Signora Infante wasn't in a boisterous mood, given the call she'd received in the middle of the night, but she knew better than to spoil the first day of summer for her troop of hungry tree-house sailors. "Happy summer everybody. Who's hungry?"

"Can the crew sleep over tonight?" Guillermo asked.

"I don't see why not, as long as it's OK with everyone's parents."

"It is," everyone said at the same time.

"Did you all leave your bicycles in the middle of the driveway again? How many times—"

"Can we stay out at Mariner's Fort?" Guillermo interrupted.

"If you promise to get some sleep and not stay up all night yelling like a bunch of swashbucklers, then you may. But make sure you're back early. They say a storm might blow through."

"Guillermo wouldn't let me play Captains and Pirates with everyone at school today," Piccola complained.

"Guillermo?" Signora Infante's thick eyebrows rose ever so slightly as she looked down on her son.

"She's too little, mama."

Signora Infante kissed her daughter's head and smiled. "Well, you *are* little. You're my little *Marzipan*."

"Mama!" Piccola protested.

"Told you," Guillermo said.

"You can play with them tonight," Signora Infante said.

"Whaaat?!" Guillermo bellowed.

"I second that idea," Mario interjected, filled with hope.

"Mama!" Guillermo implored to no avail. Piccola flashed him a big grin.

"Now, come on in sailors, I hope you like aubergine, I'm making *Rollatini di Melanzane*."

"Signora Infante, as it happens, I've been meaning to talk to you about your *Rollatini*..." Mario followed her into the kitchen.

"Come men, let's go outside," Guillermo said as he headed to the closet to grab a pile of towels.

Enzo, Luca and Tony flew out the door. In the living room Guillermo stopped briefly to gaze at his father's favorite painting, a portrait of his distant relative, Lorenzo. To his father, Lorenzo exemplified courage and bravery. When Guillermo had trouble sleeping at night he would listen to the waves crash against the stone wall below his bedroom window and imagine himself in the cabin of a great ship, sailing the open seas with the intrepid Lorenzo Infante. His father had told him how Lorenzo had brought honor to his country and while he had died young, he had lived more than most people twice his age. Guillermo hoped he could muster such courage when the time came to leave behind all he knew.

From down on the beach, Guillermo could hear his friends calling for him. He grabbed the towels but with one foot already out the door, something curious caught his eye: an old-fashioned crate roughly twice the size of a shoebox was sitting in the hallway. He'd never seen such a package before, and certainly not in his own home. He leaned in for a better look. The box was tied up with the kind of coarse rope you'd find on a ship, and wax was melted over the knot. He was about to investigate it further when he heard Enzo scream, "Captain, man overboard!"

Guillermo pushed the crate into the corner and ran down to the beach, hurtling his wooden dinghy before cannon-balling into the water off the pier. Mario had also heard Enzo's call, although it took him somewhat longer to stagger down from the kitchen. His belly flop displaced enough of the Mediterranean to irrigate a small farm and to completely drench Luca, who had stayed on the pier.

"Hey Guillermo," Luca asked once the boys regrouped on the beach, "when is your father returning from Rome? He promised to bring me a legionnaire's sword."

"He's bringing Roman breadsticks with sesame seeds for me," Mario added with a greedy grin.

Guillermo gazed down at the water. The sun's rays glared off the golden anchor on his captain's ring, which his father had given him for his last birthday. Despite the warm breeze Guillermo had goose bumps. "He'll be back any day now," he responded softly. "But without a new ship. And probably without your swords or breadsticks either."

"What do you mean?" everyone asked.

Guillermo could no longer contain what he'd overheard the night before. He took a deep breath and explained how his family would have to move in with relatives all the way across the island in Siracusa.

Mario seemed genuinely concerned. "So... no breadsticks?"

"Simmer down jelly-belly, this is serious," Luca snapped.

Mario eyed Luca, "Look who's talking."

Enzo slouched down and rested his head in his palm, "This is not good."

"Who will steer the ship?" Tony wondered aloud.

The boys fell silent, knowing that Tony's question held more weight than just captaining a make-believe boat.

Guillermo felt his eyes moistening and realized a tear might not be far behind. He quickly turned away and began trudging up to the house. Inside his mother and sister were in the kitchen.

"Not with your wet feet you don't," Signora Infante called out, intuitively knowing from two rooms over that he'd forgotten to dry off properly.

Guillermo perfunctorily ran his feet over the rug and headed toward the kitchen. But en route the mysterious package caught his eye again. This time his curiosity pushed him relentlessly toward the box. When he flipped it over his spine straightened and his eyebrows furrowed. In bold red letters the name 'Guillermo Infante' was printed across the crate.

"Mama? Who is this package from?"

"It's the strangest thing," she yelled back from the kitchen, "It was sitting at the front door when I came home today. No return address, no postage, no note. Nothing."

Guillermo grabbed the crate and rushed off to his room, his imagination racing and his curiosity burning. "Is it for me or papa?" he asked without bothering to wait for an answer. He scraped the wax away and untied the ropes securing the crate. The inside of the box was marked with an inscription: '*Caute: navis crescit en aqua*', and it contained an exquisite model warship. He carefully extracted the ship, paying no attention to the two velvet pouches also housed inside, or to the mysterious inscription.

The ship had three lofty sail masts, a protruding bowsprit, a polished gun deck, an eight-pronged wooden steering wheel, and dozens of miniature cannons. Inside the ship were rows of corridors, kitchens and storage rooms. Its beauty and craftsmanship were far superior to any model ship he'd ever laid his eyes on.

Guillermo turned the ship around to examine the stern. The letters comprising the vessel's name were too small to make out. Nor could he recognize its minuscule red and white flag. He flipped it over to inspect the hull. There, engraved in the wood and big enough to read, was the same bizarre phrase: '*Caute: navis crescit en aqua*'.

Over in the kitchen, Piccola was helping her mother with the dinner preparations. "I hope Papa comes home soon," she said, probing for a reaction regarding the call she'd overheard the previous night.

"He'll be home soon *bella*. And there will be things to talk about…"

"What do you mean?"

"All in good time *bella*."

While watching her mother take the *Rollatinis* out of the oven Piccola decided to try another angle. "I laid out the chess board just the way Papa and I left it before he went on his trip. Do you think he'll want to finish the game when he gets home?"

"I think he'll probably be tired from the journey," she said, looking more than a little exhausted herself.

"But if he doesn't play as soon as he gets home, Guillermo will change all the pieces around and I'll lose. I hate it when he changes the board. Last time it almost worked!"

Signora Infante reached over and put her hands on Piccola's gumdrop cheeks. "Sometimes change is good, *bella*. Sometimes facing a new challenge helps you grow. You'll see."

"But I don't want anything to change, mama. I want everything to stay as it is," she huffed as she threw the warm oven mitts onto the floor and folded her arms. On a normal day this little tantrum might have earned Piccola a one-way ticket to her room, but this wasn't a normal day and both she and her mother knew it.

Running back outside to share his discovery, Guillermo nearly collided with his mother who had just delivered a tray of steaming hot *Melanzane* to his friends. He hid the vessel from her view at the last moment, still unsure if the mysterious package had been intended for him or his father. Once she retired to the kitchen Guillermo slipped the ship out from underneath his towel.

"Wow! A pirate ship," Enzo exclaimed.

"No, it's some sort of galleon," Luca said. "A first-rate galleon, I think. It looks like the type of ship that Britain's Admiral Nelson captained against France during the Napoleonic Wars."

"It's incredible how you know stuff like that," Tony said to Luca.

Mario spoke with a mouthful of cheese, "He doesn't. He makes it up."

"I guess I'm just a military buff," Luca replied.

"One day you'll be a soldier in the *Alpini Corps* just like your brother, right Luca?" Guillermo patted him on the shoulder.

"Yes captain," Luca replied in a rigid, militaristic voice.

"Where did you get the ship?" Enzo asked.

"Someone left it for... me... I think…"

Mario had paid little attention to the excitement generated by the model ship, but Piccola coming down the path to their table did pique his interest. His smile was hard to recognize beneath the spoonful of sauce dripping off his face.

Piccola reached the table with the black velvet pouches in her hand. She pointed to the model ship, "Can I see it?"

"Sure," Mario said eagerly, as if it were his.

"No way. You're too little and you could break it," Guillermo countered.

"I will not!"

"Let's see if it floats," Luca suggested.

"I'd be careful if you want to put it in the water," Piccola warned.

"Why?" Guillermo asked.

She put her hands on her hips and raised her eyebrows as if to say something the boys should have already figured out for themselves, "*Caute: navis crescit en aqua.*"

"What does that mean?" Tony asked.

Guillermo glared at his sister, "It means stay away from my side of the room."

"It's Latin. It means 'Caution: ship grows in water.'"

Nobody was sure whether to be more impressed by Piccola's grasp of a nearly extinct language or by the fact that they might have a growing ship in their possession. Guillermo led the sprint back down to the water. Even Mario mobilized for the spectacle of a growing ship.

"Wait for me," Piccola yelled, trying to keep up.

"How big do you think it'll get?" Tony asked. "A few inches larger? Or like the size of a dog?"

"Maybe it'll grow to be the size of an inflatable pool raft," Enzo suggested.

"Wait," Tony pulled a waterproof case over his iPad. "Just in case there's a splash."

"If it gets to be the size of a raft we can use *it* instead of the dinghy to get to Mariner's Fort," Luca said.

"Maybe it gets even bigger, like the size of a real ship," Guillermo suggested as he scurried out to the edge of the sea. "Maybe even big enough to replace my father's ship and then we won't have to move."

Piccola grew more excited and hopeful with every word from Guillermo's mouth.

Before releasing the ship into the water, Guillermo gave it a final dash of preparation by unfurling its sails and untying its tiny rudder. The sun was slowly trending toward the western sky but it delivered plenty of light for the moment of truth. The crew brimmed with expectation as Guillermo placed it in the water. Everyone's bulging pupils zeroed in on the ship. But nothing happened. Nothing at all.

"It's not working," Mario observed.

"I'm getting that," Tony said.

"Sorry Guillermo," Luca offered.

"It was foolish of me to think that this could work," Guillermo lamented as he picked up the ship.

"It's OK, Guillermo. We'll think of something. You're not going to have to move." Luca put his arm around Guillermo's shoulder.

"Let's just get going," Tony suggested. "I'll get the dinghy and our clothes."

Mario ran back up to the table to collect the plate of food as Piccola jostled the model ship from her brother's hands. "Let me try to figure out how to make it grow," she begged.

"Fine, but be careful with it," Guillermo warned with a tone of resignation. "It's pretty amazing even if it doesn't grow like it's supposed to."

Piccola grabbed the ship and rotated it above her head to view it from all angles. Then she put it back down in the water and shifted her attention to the velvet pouches she'd brought out from the house.

As always, Luca made sure to avoid contact with the water as he boarded the dinghy. Tony, Mario, Enzo and Guillermo piled in and used a wooden oar to push back from the shore.

"Piccola, aren't you coming?" Mario called out, inviting a harsh look from Guillermo.

Realizing she was about to be left behind she scooped up the model ship and darted for the dinghy. Guillermo gritted his teeth as Mario and Luca helped her aboard. Just then Signora Infante came out from the house and offered the group a satisfied and warm smile as she watched Piccola getting onto the dinghy. Everyone waved goodbye to her.

Before the long hand of Guillermo's watch had clicked ten notches forward, the crew pulled the dinghy up onto the beach at Mariner's Fort. The island was small enough to hike across—north to south or east to west—in less than 152 seconds (Tony had timed it on his iPad). On the far side was an ailing wooden shack that a fisherman was said to have built a half century ago to shield himself from the elements. That's where the group always slept when they stayed overnight. Guillermo had discovered it with his father when he was younger and had immediately noted its strategic potential, which inspired him to name the whole island Mariner's Fort. Surely the person who'd originally built the shack would be impressed to learn that his ramshackle creation now served as a proud fort of any kind.

While the boys went about their usual routine of collecting twigs and driftwood for the evening fire, Piccola scampered off to a nearby rock to further assess the model ship and the velvet pouches dangling from her hand.

Luca put his arm around his best friend, "Hey, my brother is going to be in the *Corps* for another two years. I can ask my parents if you can take his bedroom, whenever he's not visiting."

Enzo also turned to the captain, his chin intruding on Guillermo's personal space. "Maybe you can live with me. My sister is getting married in the fall and when she leaves her room will be empty."

"Thanks mates," Guillermo said, his voice conveying the unlikelihood of such a scenario actually working out. "But I don't think there's any way my family would leave me behind."

"I wish we *could* leave you behind," Piccola's voice piped up as she approached the group with a grin almost as wide as the model ship in her hands. "But maybe we won't have to move after all."

"What's *that* supposed to mean?" Guillermo prodded.

"Quam mihi nota evolvant," she said with fire in her eyes.

The gang looked at her expressionless.

Piccola shook her head, "I think I figured out how to make it grow."

—Chapter 3—

Arrivederci

Piccola stood knee deep in the water off of Mariner's Fort exuding confidence. "Boys never pay attention to details. Sometimes it takes the patience of a woman."

"Then be sure to let us know if one shows up," Enzo shot back.

All the boys—except for Luca who as usual stayed on dry land—gathered around her in the water, each one more confused and impatient than the next.

She leaned over and showed them the ribbon that had kept the velvet pouches tied together. The words written on it were in Latin, and so she translated as she read:

From the ocean's floor to heaven's door,
grow until you can grow no more.
Should you lay this powder round' and round',
to the seven seas she shall be bound.

"I'm taking this to be a pretty simple instruction that the boat needs the powder concealed in this pouch to be put around it for it to grow." She brought the model ship out a bit

19

further into the water and began to sprinkle the white powder in a circle around it. The ship floated lazily on the calm sea, as did the powder until it began to dissolve.

"What is that stuff?" Guillermo asked.

"It came in the box with the ship. You were in such a rush you didn't even notice it, dummy. There was a golden key, too", she flashed it to the boys, "but I haven't figured out what it's for. Yet..."

To nobody's surprise though, Piccola's efforts produced no result. The small vessel continued to bob calmly up and down with no discernible change in size.

"Good job Piccola you little 5th grade medieval alchemist," Enzo chided.

"I'm going into 6th grade now Enzo, and I'll get older, but you'll always be funny looking."

His hopes dashed, Guillermo leaned backwards until his head disappeared under the water.

Enzo and Tony gathered to have a laugh at Piccola's expense. Luca went back to building the fire on shore. Meanwhile Mario started swimming closer to Piccola, who stood stoically watching over the floating ship surrounded by the disappearing powder. As Mario approached, the ripples he created pushed some of the powder against the ship. The first sound was so faint no one was sure if it even came from the ship: an ever-so-slight creak, or crack. Guillermo looked at everyone in disbelief.

"You don't think—" Enzo started.

The second explosive sound was unmistakable. A puff of smoke shot into the air as the model ship gargled and groaned with spontaneous gusto. The sea began rocking from side to side, each wave knocking everyone off their feet. Piccola fell backwards as the second pouch of powder was flung from her grasp. Thick smoke screened the area around the boat, making it difficult to see what was happening. Panicked,

Guillermo stumbled backwards onto the shore before remembering that Piccola was at the center of the storm. He leaped back into the water to try and bring her to land. But in the chaos of the smoke, waves and cacophony of sounds it was impossible to find her.

"Run!" shouted Tony as he hastily sprinted back toward the sand while trying to shield his iPad.

"What's going on?" cried Luca.

"It's working!" shouted Guillermo before a massive wave knocked him under and pinned him to the sandy bottom. The impact sent sand torpedoing deep into his ears and up through his nose. He struggled desperately to get his head above the surface to gasp for air but couldn't. He couldn't even figure out which way was up. As the surf threw him around like a fish beneath a waterfall he wondered how much longer he could hold onto the small pocket of air he had left in him. His heart had never beaten so fast.

And then from underneath him he felt something pushing up hard against his chest. Whatever it was, it thrust him upwards in halting fits, first through the water and then out of it. For a split second he wondered if he'd drowned and was ascending to heaven. Beneath him were polished wooden boards, and it was as if they were being hoisted vertically by a crane. He had somehow been scooped up onto the deck of a ship, a fast growing ship. The 'caution' part of the warning started to make a whole lot of sense.

The ship trembled violently as it sustained its slapping pace of growth. Cascades of seawater tumbled back into the bubbling sea below from the ever-higher decks. The thunderous cackle continued unabated as the ship expanded upwards and outwards. Each plank, slab and beam, each bar, hinge and screw growing fast and proportionally. Guillermo was flung to the deck boards twice while attempting to get to his feet. Sitting was just fine, he concluded. He had a reservoir of seawater to cough up.

And then the expansion stopped. Just as quickly as it had all begun, it all ended. An eerie silence fell over the ship as its size stabilized. It took nearly a minute for the smoke to dissipate and for the sea's swell to subside sufficiently for Guillermo to get a good look. He was able to make out Tony, Mario, Enzo and Piccola scattered on the deck near the bow. He called out to make sure they were safe.

"I think we're OK," Tony moaned.

"I think I had an accident," Mario sheepishly replied. "Piccola, are you all right?"

"I'm fine, Mario."

Guillermo started to wring out his drenched clothes but then froze when he heard Luca's faint call for help. Everyone scanned the deck and the island but he was nowhere to be seen.

"Er, captain," Enzo said pointing to the stern of the ship, "take a look up there."

Luca looked down at everyone with a confused grimace. He was hanging by his shorts fifteen feet up in the air on the ship's flagpole. "I was running and this flag pole came out of nowhere and hooked me like a fish," he called down.

Luca finally managed to break free of the pole's grip and he slid down while everyone hovered at the base of the pole to try and catch him if he fell. On deck the crew reunited, remarkably all in one piece.

Everybody gazed out at the full splendor of their vessel. It was simply enormous. The model ship that had minutes before been resting idly in an old crate had preserved every inch of its wondrous craftsmanship as it morphed into a seaworthy vessel: a seaworthy vessel even larger than Captain Infante's famed ship.

The kids leaned back against a wooden bench, too tired to start analyzing what had just happened. Or to begin discussing if what had just happened had really just happened. It was only when everyone felt a giant thud, and looked over the side to see that their ship had drifted into the harbor and rammed straight into a tugboat, that they realized how big and powerful their vessel was. Its design may have looked centuries old, but its breadth and scope left it towering over every other ship in the harbor. Guillermo thought it was probably the biggest ship he'd ever seen. He ran to the helm.

"Oh no, we just crushed Rumrino's boat," Enzo yelled.

Piccola and Guillermo tried to impart a responsible look of concern, but the corners of their mouths, spiking upward ever so slightly, briefly revealed their inner joy.

"We need to turn around," cried Tony as the ship drifted past other boats, its monstrous sails beginning to suck up the wind.

"The ship's too big! If we turn around now we're going to destroy every boat in the harbor!" Luca countered. "We need to get out into the open water to turn around."

"I don't think we'll make it out of the harbor!" Mario bellowed.

Ten panicked eyes flashed to Guillermo who quickly realized that everyone expected him to start making real decisions. The color drained from his face and his stomach began to churn.

"What should we do?" Enzo cried to Guillermo.

"How am I supposed to know?"

"Well, you're the captain," Mario gasped as the ship clipped the stern of a moored fishing boat and flung it around.

"I'm the captain of a tree house! I've only been on a sailboat once, and *that* had a motor on it."

"Well, we better do something fast!" Piccola implored, as she pointed to the local fireboat directly in their path.

Beads of sweat dripped down Guillermo's cheeks as he did his best to survey the situation and feign some degree of confidence. He struggled to muster his voice, which cracked as soon as he began to speak. "Let's try and steer out before turning to come back in. Otherwise we'll destroy half the boats in Pizzolungo." If he had grasped the wheel any tighter he would have left imprints in the wood.

"We'll make it!" Luca exclaimed.

"It's going to be tight!" cried Guillermo, as he swung the wheel downwards with all his might, only just managing to avoid a major collision, if not a slight exchange of side paint, with Captain Milioto's crabbing vessel. Everyone breathed a giant sigh of relief as the ship snuck past the remaining boats in the harbor and eventually made it to the open sea without further destruction.

Guillermo knelt down next to the wheel to regain his composure. He knew his dizziness had nothing to do with the rocking of the ship.

Mario started climbing below deck.

"Where are you going?" Luca asked.

"Downstairs to have another accident."

Meanwhile on land, Captain Rumrino stumbled out of the local pub with a bottle of fermented grapes. The bottle fell from his hand and shattered when he saw his tugboat drinking heavily through the gigantic hole on its starboard side.

Judging by how small Pizzolungo now looked from the deck, Guillermo estimated the ship was well over a mile out to sea. He guessed it would take a good spin of the clock to steer her back in. But he could barely summon the strength to stand up.

"*Arrivederci* Pizzolungo," Tony whispered helplessly.

Guillermo struggled to his feet in order to address his motley crew, "I guess that's about enough fun for one day."

"It's starting to get pretty dark," Piccola pointed out, "let's try and get back."

Just then an abrupt gust of wind seized the mammoth sails and pushed the ship even further out toward the open sea.

"Terrific," moaned Tony.

Guillermo took a deep breath and cleared his throat. "All hands on deck..." he phrased as more of a question than a command. Everyone gathered around anyway. "Uh, guys, I think we need to turn into the wind to get back. Which means..." he paused and examined his expressionless crew, "which means that we need to turn the ship into the wind... to get back." His words trailed off as he realized he didn't know how to implement his own command. "Any suggestions on how to do that?"

Nobody moved or said a word.

Guillermo stood up a little straighter. "OK, we need a plan." He recalled a story his father had once told him about 40 foot swells he'd battled in the North Sea. Everyone on the *Coraggio* had lost hope of surviving, including his father. But Captain Infante had told Guillermo that it had been his duty to project confidence and strength in the face of such adversity. And it was that gritty determination that kept his father's crew motivated enough to eventually persevere and reach safety. Guillermo eyed his crew. "So here's what I suggest..." Everyone huddled together to await their instructions. "The wind's pushing us out. Fast. So maybe we need to re-angle the sails to the sides. That might make it possible for us to tack left and right to head back toward Pizzolungo?"

"Are you asking or telling?" Luca demanded of Guillermo, who was wondering the same thing himself.

Guillermo projected his voice to be heard clearly above the blustering wind, "I'm telling."

"That makes sense," Tony uttered, doing his best to sound upbeat.

"Yeah," Enzo agreed. "How are we going to shift those sails around though?"

Everyone peered up at the sails towering above their heads. The mainmast seemed high enough to scrape the moon.

"There are stairs running up the masts, so Luca, uh, you take the mainmast, Tony and Enzo, you two take the mizzenmast and the foremast. Push the sheets as far to the right as you can, ok?"

"What can I do?" Piccola shouted.

"You can stay out of the way," Guillermo offered.

"You can check the galley for food with me," Mario suggested as he lumbered over to the cabin stairs and then disappeared.

"How does one shift sails around? Those things must be heavy and—" Enzo began but was interrupted by Luca, whose panicked voice grabbed everyone's attention: "Captain, you might want to check the bow!"

"Oh no!" Piccola cried.

Tony started typing manically on his iPad. *"Oh Dio mio,* this must be the storm your mother was talking about."

"Oh you think?" Enzo said dryly.

Guillermo spun around; the look on his face said it all. Terror. Coal-colored clouds were gathering fast on the horizon, blackening the sky. Radical bursts of lightning and thunder piggybacked off each other in the distance.

"That's the worst looking storm I've ever seen," Tony muttered.

Fear seemed to dislodge Enzo's chin slightly further from his face.

"When it rains it pours," Guillermo said to no one in particular.

Mario was already talking as he came out from the galley stairs, "Hey guys, we have pasta: Spaghetti, Linguini, even Fettu—" Just then he caught sight of the storm up ahead. "Oh, this is not good," he whimpered as he swiftly retreated downstairs.

"Do you think we can outrun it?" Luca asked. "Maybe we can harness this gale to get back into port before the storm hits us."

A massive bolt of lightning sizzled down from the sky to the water in front of them, the thunder following in tandem. It was so loud it left everyone's ears ringing. Piccola sidled up next to her brother in fear.

Guillermo evaluated the situation, "I don't think so."

"What should we do? Are there any life jackets on this ship?" Enzo asked.

"I think our only option is to go downstairs and batten down the hatches," Guillermo said.

The ship rocked back and forth as the storm's initial swells crashed up against the bow. Volley after volley of rough sea shot onto and over the top deck. Everyone ran for cover down in the cabin of the ship. Only Guillermo stayed on deck to secure the wheel by tying it in place with a nearby rope. He also quickly ascended the foremast's low yard to make sure they weren't encroaching on any dangerous rocks. Not that he had any idea of what to do if there were rocks ahead. What he did know was that the crew would be in far greater danger if not for the ship's impressive size. But the storm seemed to be only gaining in strength.

While finally running for the cabin stairs a splash of sea surprised him from behind and sent him tumbling toward the railing and the open sea. His bare feet offered no traction on the wet boards but with his arms extended to their breaking point his fingers just managed to snag a metal docking loop seconds before it would have been curtains for him. It wasn't until the ship was tossed back on its other side that he could pull himself upright. He breathed a heavy sigh of relief, knowing that if he'd gone over his friends would have never heard his screams amidst the chaos of the storm. He frantically descended into the lower cabin area, sopping wet and nearly in shock. Luca, Piccola, Tony and Enzo were there waiting for him.

"Looking any better captain?" Luca asked, trying to mask his own panic but doing an awful job.

It took what seemed like minutes before Guillermo could speak. "Worse actually, the waves are getting higher and who knows how long this drifting pile of wood can take it." He paused to catch his breath. "We're going to have to wait it out down here."

"We should look for those life jackets," Piccola stressed, "and try to figure out the most practical way to turn the ship around to head back home."

"How are we even out here?" Tony cried, shivering from a mix of cold rain and fear. "What kind of ship grows like this, sails you out to the middle of the ocean and drops a storm on you?"

"I think the storm would have been here one way or another," Enzo countered as Tony looked at him as if he had three heads. "Well, it would have."

Mario stuck his head into the corridor. "Captain, you have got to see this galley downstairs. We've got like twenty pounds of pasta in sealed jars and all sorts of exotic spices. There's also lots of fresh water. No sauce, though. I was going to cook us up a huge meal but there's no sauce."

"No sauce?" Enzo asked.

"No sauce," Mario sighed.

"Are you all insane?" Tony yelled. "Storms, sauce, spices? We're in the cabin of a toy boat right now, out in the middle of the ocean! Who made this boat? Who gave it to you, Guillermo?! How are we going to get home?"

"I don't know how we are here, but we are here." Guillermo put his hands on Tony's shoulders. "I don't know how it grew to be so big, or why there are exotic spices on board, or who designed it. But it's a pretty big ship, isn't it?" Tony acknowledged its size. "So I think as long as we stay down here in the cabin we should be safe. But I need you to help us figure out how to navigate out of here. Do you think you can do that?"

Tony finally lifted his teeth from his lip and stopped his knees from knocking together. He nodded his head.

"Good." Guillermo let go of Tony's shoulders. "Luca, you and Enzo take a look down the corridor to try to find us some life jackets. Just in case."

"Already on it, captain," Luca said, pushing Enzo down the hall.

"Well, Tony, I don't know how any of these ingredients got on the ship either," Mario said, "but my mother always tells me, 'shut up and eat'. So in a little while I'm going to cook up whatever I can."

It wasn't long before Luca and Enzo rushed back into the corridor holding candle lanterns. They carried with them folded sailing uniforms: long white pants, gray vests and blue overcoats with large white buttons down the front.

"You have to check out this beast!" Enzo gushed with frantic exuberance. "There are dozens of rooms, amazing rooms with libraries, kitchens, everything. We found all sorts of tools and weapons too."

"And clothes," Guillermo observed.

"Yeah, there are enough uniforms to go around. If we find a pair of scissors we can get them to fit, too."

"Any life jackets?" Guillermo asked as a strong swell sent the ship up and down at a harrowing angle that would capsize many a smaller vessel.

Luca shook his head. "Negative captain, we'll have to keep looking for those. The ship is enormous; it would take hours to fully search. Maybe even longer. It's definitely big enough to replace your father's ship."

"There's no motor, motorhead," Piccola interjected. "Our father," she glanced proudly at her brother "is one of the world's best captains. But it's the twenty-first century, not the sixteenth. He can't run his business from this ancient sailing ship."

"I know," Guillermo admitted. "But maybe we can sell it and Papa can buy a new ship."

"You think people are lining up to buy ancient sailing ships these days?" Enzo asked before imitating a potential buyer. "Hmmm, what should I buy, that fancy new ship with the powerful engine, or the giant, floating museum exhibit?"

Guillermo didn't bother with a response. "All right everyone, why don't we do some exploring while we wait out this storm."

The six young crew members descended another two floors down the cabin stairs and headed off along the first corridor they found. Guillermo stopped to take in the scent of the vessel. The smell of oak and pine from the hull wafted heavily in the air. It was as if the trees from which it was made had been cut down just the day before. The stairs, railings and walkways were smooth and polished, like the façade of the violin his father had once bartered in exchange for a deck of Tally-Ho playing cards and a bottle of Chianti wine from a Maltese captain. The ship's wood trimming emitted a reddish hue that made Guillermo think of ripe cherries. He was about to ask Mario if he'd spotted any cherries in the kitchen when another strong wave threw everyone against the corridor wall, hard.

"I think I'm gonna be sick," Mario moaned.

"We better find those life jackets," Piccola exclaimed.

It was dark in the first room the crew entered but there were additional lanterns by the entrance. Enzo used his flame to light them.

"What is this, a gym?" Mario asked. "I hate gyms."

Lined up on a rack were half a dozen bicycles. But no Treks, Cannondales or Schwinns. Rather, bicycles with really big front wheels, and small rear ones. Luca pulled the bikes off the rack and inspected them further. Their wheels were made of metal and were covered with thick wax. There were no gears, reflectors or brakes. They didn't even have the standard GPS trackers that normally indicate speed and distance.

"This looks like fun," Piccola said. She grabbed the smallest bike and climbed up with Mario's help, but her feet couldn't reach the pedals. Mario pushed her and she steered in circles until another healthy wave rocked the ship causing her to careen into a shelf and fall over. From the shelf a stack of yellow envelopes rained down on her. She picked herself up and grabbed the envelopes for closer inspection.

"Maybe we can use the bikes to get around the ship," Tony suggested, the color coming back to his face. "Otherwise who knows how long it would take just to walk from bow to stern?"

"I wonder if that's why the bikes were originally put here?" Guillermo said.

Tony and Enzo were the first out of the room on their new bikes. They pedaled down the corridor with the lanterns swinging off the handlebars. The wheels responded

31

hesitantly, and only after some time propelled them forward slightly faster than they normally walked.

"Stop!" Tony yelled. "Check this out", he pointed into a room that had been painted, 360 degrees around, with a giant map of the world. The two entered, mouths agape. "*Mamma mia*, this map is *really* old. Whoever painted it must have done so before most of the Americas were discovered. And a lot of the Pacific islands are missing, too, so it even predates Magellan and Cook."

"How do you know all this stuff?" Enzo asked.

"In case you don't remember, Guillermo made me our chief navigator in the 5th grade because I got an 'A' on my Vasco da Gama presentation. I can get us from Pizzolungo to Marsala and back with my eyes closed, any time."

"Just get us back to Pizzolungo from here and I'll be happy."

Guillermo and Luca made their way down the corridor. A library with books shelved from floor to ceiling caught the captain's eye and he wandered in while Luca held up a lantern. Guillermo pulled a heavy book off the shelf. It was half the size of his kitchen table back home and weighed more than Piccola. He let its weight pull his hands to the ground where he flipped it open to the title page. In large, italicized font it read, '*Magister Mari*' in Latin, but sounded close enough to the Italian words '*Maestro del Mare*' to be understandable: 'Master of the Sea'. He leafed through a random selection of pages and saw that it contained hundreds of diagrams of sail positions, rope and knot usage, and other seafaring techniques. He pushed the book into the corner of the room.

Enzo and Tony were in the map room when Guillermo and Luca joined them.

"Mario went back to start cooking pasta without sauce," Enzo said. "He'll call us when it's ready."

Luca's eyes caught sight of the wall map. "Whoa!"

Guillermo surveyed the enormous cartographic wall. With his arm extended he was just tall enough to reach the island of Sicily. He traced his finger around the waters off the coast of Pizzolungo where the storm was tossing around their ship. Off to the right of the map Guillermo opened a cabinet to see what else he could find and pulled out a handful of rolled up dockets. He unfolded them as everyone looked over his shoulders. "What are these things?" he asked aloud, pointing to dozens of sketches drawn in fine pencil over the frail paper.

"I'm not sure," Luca responded, "they look like blueprints for inventions." He pointed to the bottom of the page, "But the date here says 1497. Some of these things, like smoothbore cannons, dual periscopes and deep-sea diving equipment wouldn't have been invented until way after 1497, like the bicycles. Some of these other devices I don't recognize at all; they probably *still* haven't been invented.

"What's a dual periscope?" Tony asked.

"I guess it's a periscope that can be used to examine things over *and* under water," Luca said. "But even traditional periscopes on submarines weren't invented until much, much later. Same goes for the smoothbore cannon designs shown here, which I think are from the nineteenth century."

The kids marveled at all the designs. Meanwhile Luca retreated backwards to scope out the next room. "*Allora!*" his faint voice echoed from across the corridor. "Now this is my kind of room!"

Guillermo, Enzo and Tony hurried over, passing Piccola in the corridor, who was studying the documents she'd collected in the room with the bicycles. Upon entry, Guillermo could see where Luca's enthusiasm was coming from. Gun port windows lined the room and the lanterns offered enough light for everyone to see that it was unlike anything they'd ever seen. Many of the weapons and inventions that were mere sketches in the map room were the real thing in this room.

"What are these things?" Guillermo asked.

"I don't know," Enzo said, mystified.

"I've read about all these kinds of weapons," Luca said as he scanned the room of his dreams. "Those cannons pointing out to sea are cast-iron smoothbores. And those over there are short-range carronades." He stepped back to admire the wider collection. The room was filled from floor to ceiling with weapons and other contraptions: dozens of cannonballs were stored in thick wooden bins marked '42', '32' and '24', and bag upon bag of black gunpowder lay at their side. A catapult system on wheels faced the wall and in the corner there were two bell-dive suits – the kind the crew had only read about in Jules Verne novels. There were dozens of lockers and cubbies with other gadgets and weapons that nobody recognized.

"Those are some seriously heavy cannonballs," Luca noted. "A 42-pound armament like this one could blast a hole through two wooden ships simultaneously." He walked over to the cannon bores. "If we fill these cannons with the gunpowder from those bags and load up the cannonballs, we'll be prepared for any dangers out here at sea."

"You mean like this storm, General Brizzi? Or against things like sharks and seasickness? Or pasta dishes without sauce?" Enzo laughed.

"Did you say sharks?" Luca asked fearfully. With those words, everyone went airborne as the waves hoisted the ship above the crest line and back down furiously.

"I think the storm is getting worse, if that's possible," Tony said, holding his stomach.

"Linguini *con olio*!" Mario bellowed from the kitchen, his drained voice rumbling down the ship's hallway. "I found some olive oil in a spice cabinet."

The kids made their way over to where Mario was lethargically dishing out the pasta. Sweat was falling off his forehead and his complexion had turned green. "I vomited twice trying to prepare this meal; I've got to get off this ship!"

Nobody touched their food.

"I'm worried about this storm. The wind is—" Guillermo began, adopting a more serious tone.

"We're fine down here," Luca interrupted. "This ship is so big that it should be able to withstand it."

"That's not the only problem," Piccola explained, pushing aside the document she'd been reviewing. We've been down here for a long time. If it's too rough to get outside and steer then by the time the storm is over we might not know where we are."

"I just checked," Tony said hesitantly, "and the storm must be interfering with my Internet connection, I can't pull up our location.

"Don't worry," Luca explained, "we found the map room. We'll be home before Mario's hungry again."

"That soon?" chided Enzo.

They looked over at Mario who had gone from green to yellow and was about to vomit again.

"This storm can't last forever," Luca said.

"That map downstairs is so old it's one step up from useless," Tony lamented. "If we can't spot land after the storm we'll have no way of knowing where we are."

Thunder shouted over the wind from outside the ship as Guillermo turned to Tony, his face gravely serious. "What are you saying Tony?"

"We have to turn back now captain, or we might end up lost at sea."

—Chapter 4—

Inflecto!

Giant waves bullied the frame of the ship as a charge of lightning fragmented the sky. Mario held onto the entranceway railing of the upper deck with one hand and onto Piccola's hand with his other. Piccola held onto Enzo, and Enzo onto Luca. The crew formed a train until Tony clutched Guillermo's left hand. Guillermo tried to navigate with his right hand.

"It's not working," Guillermo cried. "The storm is too strong. I don't think I can hold on."

"We're already so far out that we don't even know which way to steer," Tony hollered.

"Captain, what happens if lightning hits a wooden ship?" Enzo shouted above the din of the storm.

"No idea, but it can't be good," Guillermo screamed back as the fiercest wave of the day slammed into the vessel and nearly sent it over on its side. The human chain from the railing to the ship's wheel fell apart like a wet paper bag.

"I'm not having fun anymore," Mario whimpered as he coughed up a fountain of salty water.

"Everyone go downstairs," Guillermo ordered. "I'll stay up here with Tony to try to steer." He looped a safety rope around his and Tony's waist and tied it to the wheel. "Let's try that way!" he bellowed, pointing into the black abyss.

Tony helped Guillermo manage the wheel, "Are you sure this is a good idea, captain?"

The next wave crashed down onto the deck from twenty feet above. Piccola, Mario, Enzo and Luca nearly swam down the cabin stairs.

"He must know what he's doing," Luca offered, as if saying it aloud would somehow make it true.

Downstairs Piccola crossed the room and dried her hands before picking up the document she'd previously been studying. She homed in on a small section of the paper and drew a circle around it with a fountain pen she'd discovered in one of the drawers. "*Inflecto*" she repeated twice out loud.

"Piccola's talking to herself, loverboy," Enzo whispered to Mario who was too ill to respond.

"*Converte me et tuere me venire voluisset seris velocius aevo,*" Piccola continued. "*Inflecto... Inflecto.*" She paused to think and then leapt to her feet, "Guillermo! Guillermo!" she hollered as she trampled over Enzo, Mario and Luca who were lying in the pond of water they'd brought in from the deck. She flew up the stairs.

"Be careful *amore mio* ... I mean, *amica mia,*" Mario shouted.

"Guillermo!" Piccola slid across the wet deck and then crawled between his and Tony's legs searching for something below the ship's wheel.

"Get down below with the others," Guillermo barked. "Are you crazy? You'll get blown right off the ship."

The first thing she saw was a sand-filled hourglass off to the side. It was long and thin and the top chamber was completely full, the bottom empty. The glass neck between the two chambers was infinitely narrow. Then off to the side she spotted what she'd been searching for. "Yes!" she screamed with delight. "*Inflecto!*"

"What are you screaming about?" Guillermo asked, swiping water away from his eyes. The rain wasn't coming down in sheets anymore. It was coming down in blankets.

"*Inflecto* means 'warp' in Latin. On the ship's blueprint," she continued, spitting out her words in rapid succession, "it said the word '*inflecto*' beneath the wheel. Then I remembered the golden key that came in the crate with the ship." She pulled the golden key from her pocket. Everyone had forgotten about it.

"What are you talking about?" Tony asked.

She pointed to a shiny brass-ringed keyhole underneath the wheel. "*Inflecto!*"

Sure enough, inscribed under the keyhole was the word '*Inflecto*'. To Guillermo and Tony's surprise she then pointed to the inscription on the key: '*Inflecto*'.

"Get it?" she asked.

"No," Guillermo answered testily.

Another huge wave rocked the ship, nearly dislodging Piccola from under Guillermo and Tony's legs. Guillermo swung the remainder of the rope he and Tony were using around Piccola's waist and tied it tight.

"There must be some kind of motor. Something to give the ship more speed. Warp speed!"

"Whatever it is it can't leave us worse off than we are now!" Tony exclaimed.

Guillermo scanned the ferocious waves against the backdrop of the black sky. The salty water splattering across his face stung and he wondered if it would eventually cut through his skin. He motioned for Piccola to try the key.

Before inserting it into the keyhole she repeated the words *"Converte me et tuere me venire voluisset seris velocius aevo."*

39

"What's that?"

"I identified this keyhole using the ship's blueprint which I found downstairs. It said *Inflecto: Converte me et tuere me venire voluisset seris velocius aevo,"* which means "*lock and turn if so inclined and I'll move faster than space and time.*"

She turned the key. The three of them waited impatiently but the ship's speed didn't seem to increase. Another giant wave pummeled them and Guillermo eyed her anxiously.

Piccola slid down the panel that the key unlocked; it revealed a metal box fastened to the steering console with four numbered dials on it. Each dial was set to zero and resembled the combination lock of a briefcase. Their eyes fixated on the words engraved beneath the zeros. Again, Piccola read out loud, translating from Latin:

> *From you to me, and me to you,*
> *Just this one time, you may pass through.*
> *My greatest masterpiece at hand,*
> *Created specially for the Grande.*
> *Dial the numerals left to right,*
> *And Inflecto shall guide your flight.*
> *But be so warned before you fly,*
> *You're offered only this one try.*
> *Inverse to Reverse.*

> **Dial 1:** *Ancient wonders of the world.*
> **Dial 2:** *Time to be born.*
> **Dial 3:** *Corners of the globe.*
> **Dial 4:** *Life.*

"Inverse to reverse," she repeated. "That doesn't rhyme with anything. What do you think that means?"

"What's any of it supposed to mean?" Tony asked.

Guillermo held his stomach as the ship rose high onto a pugnacious crest. "I don't know, maybe it's a puzzle or something."

Piccola stared at the words and the dials. "Pass on through… Guide your flight… I think it's just confirming that we'll get some kind of warp speed from this machine, some kind of *inflecto*. But what are these dials for?"

"There are four dials and four clues," Guillermo said.

"Maybe it's an old fashioned version of a password," Tony yelled through a spray of water. "Let's try it. The first one's easy, we know from history class that there are seven wonders of the ancient world."

Piccola spun the first dial to the number seven. She could feel her pulse race.

"Time to be born?" Tony asked out loud. "Someone can be born at any time, really. How can we guess that?"

"It takes someone nine months to be born, last time I checked," Piccola said evenly.

"Right," Tony conceded. She spun the dial to nine.

"OK, this one's simple," Guillermo shouted, "there are four corners of the globe."

Piccola and Tony agreed and she moved the third dial to the number four.

"Life?" Piccola said out loud, her voice indicating uncertainty.

"Hmm, what about Life?" Guillermo asked. "Maybe how long you live?"

"Those numbers are too big for our dial. It only goes up to nine," she said.

"And besides, people live to all different ages. All different numbers," Guillermo offered.

"Maybe nine is the answer then, because it's the biggest number there," Tony proposed.

Suddenly Piccola's eyebrows shot upwards and her pupils doubled in size.

"What's with the face?" Guillermo asked.

"Do you trust me?"

"Do I have a choice?"

"Well, whatever you are going to do, do it fast or we are going to die out here," Tony cried.

"It says we only get one shot at this Piccola," Guillermo warned. "Just one."

She inhaled deeply and rolled the last dial to the number one.

All of a sudden a great flash of white light enveloped the vessel and the numbered dials all reverted to zero, locking back into place with a loud clack. A giant whirlpool formed right below the bow as the ship began spinning like a bathtub toy circling a drain.

"I think we're going down," Guillermo roared. He frantically untied the safety rope and grabbed Piccola by the hand, pulling her down the cabin stairs toward the belly of the ship. Tony followed right behind. "Everybody hold onto something!"

"What's happe—" Mario tried to utter, but the ship started plunging downwards, under water.

Everyone swallowed the biggest breath of oxygen they could gasp. All twelve cheeks bulged like swollen balloons. The ship seemed to be plunging repeatedly over and on top of itself. The centrifugal force whisked the kids up against the walls of the room, flattening their cheeks and pulling back their hair. Hurricane-force winds tossed the crew around and a wickedly bright light pierced everyone's retinas even though their eyes were fastened shut. The upside-down terror lasted only a few seconds though, before the ship stopped spinning and seemed to stabilize, right side up.

Everyone fell onto the floorboards and cautiously eyed each other. Strangely, no water had flooded into the cabin.

"It feels like the waves have stopped," Guillermo moaned as he rolled onto his back. "Like... completely."

Bright light snuck into the room from below the hatch and through every small crack in the wood. Guillermo listened to the soft interplay between the ship's outer boards and the seemingly placid water beneath them.

"That was insane," Luca sighed as he pulled himself to his feet. "Really insane."

"Did that code turn the storm off?" Guillermo asked Piccola.

"Umm, I don't know what it did."

"What code?" Mario asked.

Guillermo hobbled over to the cabin stairs and opened the hatch. The sun was blinding, and hot. The crew piled up behind him on the stairs like troops ready to rush into combat. Only there was nothing to fear up ahead. The seas were indeed perfectly calm. The water drifted by so peacefully that it looked like a stagnant pond on a windless day. Miraculously, it was broad daylight. A minute earlier Guillermo had wished for a poncho and a pair of goggles. Sunglasses and sunscreen seemed more appropriate now.

Everyone climbed up onto the deck and looked out at the beautiful sea in awe.

"What just happened?" Guillermo asked.

"I don't know," Piccola replied as she wrung out her drenched uniform. "But you're welcome."

"How did you know the answer was one?"

She grinned proudly, "Papa always says 'you only get one life to live, so make it count'."

Guillermo and Tony shrugged, surprised by their obvious oversight.

"Not bad," Guillermo said.

43

"Why is it daylight?" "Where are we?" Mario and Tony's questions overlapped.

"And what's that ship out there called the *Black Bass*?" Enzo motioned off the portside of the vessel. Everyone turned and stared at a far smaller and seemingly even older ship.

"How can you see its name all the way from here?" Guillermo asked.

Enzo tried to conceal his smirk but truthfully he never minded impressing his friends with his sensory abilities. (It was much to his chagrin that "Enzo the *En*credible" was a nickname that didn't stick, which was all the more upsetting to him since the nickname was, of course, his idea.)

"Isn't that the kind of ship that pirates used to use?" Tony slowly asked.

"Affirmative," Luca responded. "That's a fifteenth century pirate ship if ever I've seen one."

"Why is it daylight?" Mario still demanded to know.

The *Black Bass* began turning around and tacking directly in the kids' direction. The crews of both ships gathered on their respective forecastle decks to size each other up.

"Why are they all wearing pirate costumes?" Piccola asked.

"Yeah, that is kind of weird," Guillermo conceded. "Who would want to dress up like that in this heat?"

"Tony, take a picture of them with your iPad," Luca said.

"I wish I could. I tried getting a shot of the map room downstairs but I think the camera broke when I dropped it during the ship's transformation."

Just then a loud bang echoed from the *Black Bass* and a puff of smoke floated up off its starboard. A cannonball plowed into the water just in front of the kids' ship, sending a splash of water high onto the top deck. The young sailors backed up in fear.

44

The men dressed like pirates donned a hodgepodge of well-worn threads, mainly black and white, and most had their anchor-raising muscles fully exposed. Shaving didn't seem to be popular among the group, and neither did smiling. Their skin was a mix of leather and boils from, Guillermo guessed, years of exposure to the sun.

"That was a warning! We're boarding your craft," one of the men dressed as a pirate barked to the flabbergasted kids as the relatively modest *Black Bass* pulled up alongside their behemoth.

The men lowered their swords as they struggled with how to react to their discovery of a crew of children, and the challenge of how to board a ship that was *much* higher than theirs. They began arguing amongst themselves.

"Maybe they're, like, real pirates," Luca said, barely believing his own words.

"Do we even have real pirates anymore?" Tony asked, grabbing his iPad to check. "I still can't get any signal. Now that the storm's over we should get a signal."

Guillermo studied the pirate ship with alarm. "Guys, where *are* we?"

—Chapter 5—

Fleury

"Throw down the sea dog or we'll sink ya straight away." The threat came from one of the men dressed as a pirate.

The top deck of the *Black Bass* only reached the lower portholes of the kids' ship and everyone had to strain to hear what the man was saying.

"We can spit down on their heads if we want," Mario observed.

"Who are you and why are you dressed as pirates?" Guillermo fired back. "And what's a sea dog?"

"What'cha mean why are we dressed as pirates? We *are* pirates!" The man speaking raised his sword. The sun shone off it almost blinding Guillermo. "I'm Philippe Gascon, the *Bass'* boatswain, 'n me crew will be boardin' yer vessel, so deploy the sea dog or pay the price."

"I think they mean the rope ladder," Luca suggested.

"They sound like they mean business," Tony trembled. "Maybe we should throw down a rope."

"OK," Guillermo instructed, "Luca, lower them the rope."

"Don't do it," Piccola protested. "Something's wrong about all this."

"What should we do?" Guillermo fretted. "They're adults."

Piccola looked down at Gascon. "I am going to tell my father about this and he'll send the Coast Guard to arrest you all if you try anything funny."

"Coast guard?" one pirate asked another. The other pirate shrugged his shoulders.

Luca flung the rope down onto the deck of to the *Black Bass*, trying his best to hit Gascon on the head.

Gascon glared at him. "I said the sea dog: the rope *ladder!*"

"Well, that's all we have," Guillermo retorted, "We just got this ship today and we don't know where everything's stored. You wanted a rope, here's a rope." He hoped his words conveyed authority and not the paralyzing fear he was actually feeling.

Gascon conferred with his men. "All right ya little devils, we've decided yer' comin' down here instead."

"Oh, no thanks. We're fine up here," declared Mario, backing away.

"T'wasn't a request," Gascon said with a hardened tone. "Board our ship or we'll sink ya where ya stand."

The kids felt their palms getting sweatier as they weighed their options of either sliding down or being sunk by the pirates. Finally Guillermo clutched the rope and reluctantly slid down. The others followed.

The small pirate ship offered no smell of oak or pine, only the stench of rotting food and something else so foul that nobody could even place the scent.

"What *is* that?" Luca gasped.

"Just hold your breath like I'm doing," Piccola suggested.

The *Black Bass* had a single main deck, two stout sail masts, and a cracked bowsprit. Its wooden planks were warped and fractured, making it hard to stand, and the paint

47

seemed to have been completely seared off by the sun. Guillermo figured the pirate crew had more pressing priorities than the upkeep of their vessel. Sure enough, at the rear there was a plank.

"What ship is that?" Gascon asked, pointing his steel sword upwards toward their craft. He was weathered but, unlike the rest of the crew, pale as chalk. His right eye twitched spastically whenever he spoke.

"We haven't checked to see if it has a name yet," Mario whispered to Guillermo.

Guillermo thought about it. "The *Infante*," he declared.

"Where's the Capt'n?" Gascon asked.

Everyone looked at Guillermo who for the second time that day wished he wasn't the captain. "I am," he said with as much bravado as he could muster.

"A li'l small to be a captain ain't ya?" The other pirates laughed.

"A little small for a pirate ship isn't it?" Guillermo retorted.

Gascon stopped laughing and gazed down on his little visitor. "Well, come on in. Captain Fleury wants to see ya and he don't like to be kept waitin'."

"Fleury. That name sounds *really* familiar," Tony said, repeating the name out loud.

Enzo poked Tony, "You know a Captain Fleury?"

"What did you say?" Gascon stared at Enzo. His eye twitched again as the wrinkles above his forehead tightened. "And why ya looking at me like that?"

"Like what?"

"Like *that*," Gascon edged the blade of his sword up against Enzo's chin, currently protruding proudly against his will as if to challenge the angry pirate. "Square off on me like that again and I'll bleed ya."

Enzo trembled but slowly found enough fortitude to explain. "I'm not doing anything, I swear. That's why I have these braces, to correct my overbite." Enzo showed Gascon his braces.

Gascon and his men leaned in for a closer look. "You may wear silver on yers but 'ave a look at these." Gascon flashed his six gold teeth. They were his only teeth.

"OK, I'm pretty convinced they're real pirates," Piccola said to her brother as everyone swallowed hard.

Gascon and his squadron shoved the kids through a dingy corridor and up to the main station where Captain Fleury sat with his legs up against an oak desk. Fleury leaned forward and fixed his eyes on them sharply. His just-blossoming mustache pointed down from the sides of his cheeks. The curls of his jet-black hair were faded and oily. He appeared to be in his early twenties, which might as well have been his early fifties to Guillermo. Only Fleury's red cloak uniform gave any indication of his seniority on the ship. He stroked his broad-brimmed hat that lay on the table next to him. It had a lone gray feather sticking out from it.

"I asked to speak *wiss ze* captain, not his son," Fleury said with a thick French accent and a mouthful of meat. From the spittle of semi-ingested food that landed on Guillermo's shirt, he guessed turkey.

"I am the captain," Guillermo affirmed.

"A little small to be *ze* captain of such a big ship, no?" Fleury put his hat on.

"Well, I'm just trying to get us home. We came through that massive storm earlier and now we can't even get an Internet signal to help us navigate back to Pizzolungo."

The pirates looked at each other. "What storm? Been quiet as a cornfield out here for weeks," one of them said. "What's an inranet?" asked another.

"In-ter-net," Tony corrected him. "You know, to use Google and Facebook and all that. Actually, GPS would be sufficient to chart our course home. Your boat wouldn't be equipped with WiFi by any chance, would it?"

Fleury rose from his seat and glared at Tony who immediately shut up.

"You know, you should all be using sunscreen," Mario said to the pirate with the most boils. "SPF 80 really wouldn't hurt anyone on this ship."

"Who else is on *zis* vessel of yours?" Fleury probed. "And where is *ze* real crew?"

"We *are* the real crew. It's just the five of us, and my sister," Guillermo said, backing away.

Piccola jumped slightly when Guillermo identified her to Fleury. Her lips parted, and she exposed her clenched teeth to the pirate boss. Guillermo knew that the grimace on her face was an attempt at faking a smile—and that it wasn't hard to tell.

"About *zis* ship of yours... why is she called *ze Grande Infante*?" Fleury pointed to the back of Guillermo's ship.

"No, I was just... My last name is Infan—" Guillermo started but lost his words as his eyes turned in the direction Fleury was pointing to. Upon seeing the stern of his ship for the first time he nearly fell over. The ornate, mustard-colored lettering read:

'Grande Infante'

"Infante?" Guillermo and Piccola said out loud together as the rest of the crew stared at the name wide eyed.

Gascon took a step toward them and let his eye do its twitching. "You told us the ship's name was the Infante back on the forecastle."

"Um, sorry," Tony interrupted with urgency, "but can I quickly ask where the bathroom is?"

"What's a bathroom?" Fleury asked.

"It's like a place... where you go to the toilet..." Tony explained.

Piccola couldn't hold back her frustration any longer, "Look, just because we are young doesn't mean that we are stupid enough to believe you've never heard of a bathroom"

Guillermo shot her a worried look.

Fleury walked over to Piccola and raised his voice. "*Ze* last time a seafarer talked back to me we used his arm bone to stir our stew. And he was *a lot* bigger *zan* you, *ma petite*, so I suggest you shut your mouth."

"You don't scare me," Piccola replied.

"You scare *me*," Mario assured.

"I know what the kid's looking for *patron*," one of the pirates said to Fleury, pushing Tony back through two corridors and out to the plank. "That's for interrupting the *patron*," the man said as he smashed the heel of his boot into the small of Tony's back, knocking him to the ground.

Tony peeled himself off the rough floorboards, wishing he'd simply relieved himself in his clothes instead of opening his big mouth about a bathroom. A displaced nerve in his back made it feel like electric eels had nestled inside his body. He struggled to contain his fear and desperation to get off the ship.

"Don't get lost on your way back," the pirate said, pointing to the ship's bathroom—the plank. He headed back toward the main station.

Tony slithered out onto the plank, all four of his arms and legs drooped over the side of the wooden board. "*Madonna mia*," he said, looking down at the empty sea beneath him.

Up on the main station Fleury eyed the other visitors evenly. "All right, so what is it going to be?"

"What's what going to be?" Guillermo asked.

"Are you going to cooperate or are you going to make my afternoon a little more fun? We shall make your ship a bit lighter for you, so *zat* you can get home a bit quicker... to wherever you're from." Fleury coughed up a wad of phlegm and spit it down onto the floorboards. "So, *petit capitaine,* show us *ze* valuables *zat* you have on board. Show us your shiny metals and polished stones...."

"We don't have any of those things," Luca explained.

"Yeah, there's just a bunch of cannons, scientific tools and bicycles but no precious metals or shiny stones of any kind," Mario said.

The pirates' eyes widened.

Mario could sense his friends' burning stares upon him. He corrected himself, "I meant, there's basically nothing on board. We don't even have pasta sauce."

"We'll have a look for ourselves anyway, right *patron?"* Gascon said, turning to Fleury.

"I have a better idea, we shall confiscate *zer* whole ship. We'll treat *zem* like *ze* Englishmen from whom we confiscated our fine maiden." Fleury caressed the wooden boards of the *Black Bass*. "With *zeez* two ships in our pocket we'll have *ze* makings of our very own armada." He looked straight at the kids. "What do you *sink?* Perhaps you fancy becoming our rowers... We could use some extra deck hands for our next mission out in *ze* Atlantic."

The young sailors were speechless. Guillermo thought back to the time in 4th grade when he convinced 6th grader Alfonse Stracci not to beat him up by telling him he was infested with lice and that touching him would result in Alfonse spending the next three weeks bathing in olive oil to kill them off. But nothing he'd ever experienced had prepared him for how to defend against, or negotiate with, real life adult pirates.

"I can tell by your silence you are hoping *zer is* an option B. Well you're in luck," Fleury said with a grin that would break a camera lens. *"Zer's* an option B."

"What's option B?" Guillermo asked, relieved that any other option existed.

"We take your ship and leave you in *ze* water."

The pirates all laughed creepily.

"Is there an option C?" Mario inquired desperately. "Because I'm sure whatever that is, we'll take it."

Gascon reached for his dagger as Luca hit Mario on the arm.

Meanwhile, Tony started making his way back toward the main station, nursing his lower back and fretting what the pirates would do with him and the crew. En route a poorly fixed wooden deck board got in his way and, already unbalanced and in pain, he tumbled to the ground. While getting up he noticed a map hanging off a desk in what he figured to be the captain's quarters. Making sure no one was looking, he gingerly slipped into the entranceway for a closer look. Inside, a single bed made of warped planks was shoved into the corner; next to it, propped up against the wall, rested a crooked desk with one drawer missing. The sun's rays fired into the room through an unevenly carved porthole.

"Oh Dio mio," Tony whispered aloud.

He stared at the map in panicked excitement and then double checked that nobody was coming before he took it off the desk, folded it up and slid it into his back pocket. His hands were so clammy he had to use Fleury's mangled pillow to wipe them off. He crawled back out into the hallway, but made a wrong turn and ended up in a dimly lit room filled with cannons. A small wave jostled the ship and Tony fell over again and banged his knee against one of the cannons. The lantern on top of it slipped off and lit the fuse. Seconds later, to his absolute horror, a cannonball rocketed out into the open sea as a tower of smoke mushroomed into the sky.

"Oh no, oh no," he anxiously panted. He sprang to his feet and instinctively dashed off toward the main station to explain the accidental cannon fire. He knew he was almost certainly running toward his death, but he also knew there was nowhere else to run.

On deck the stunned pirates watched the smoke rise in disbelief. "What's *zat*–?" Fleury began.

Guillermo noticed the distracted pirates. "Run!" The kids fled back down the dingy corridor, seconds later colliding into Tony who was running from the other direction. They spun him around and everyone headed for the rope. Enzo was the first to start climbing, followed closely by Tony, Piccola, Guillermo and Mario. Luca was last. Gascon lunged at him with his sword. The blade moved so fast that Luca could hear it whistle as it sliced through the air, just before it smashed up against his shoe. Luca looked down, morbidly thinking he'd just lost his left foot. Instead, though, he watched the completely severed heel of his shoe tumbling back down to the pirate ship's deck. As Gascon repositioned himself to swing again Luca heaved himself upwards with every mineral he could muster. Gascon's second slash at him was too late; Luca's feet were out of reach and the lower rope got tangled around the blade.

Finally Luca's head collided into Mario's cushiony bottom. His impact helped propel Mario over the railing and back onto the *Grande Infante*. Luca leaped over as well and looked down to see two pirates struggling up the rope in hot pursuit, daggers in their mouths. "Stand back!" he yelled as he released the pulley system and let the rope go, returning the pirates to their ship with a thunderous thump.

The *Grande Infante* started drifting away from the *Black Bass*. "All hands on deck," Guillermo commanded with a decisiveness that even he was surprised to hear. "Tony, swing the jib off to the right. Luca, Mario, the three of us are going to re-position the mainmast to catch ourselves a breeze. Enzo, head up the foremast to stand lookout."

"What about me, Guillermo?" Piccola asked.

"Um, you can hold the wheel straight."

Piccola stood up proudly, "OK captain."

"Full bore!" hollered Gascon from below as his men swung their sails into motion.

Just then a pirate ran up to Fleury, "Captain, the map is gone."

"What map?" he asked, seething.

"*The* map, captain!"

"We were going to be lenient and let *zem* little snappers row." Fleury's face darkened. "Now *zey'll* get acquainted with *ze* plank, and we'll—" He stopped short and eyed the pirate carefully. "What were you doing in my quarters? How did you know *ze* map has gone missing?"

The pirate started quivering in front of Fleury.

On the deck of the *Grande Infante* the boys jumped on their bikes and pedaled with determination. They dismounted at the base of the mainmast and started climbing up, clutching metal handle after metal handle.

"Nobody look down," Enzo called out, ensuring that everyone immediately looked down.

"*Madonna mia,* we're high," Mario moaned.

"Keep climbing," Guillermo implored. He licked his index and middle fingers and let the breeze hit off them to discern the direction of the wind. "We're almost at the top. We just need to push the sails portside, because the wind's definitely coming from starboard."

Once they reached the top everyone collectively re-positioned the sail, relying partially on Mario's linguini belly for leverage.

The pirate ship followed slowly, its square-rigged cog sails snatching up only a fraction of the wind that the *Grande Infante*'s much larger, lateen sails swallowed.

From his lookout post, Enzo watched as Fleury lightened his ship's load by marching the quivering pirate who'd told him about the missing map—one of his own shipmates—off the plank. Despite the aggression the pirates had shown his crew, Enzo felt his stomach twisting just thinking about how scared the pirate in the water must be. Soon he'd be all alone, just him and the ocean, to die a quick death by deadly creature if he were lucky, or a slow death by drowning or dehydration if not. What kind of a person would send someone to perish like that, Enzo wondered?

"After *zem!*" Fleury commanded his mates. "I want *zat* ship."

A second later a cannonball shot out from the *Black Bass.* Its soot formed an arched, gray contrail before it descended with increasing speed directly into the lower abdomen of the *Grande Infante.* The boys hung onto the mast poles and ropes as their ship rocked to the side before steadying itself. Piccola landed flat on her back.

"What are you doing?!" Fleury howled down at the pirate responsible for the cannon fire. His voice was cracking and his face had turned bright red with fury. "You want to walk *ze* plank too? *Ze* map is on *zat* ship you idiot!" He turned to the rest of his men who stood aghast. "Charge *zat* vessel. Prepare a boarding party, get my map back and take *zer* ship!" Fleury swung the *Black Bass* around so that it pointed directly at the *Grande Infante*.

As the *Grande Infante* stabilized and the boys continued to reposition the sails Piccola observed Fleury's maneuvers, "I think they're getting into position to try and ram us," she shrieked. Nobody responded. After a moment of hesitation she ran with urgency to the main sail, still holding her bruised back. "Guillermo, Luca, come down. *Now!*"

Guillermo sensed the distress in Piccola's tone and motioned for Luca to follow him down the mast. "Tony, Enzo, you two monitor the situation from the foremast. Mario, stay with the mainmast sails." Everyone scattered into action as the wind amassing in the *Grande Infante's* sheets began to propel her forward even faster.

Luca followed Piccola on his bike to the cabin stairs, with Guillermo not far behind. They sped down to the room with all the machines. She slammed the hatch on the largest cannon she saw and lit the fuse with a lantern. There was no reaction.

"Cannons require a cannonball to be effective," Luca said as he rolled a 42 pounder over. "And some gunpowder, too." He slid the cannon out of its gunport and, with Piccola's help, tried to hoist the cannonball high enough to roll down the barrel. But its round shape and weight made it too cumbersome to lift that high.

"Need help?" Guillermo asked as he rounded the corner out of breath.

"One, two, three, *lift!*" They just managed to get the cannonball into the barrel.

"Now stuff the hole with those bags of gunpowder," Luca instructed.

Guillermo peeked out of the gun port as they rolled the weapon back into place. He could see his ship was speedily moving ahead, but he could also make out Fleury trailing not far behind. "Fire!" he ordered as Luca and Piccola set the fuse aglow. The backfire of the explosion was so powerful that it landed Guillermo and Luca against the rear wall, and Piccola out in the corridor.

The cannonball plummeted into the sea just in front of the *Black Bass*, forcing a spray of sea water up onto the deck. The ship swayed violently from the waves, sending Gascon and three crew members who had been leaning overboard into the sea. Guillermo high-fived Luca. Not to be ignored, Piccola rushed over to slap palms too.

"I've never seen such massive cannon fire," Fleury said expressionlessly to the crewmate standing next to him.

The pirates lowered their sails to fetch their mates from the sea. Fleury watched as Gascon and the others climbed up their small sea dog.

"What kind of a ship is that?" the pirate asked.

"I do not know," Fleury responded, "but we are going to find out."

The enormous sails of the *Grande Infante* continued pocketing vast amounts of wind. The ship propelled forward, crashing through the growing swells below. Luca headed down toward the lower deck to check on the damage to the ship. Guillermo and Piccola found their way back to the deck.

On the way the captain spotted a shiny brass telescope. He extended it to its full length and focused in on Mario who was doing his best to command the sails. Enzo and Tony were just visible at the top of the mainmast monitoring Fleury's movements. Down on the lowest deck Luca was hanging over the railing examining the damage inflicted by the cannonball. He shot a thumbs-up back to Guillermo. The captain smiled as he surveyed his busy crew, imagining how his father must have felt while commanding the *Coraggio*. He indicated for everyone to return to the main deck.

Guillermo shifted the telescope to the distant pirate ship. "They're really far behind us, but it doesn't look like they're giving up."

"Which direction is Pizzolungo?" Piccola asked.

"Hard to say. The sun's just starting to set, so we know *that* way is west." Guillermo pointed off the starboard side. "But I still don't know where the storm dropped us, so I'm not even sure which way to steer." He scanned the horizon through the telescope. "Hey what's that way out there? I think I see land."

"Let's aim for it," Piccola said.

Luca ran up to Guillermo, "Captain, the structural damage to the ship isn't critical; the cannonball didn't pierce the inner hull. But the damaged boards will make it difficult to steer, and it's going to slow us down. We'll have to dock soon to get it repaired."

The definition of the coast grew more distinct as they continued west. Two large bodies of land jutted toward each other, separated only by a narrow channel of water. Steep, snow-covered mountains rose to the south. To the north, tree-lined ridges traced the coastline. Through the channel lay more open sea.

Guillermo steered in toward the northern coast. Just off the beach an enormous rock seemed to punch its way out of the water. "None of this looks at all familiar," Guillermo grumbled as he put his head down on the wheel.

"What's the matter?" Luca asked.

"Everything," Guillermo muttered without looking up. "I have no idea how to get home from here or even where here is."

"Captain, you just weathered the biggest storm I've ever seen and evaded a pirate ship. An actual pirate ship! I'd say you're doing pretty well so far."

Guillermo examined the coast. "Even if I could get us home, what's the point for me? I won't even *have* a home soon."

"Don't say that," Luca pleaded as Enzo and Tony returned from lookout duty.

"Well unless there's a vault on this ship that we've overlooked, filled with enough money to buy my father a new ship and to keep our house, I'll still have to move away when we get back."

"Oh, I wouldn't say that, captain," Tony said reaching for his back pocket. "I wouldn't say that at all."

—Chapter 6—

Between a Rock and a Scarred Face

"I think it's a treasure map," Tony said as the group gathered around to look at his grab.

The map showed the western coastline of Europe and Africa. Right off the coast of the Canary Islands there was a small depiction of a treasure chest overflowing with gold bars.

"What gave it away?" Enzo asked dryly.

Above the treasure chest were numerical inscriptions detailing the precise location of something. Scattered across the ocean were depictions of puffed faces emptying their lungs, indicating wind directions. Geometric lines ran across the page, intersecting dozens of times, forming triangles, hexagons and trapezoids before running out of space at the edge of the map. Tony noticed that for some odd reason the mapmaker had drawn pictures of dogs on the islands, not birds.

"Do you think it's real?" Guillermo asked.

"I got it from Fleury's cabin," Tony explained. "It must show the location of a shipwreck. If we can find whatever treasure is there we'll be able to get your father a new ship."

"Then you'll be able to stay in Pizzolungo," Luca added.

"And we'll all be rich!" Enzo exclaimed.

"Fleury mentioned that they were planning a mission into the Atlantic. It must have been to get this gold." Guillermo paced as he thought. "But do you think the treasure would even still be there? This doesn't exactly look like a very modern map. And how would we even get there?"

"What about Mama and Papa? They must be really worried about us," Piccola uttered.

"Yeah, my parents too," Enzo concurred.

"But just think about it," Tony pleaded. "If we can get the treasure, then even if our parents worry a little now, we'll come home as heroes and save the captain's family from having to move away. And we'll have enough money to buy a better tree house for the school. We have to at least try, no?"

"I'm sure when we dock we can find a phone to call home," Guillermo noted.

"If we can call home then I guess it's OK with me," Enzo said.

"I don't know," Luca shook his head. "It'll be pretty tough to bring up treasure from a sunken ship, assuming it exists, and assuming we find it."

"You just don't want to go in the water," Tony teased.

"How about I throw *you* in the water right now?" Luca countered. Tony cowered behind Mario.

"If those pirates weren't after us before, and they *were*..." Mario said, "they're surely going to be after us now."

"Maybe the treasure ship just hit a rock in shallow waters and we can swim down to collect the gold," Tony speculated. "The map is really specific about the location; you can probably see the shipwreck from the surface."

"Well if that's the case," Piccola questioned, "why didn't the person who drew this map just collect all the treasure himself?"

"Maybe the mapmaker couldn't swim," Tony said.

"Maybe he didn't like getting in the water," Luca offered. "Or sharks."

"More likely is that the mapmaker wanted to secretly come back to get it alone," Piccola said.

Guillermo rose from the table. "We have a decision to make. We can try to go home or we can go for the treasure."

Everyone briefly inspected one another, trying to gauge who stood where on the big question.

"We don't know if the treasure is real," Guillermo continued. "We don't even know if the map is real. The decision we make is going to have to be ours. Our parents are going to be worried. The whole town is going to be worried. And when we get back we might arrive empty-handed. And we might be in a *lot* of trouble."

Everyone slouched, imagining defeat.

"But we also might come back with gold. And lots of it," Guillermo continued. "And if the pirates were planning on getting that treasure then I think *we* can get it."

"That's true," Piccola noted. "They could barely climb ropes, but we could."

"They tried to steal our ship, and we got away," Tony added.

"They tried to catch up with us, but they couldn't," Enzo said. "They're already completely out of sight."

Everyone scanned the horizon. Fleury's ship was nowhere to be seen.

"So what's it going to be mates? Gold, or home?" Guillermo asked.

Tony stood up, "Go for the gold." Then Enzo, followed by Luca, "The gold."

Mario had just ingested a handful of cold pasta from the untouched bowl. He swallowed everything down and looked at Guillermo. "'*Go for the gold*?' What is this, the Olympics? I want to go home."

Luca elbowed him. He begrudgingly retracted his statement. "Fine, I guess 'gold' is what you want me to say?"

Piccola and Guillermo stared at each other intensely. She stood up with the rest of the group. "Sometimes in order to get back you have to keep going forward."

"Huh?" Mario muttered.

"All right. We go for it," Guillermo exclaimed.

"These pirates have serious pirating issues," Piccola said with a renewed sense of purpose. "That's probably why Fleury wanted to make us his slaves, so that we could help him get that treasure."

"Fleury. Jean Fleury! That's his name," Tony shouted as he leapt up and down, banging his head on a wooden beam. "That pirate had the exact same name as the famous French buccaneer Jean Fleury. I included him in my 4th grade report on pirates. I knew his name sounded familiar. He used to raid all the Spanish ships filled with gold from the Aztecs and the Incas."

"Hmm, our Fleury also had a French-sounding accent," Guillermo noted. "Maybe it was like his great, great, great grandson or something."

"Maybe he's a Fleury impersonator because I remember the real Fleury sailed on a small ship just like that one, and wore a feather in his hat," Tony said.

"Hey what's that?" Guillermo shouted. Everyone looked off the starboard. They were close enough to the shore now to see ships docked in a harbor. "Every ship is made of wood. And none of them have engines. They all look about 500 years old." He scratched his head. "Tony, check to see if you get an Internet signal here, now that we're near the port."

"Negative. I've been checking the whole time, captain."
He squinted to get a better look. "It is strange that all the ships
here look so ancient."

"Maybe it's just a really poor town and they can't afford
modern boats," Enzo guessed.

"I guess so," Guillermo muttered. "All right, we need to
bring down these sails to reduce speed. We're getting close."

The crew spun into action, climbing back up the three
masts and releasing the pulley ropes governing the sails. The
sheets came down easily but the ship's momentum continued
to carry it toward the outer pier fast enough for Guillermo to
foresee a clumsy and potentially dangerous impact. He
thought fast as the crew descended back down to the main
deck with uneasy, frightened looks.

"Captain," Tony yelled, "we're going to crash!"

"What should we do?" Mario begged.

"We need to drop anchor right away!" Guillermo
commanded. He sprinted toward the bow with everyone on
his heels. "There it is!"

Guillermo and Luca fought through a knot in the thick
fiber rope and released the anchor. Gravity sent it hurtling
downwards, causing such a splash that it drenched a flock of
seagulls hovering above the ship. The anchor's enormous
iron arms chiseled into the shallow harbor seabed and the
rope connecting it to the ship pulled taught and emitted a loud
creaking sound as it stretched to its limits. Beads of water
were propelled off the rope like from a wet towel being
twisted. The ship's forward momentum swung it around 180
degrees before jolting it to a dead stop and flinging the crew
off their feet and onto the deck.

One by one they pulled themselves upright and rushed to
the side of the ship to look down; they were right up against
the stone pier facing back out to sea. The strangely dressed
dock men gazed up at them curiously. Guillermo wondered

whether it was the size of his ship or his unorthodox approach to docking that had the locals in a state of minor shock.

The kids took in their surroundings. The area behind the piers teemed with action. It was loud and smoky and the shadows draped out from the buildings and covered much of the waterfront. A more residential area stood a ways back from the harbor, on the initial slopes of the mountain range. The houses were bunched up almost in piles, and every single one was painted white and had a red clay roof. A tall spire from a Gothic cathedral towered above all the other buildings. There were no public lights other than the moon, which was beginning to make its evening ascent. The mixed scent of filth and incense hung heavy in the humid evening air. Nothing looked or smelled familiar to any of them.

A dock worker with a bushy mustache and a leather wine skin strapped over his shoulder called out for the kids to throw him down the docking ropes. Luca, Enzo and Tony lugged three ropes over to the side and dropped them over. The workers down below scrambled to secure the ship. Meanwhile the crew navigated the inner passageways to get down to the lowest deck. From there they tossed another rope onto the pier and used it to disembark.

"Why are such small children like you sailing on a giant ship such as this?" a local man asked as the kids put leg to land for the first time since accidentally setting sail.

"Don't ask," Mario responded as he stretched out his stubby arms and legs.

"Mates, we have a lot of work to do," Guillermo interrupted as the disoriented locals watched on speechlessly, "and I think we should do it fast and get out of here in case those pirates come looking for us. So let's split up. Luca and Tony, you head into town to look for a public phone so we can call home. Mario, you said you needed some tomatoes and more spices to make sauce, so why don't you find a market and get what you need; I'm starving. Enzo, go with him and make sure he doesn't spend half our money on a three-card monte hustler."

Mario snarled as Tony gave him and Luca a few of the coins he still had in his pocket from the schoolyard.

"Piccola and I will try to find someone to repair the hull. Let's meet back here in an hour."

Luca and Tony walked into the heart of town, passing throngs of curious onlookers dressed in costumes from centuries gone by. There were no cars or buses on the streets, or airplanes overhead. No buzzes or hums from telephone poles or cable wires, no trace of modern technology at all. Everyone traveled on horseback or in horse-drawn carriages and manure was spread out like polka dots on the unpaved, narrow roads. Flies danced about everywhere. Some of the men donned medieval armor, swords and shields. There were flags hanging from the buildings but none of them were of Italy, Sicily or anything else recognizable. Few were even rectangular.

"I don't see any payphones. Maybe there's one in that pub," Luca suggested. He and Tony headed past a crowd of unruly townsfolk as they made their way into the ale house.

Across town, Mario and Enzo ventured into a narrow, twisting bazaar where row upon row of merchants were jockeying for the choice positions to sell their wares. Each of their wooden stalls had a lit candle hanging overhead. Foods, animals, ropes, anchors, fabrics—everything was for sale.

"*Va bene!*" Mario proclaimed. "This place is awesome."

Down by the waterfront Guillermo and Piccola searched the docks while dodging fishermen hauling in their catch. They came across a sloppily-shaven, hulkish man snoring next to a crate of ale. He seemed to be passed out with all four of his tree-trunk-sized limbs sprouting out in different directions. His arms were so long that Piccola guessed he could probably tie his shoes without having to bend over.

"*Scusa Signore?*" Guillermo said in a gentle voice so as not to startle the man, who didn't budge. "Sir?" Guillermo tried again.

Piccola palmed some water from the side of the dock and splashed the sleeping giant awake.

"I wasn't using my teeth, I was using my pigeon feathers!" The burly man got his bearings as he leaped upward, towering over Guillermo and Piccola. What's the meaning of this?"

The siblings had seen the size of the sprawled out man, but hadn't yet considered how he'd look upright. They immediately began to inch backward. "She did it," Guillermo said, pointing to his sister.

"Sorry about the bath but..." Piccola smelled him, "quite honestly, you could use it."

Guillermo shouldered his sister out of the way before the man completely lost his temper. "We're looking for the Admiral, Juan Cruz. An old man down the pier told us he hangs out around here. We have a ship docked nearby with a damaged outer hull. We need someone to fix it."

"What's an *outer* hull?"

"It's the other hull on a double... listen, can you just tell me where we can find him?"

The man raised a suspicious eyebrow, "Never heard of the Admiral."

"Well, can you point us in the direction of someone who can help us? We have some money. We're willing to pay for…"

The man fixed his hair and grabbed his mug from the top of the crate. He took a long glug, which he followed up with an even longer belch. "I told you, I don't know any Admiral! Now beat it before I use your nails to scrape the pier free of barnacles." He let out another belch as Guillermo and Piccola observed the man with heads sideways. "And word to the wise, don't be telling anyone around here you have money to pay people. After dark, this town is no place for a couple of children to go round' announcing they have money to give away. Now get!"

Guillermo and Piccola were already on their way. The man got back into his napping position, one eye open to make sure they left him alone. He continued watching as two drunken men followed the siblings off the pier. "Stupid kids," he said under his breath.

Luca and Tony walked into the boisterous pub. Torches with long flames were spaced out at intervals along its interior stone walls, providing the only form of illumination. In the back, through the smoky haze, they saw two men slashing at each other with swords. Each time their weapons collided a harsh slicing sound echoed off the cavernous walls. Tony covered his ears as Luca nudged him toward the bar and away from the fight. Seconds later someone hurled a mug across the bar in the direction of Luca's head. If not for his rapid maneuvering, it might have been the last thing he ever saw. An expressionless man behind him knocked the mug to the ground with an iron shield before casually resuming a conversation with a husky fellow sporting an archer's bow across his chest. The bartender didn't seem to find any of this strange. And why would he, Luca thought. *He* wore a metal-laced vest, carried a flanged mace and had a deep, purple scar across his right cheek.

Luca got his balance as the blood rushed back to his pale face. He scanned the chaotic scene for other signs of danger before turning to Tony, "I didn't know pubs were like this."

"I've never been to one either."

Tony timidly got the bartender's attention. "*Scusa Signore*, do you have a phone?"

"If you like," the bartender said while scratching his scar "but it's still going to cost you a penny."

Tony tried to look away but found himself morbidly mesmerized by the deep, purple gash. Luca produced a penny from his pocket.

The man took a mug and filled it with ale from a large metal canister. He then spilled the ale out leaving only the foam. "Little young to be in here aren't ya?"

Tony looked at the mug quizzically. "Not foam, *phone*."

"What's *phone*?" The bartender looked down at the coin. "And what's this? Are you trying to cheat me, child? We don't take counterfeit money."

Luca and Tony looked down at the one-cent Euro coin on the bar.

"I won't be made to look a fool in my own establishment," the angered barkeep said as he flicked the coin back at Tony who still couldn't look away. "How'd ya like a scar bigger than mine?"

"We're just trying to call home," Luca explained. "If you could simply point us in the direction of a phone, we'll be on our way."

"*Mira!* I don't know what this phone thing is, but this *taberna* has been standing here five long years and I've yet to have someone slip a fast one past me to get a free drink. If you don't have the money to pay, I suggest you shove off."

70

"I don't think he knows what a phone is," Luca whispered to Tony.

"I'm getting that too."

Back near the pier, Guillermo and Piccola headed in the direction of their ship, keeping a close eye over their shoulders at the two men following them.

"I don't like this," Piccola said, taking faster steps.

"Just keep walking. Don't look back."

Then from an alleyway they heard a soft voice. "*Amigos,* you're looking for the man who fixes boats, *si*?"

Guillermo grabbed Piccola by her shirt and pulled her into the alley. "Yes, we're looking for the Admiral. Are you him?"

"That's a nice ring you have there, *amigo*," the man said as the kindness disappeared from his voice and he took a labored drag off his tobacco stick. He exhaled a cloud of smoke in Guillermo's face, then grabbed his wrist and twisted his hand around to get a closer look at the band, the golden anchor's gleam in particular catching his eye.

"Oscar, Federico!" the boss called out as the two men who had been following Guillermo and Piccola joined them in the alley. "What do you think a ring like this trades for?"

"A pretty coin, I'd say. They have money too," Oscar said, as spittle sprayed across Piccola's petrified face.

"Take our money," Guillermo said, his voice trembling. "Just leave us alone."

"I want the ring too," the boss said as he pulled out a jagged knife.

"My father gave me this ring. It isn't worth anything to anyone else."

"I'll be the judge of that," the boss said raising the knife. "I just want the ring. It's up to you if I get the finger that comes with it." He exhaled another ring of smoke.

Guillermo looked at the razor-sharp knife. As much as it would break his heart to give up the ring, it was a far more appealing alternative to giving up his finger. He removed the ring and passed it over to the thief.

"Now hand over the money before I—" Federico began, but his speech was interrupted by a giant wooden oar landing squarely on the top his head. Only his two front teeth beat his fall to the ground. By the time Oscar had turned around all he saw was a giant fist coming at him. Guillermo and Piccola flushed their bodies up against the stone wall and ducked down to stay clear of the swinging oars and arms. They clasped each other's hands tightly and Piccola pressed her eyelids closed.

Guillermo could make out the silhouette of a large man rubbing his hands together in eager anticipation of his final adversary. The boss threw his tobacco stick to the ground and lunged at the looming giant, who dodged the charge and tried to lay on a heavy kick of his own. But he lost his balance and fell on his back with a loud crash, rupturing the wooden docking boards.

"Looks like it's my lucky day you clumsy old drunk," the boss said, kneeling over the giant man with his glimmering knife drawn.

Piccola wiggled out of Guillermo's arms.

"Come back here!" Guillermo whispered.

She grabbed the smoldering tobacco stick off the ground and tiptoed over to the boss man who was still kneeling over the fallen giant like a lion toying with its prey.

"I'm going to enjoy this," the boss said as he bent down further with his knife. Fortunately for Piccola, he didn't notice the burning tobacco about to be shoved into his eardrum. And as much as the man could taunt, he could scream even better. He sprung to his feet with both hands protecting his smoldering ear. The fallen giant seized the opportunity and grabbed his oar back, quickly knocking out the tortured man with a swift blow to his smoky ear.

Guillermo rushed over to rummage through the pockets of the slumbering boss. He pulled out his ring and, before putting it back on, read the inscription on its inner band, '*To Pizzolungo's next great seafarer, Love Papa.*' It was the first time the ring had been off his finger since his father had gifted it to him.

The man took Guillermo by the arm and lifted him upright. Once standing, Guillermo could see it was the hulking man who had been sleeping beside the crate of ale.

"Are you OK?" the big man asked.

"I think so," Guillermo said as he ran over to check on Piccola.

"I'm fine," Piccola said, observing the wreckage the giant man had left in his wake.

"Well two out of three isn't bad I guess," the man said while he wrapped his bleeding leg with some tattered rags from the ground. "I'm not as fast as I used to be I guess."

"Sir," Piccola said, "we owe you an enormous thank you. If there's any way we can repay you—"

"I could say the same of you, young lady. But when these boys wake up they're going to be plenty angry and I'm going to have a lot of explaining to do."

"Why don't you just tell the police you were saving us from *them*? They'll get in trouble, not you," Piccola said.

"That's not as straightforward as you think."

"Why not?" Guillermo asked.

He peered down at the three semi-conscious men on the ground. "They *are* the *policía*."

73

Piccola retook Guillermo's hand and squeezed it firmly. The big man ushered them out of the alleyway. "You say you're in my debt. So I won't argue with you. You also say you have a boat. Well it seems I'll be in need of a lift out of town as quickly as possible."

"We'd give you a ride but our hull is damaged."

"I'll make a deal with you. I'll have the *Almirante* repair your ship if you sail me to the next port." The man watched as the three thieves began to stir. "Do we have a deal?"

"So you *do* know Juan Cruz, the Admiral," Guillermo said, with a glimmer of hope.

"Know him?" the man asked as he slapped Guillermo on the shoulder with the force of an oak tree. "I *am* him."

Back at the bazaar, Enzo was frantically searching for Mario who had disappeared. He was about to give up and head for the ship when a stranger beckoned his attention. The middle-aged man was dressed in a crimson robe and had flowing light hair and big rounded fish eyes. He carried a square canvas and a pallet of paint.

"Young man, would you mind sitting for a quick portrait?"

"You want to paint *me*?" Enzo asked, pointing to himself.

"Indeed I do."

The man's pleasant and earnest smile convinced Enzo that the uncanny offer was genuine. "Every summer at the Pizzolungo festival I ask my mother if I could get a caricature done but she always reminds me of how expensive they are, and of how my father had to give up eating meat for two years to be able to save up for my braces." He paused to ponder the sacrifices being made on account of his ambitious jaw. "I know that if we could afford it my mother would love a

74

portrait of me on her wall. So I'd like to say yes, but my friend is missing and I need to find him."

"Sounds like quite a predicament, my young friend."

Enzo felt the artist's eyes hovering over his wrist.

"I'm intrigued by the miniature clock you keep on your wrist," the artist said.

"My watch? It was supposed to be water resistant but I guess it wasn't. Until I get it fixed it's only giving me the right time twice a day."

"That's twice more than mine," the artist said, pointing to his bare wrists. "Anyway, I've come a long way to get here for a special client, and I have to travel back to my country tomorrow. But I find your features most remarkable and I would regret it if I didn't manage to paint you."

"Well, I guess it's ok," Enzo said, sitting down where the man instructed him to do so.

"I'm Sandro," the artist said, as he began to apply paint to canvas. "Tell me, were you born this way or have you been in some physical altercation?"

Enzo laughed, "I was just in a physical altercation with a pirate who also admired my features, but I was born like this." He smiled broadly at Sandro, "These braces are supposed to help correct my chin."

"Young man, I don't know how you covered your teeth in that metal, but I surely do hope that your chin doesn't get 'corrected'." Sandro leaned in as if to share something confidential. "Your chin *is* your character."

"Yeah," Enzo said proudly, "I think so too."

Sandro painted quickly.

"Enzo, Enzo!" he heard Mario shouting a few minutes later. Mario pushed toward him through the crowd, but he wasn't alone. Attached to the rope in his hands was a cream-colored, puppy-sized piglet. They both waddled over.

"What the heck is that?" Enzo asked pointing to the pig.

"It's Romeo," Mario answered before he fully absorbed that Enzo was posing for a portrait. "What are you doing, trying to start a modeling career?"

Sandro the painter laughed. "Your friend is a fine model, and you could be too, some day." He turned back to Enzo, "Now sit still for one more minute while I finish."

Mario looked sideways at Sandro and then back at Enzo. "Anyway, after I bought the vegetables from an old lady she threw in a piglet for an extra coin. She must have thought the coins I gave her were worth a lot more than they really are if she gave me this whole pig. And the leash."

"You spent our last coins on a pig?"

Sandro broke into hysterical laughter. Mario scratched his head.

"Of course I did," Mario said matter-of-factly. "You're acting like buying a pig wasn't the most awesome thing I could have done with the rest of our money."

Enzo shook his head.

"It's funny though," Mario continued, "the lady told me the strangest thing about the tomatoes. She said it's the first good crop since the floods of 1495."

"That's true," Sandro asserted as he completed the portrait and handed it to Enzo.

Enzo, Mario and Sandro crowded together to jointly review the painting.

"Great job," Enzo marveled.

"I've seen better," Mario said.

Enzo shook Sandro's hand. "I will give this to my mother when I get home." He slipped his watch off his wrist and gave it to Sandro. "And this is from me to you. Now *you* can have the right time twice a day."

Sandro thanked Enzo profusely and handed him a tube in which to keep the portrait rolled up once it dried. "I shall remember your face and paint you again from memory," he said. "I mean, with your permission."

"*Va bene!*" Enzo said, showing his braces to the world.

Mario and Enzo bid farewell to the friendly painter and started walking toward the ship, piglet and portrait in tow.

"Who was that guy?" Mario asked.

"I think he said his name was something like Sandro Bowl of Jelly, but I'm not sure."

"What a delicious sounding name." Mario licked his lips, "I don't know who keeps records about things like that, but I've been eating tomatoes since the morning I was born and they've all tasted pretty good to me."

Enzo briefly pondered this statement and then stopped walking. He put his finger in his mouth and bit down onto his nail. "I think we should get back to the ship."

On the dock, where the *Grande Infante* towered above all the other ships, Guillermo, Piccola and Juan Cruz stared up at the deck.

"What are children so small doing with a ship so big?" Juan asked, mystified.

"We've been getting that question a lot," Guillermo replied. He and Piccola started climbing the rope to get up to the deck. Juan stayed put. "Aren't you coming?" Guillermo asked.

"Not that way I'm not." Juan about faced and walked over to the next ship. He borrowed the ladder resting against it and brought it back to the *Grande Infante*. Juan climbed aboard and headed down toward the hull, stopping to curiously examine everything along his way.

"Wow! She is *increíble. In-cre-í-ble.*" Guillermo and Piccola could hear Juan Cruz repeating the word over and over to himself.

Near the bazaar, Enzo, Mario and Romeo stared at a maze of tiny streets leading in every direction. "I think it was back this way," Mario suggested, pointing down a narrow alleyway.

"I know... where the ship is," Enzo responded, distracted by other thoughts.

"Then where are you going?" Mario asked.

Just then a man on a horse came galloping down the alleyway toward them. The horse was draped with a green and white robe and decorated with a coat of arms depicting the tower of a castle fortification. The horseman carried a sword in his sheath. Enzo motioned for him to stop. There wasn't enough room for him to pass without bowling them over anyway.

Enzo looked up at the man, "*Scuza*, can you please tell me today's date?"

"The 8th of July," the knight grumbled.

"And uh, the year?"

The man looked at him quizzically and motioned for the young strangers to clear the way.

"Please. We've been out at sea for a long time," Enzo explained.

"Well, squire, last time I checked it was the Year of the Lord 1497. Now out of my way, the king's representative will be arriving shortly from Toledo." The man gently pushed past them with his horse and galloped ahead.

Enzo and Mario looked at each other perplexed. "Did he just say..." Mario couldn't get the rest of the sentence out.

"Yes," Enzo replied, dumbstruck.

The two wrestled with this a little longer before finally breaking into a sprint in search of the ship.

"Come on, Romeo, *andiamo!*" Mario pleaded as the short-legged piglet struggled to keep up.

At the pub, Luca and Tony had just been ejected by a burly regular. Luca dusted himself off.

"You must feel real big tossing around two children, huh?" Tony hollered at the man.

"Hey, how long did that bartender say this place has been around?"

"Five years, why?"

Luca turned Tony's head in the direction of the sign above the pub. It read: '*Taberna Gran Roca – Est. 1492.*' Both boys' eyes went wide. They also took off running.

On the ship Guillermo and Piccola observed Juan Cruz at work.

"I've never seen a hull like this," Juan said. "I've never seen a ship like this. A double hull. Ingenious. You say she took a direct hit from a cannonball out at sea and you were still able to make your way here without sinking? *Increíble.*"

"Looks that way," Guillermo said. "But don't all ships have double hulls nowadays?"

"None that I've seen. And I've seen a lot." Juan went back to reinforcing the damaged hull.

"You're very good at your work," Guillermo said.

"I'm the best," Juan confirmed as he drove a nail into a cracked side panel. "I used to have a ship of my own. Not as grand as this one, but a beauty all the same. Sometimes problems arise and you have to fix them right away or you end up with the clams and the eels down at the bottom. I got good at fixing holes."

"Why do they call you the *Almirante*?" Piccola asked.

Juan angrily hammered another plank of wood into place. "Because I was an *Almirante*!" he said without turning around. "I had several fleets under my command. Led good men into battle. Bled for my country and my maker. But like Icarus, if you fly too high you get burned. Word of my accomplishments spread and soon I was challenged at every bay and inlet. Each man of the sea wanting the spoils of my victories and the chance to tell the story of my defeat. And finally I *was* defeated. Afterward, I was shamed and stripped of my rank. People referred to me as the *Almirante* not with respect, but as an insult. As if I didn't deserve the rank. As if all my accomplishments were erased by my one defeat."

"What happened to your ship?" Guillermo asked.

"Pirates happened." He went back to work. "Jean Fleury put a hole in my vessel that was too big to fix."

"Fleury! That's the creep who attacked our ship," Piccola said. "What's with that guy? He has a really bad attitude. Who does he think he is, Captain Hook?"

"Well, I don't know who Captain Hook is. Or even what an attitude is, but Captain Fleury is the cruelest pirate I've ever come across. But I'll have my revenge one day." Juan took a sip from his mug and pointed his finger at the sea, spilling half his ale on the deck around his feet. "I will have my *venganza,* my revenge! This I swear to the almighty!"

"Chill out Juan. You know, I always thought pirates died out in like the eighteenth century. I mean, except for in the movies," Guillermo said.

Juan stopped what he was doing and put his mug down. He fixed his cap and rubbed his chin before speaking. "I have to say, you seem like good lads, but I don't understand half of what you say." He went to pick his mug up again but slipped on the ale under his feet. His knees knocked against the side of the ship as he went down.

"Epic fail," Guillermo said to a laughing Piccola.

"LOL" Piccola giggled back.

"LOL?" Juan repeated, confused and frustrated as he got back to his feet.

"It means 'laugh out loud'," Piccola explained.

"*Niños*," Juan sneered as he got back to work. "Kids…"

Suddenly, Mario's voice piped up in the distance. "Guys, guys!"

Guillermo ran to the porthole. Mario, Tony, Enzo and Luca were all running full tilt toward the ship.

"What is it?" Piccola asked.

"It's the crew, and a pig."

Piccola rushed over to the porthole as well. "They're running fast."

Guillermo and Piccola hustled up one flight of stairs while the rest of the crew climbed the ladder and fell onto the lower deck with a thud.

"We've got to get out of here, fast!" Mario shouted. His words were hard to hear over his panicked, loud breathing.

"I'm workin' as fast as I can. It's almost sealed," Juan boasted.

Mario peeked down the stairs at Juan. "Who's that?" he asked, still speaking twice as fast as normal.

"That's Juan Cruz. People call him the *Almirante*, the Admiral. He's fixing the ship."

"Who's *that*?" Guillermo asked, motioning to the piglet.

"That's Romeo. But we don't have time for this right now."

"Listen, you are not going to believe this… we're back in—" Luca started, but was immediately interrupted by a voice yelling up to the ship from the dock.

"*Almirante!* We know you're in there."

Juan Cruz dropped his hammer, "Uh oh."

"Who are they?" Guillermo shouted down.

"*Santa Hermandad*," Juan yelled back. "The Holy Brotherhood."

"Who?" Mario asked, more confused than Guillermo.

"The police," Piccola responded with more than a little panic in her voice.

"Why don't you come down so we don't have to come up," one of Juan's visitors suggested. His face was bloody and he was rubbing his ear.

Juan surfaced onto the lower deck and scrutinized his impatient associates on the pier. "*Amigos*, I was just coming to turn myself in."

The kids all observed each other. Juan motioned for Guillermo and Luca to urgently bring up the anchor. "Time to go," he commanded under his breath.

"What the heck is going on?" Enzo asked to no one in particular.

One of the lawmen shouted up from the pier, "Juan, you have ten seconds to come down. I suggest you use them."

Juan retreated from their sight and ran frantically across the ship unhooking latches, and unwinding coils. "No problem I'm just gathering my things," he called down before turning back to the young crew with desperate eyes.

"All hands on deck!" Guillermo commanded. "Get the ship ready to sail, now!"

Juan took a knife the size of a sword out of his pants and ran down the deck cutting the three docking ropes from their pegs just as Luca raised the anchor feverishly and Tony, Mario and Enzo stormed up the mast poles to unfurl the sheets.

Finally the police grumbled loudly, "*Basta! Vamanos!* We're coming up."

Guillermo looked over the deck. The men were starting up the ladder.

"Too late, *Almirante*," one of the officers called up.

Juan rushed over to the railing and winced at the men climbing up. "*Amigos*, I bet you can't guess my favorite season. I'll give you a hint. It comes right after summer." Then with all his strength he grabbed the ladder and lifted it off the side of the ship. "Give up? It's *fall*." Sweat poured off his forehead as he muscled the ladder sideways so that it careened off the ship and onto the dock. The three officers yelled as they continued their plummet into the water.

As the *Grande Infante* drifted back from the docks and the sails filled up plump with air everyone gathered back on the main deck. Juan chuckled as he glanced at the children staring at him as if he were raging mad. He saluted the giant rock sticking out of the sea, "*Adios* Gibraltar!" He looked back at the hyperventilating kids, "So, anything to drink on this ship?"

"Gibraltar?!" everyone yelled in unison.

"We're near Spain?" Piccola asked.

"Not for long," Juan assured her.

"How the heck did we end up near Spain?" Enzo asked, a bead of sweat dripping off the tip of his nose, his chin the only thing interrupting its descent to the deck.

Everyone started shouting. Nobody could hear a thing because everyone spoke at once. Finally Luca's voice rose above the others. "If you think *that's* strange, if anyone's still wondering why there's no Internet signal, why there are boatloads of creepy pirates sailing about, and why nobody knows what a bathroom or a phone is... it's because we've somehow ended up back in the fifteenth century. It's 1497!"

"What?" Guillermo and Piccola both yelled.

"It's true!" Mario confirmed.

"A bartender with a scar who poured us foam basically confirmed it to us," Tony said.

"Course it's 1497," Juan said as he brushed himself off and bid farewell to his acquaintances in the water. "That's what normally comes after 1496." He shook his head and muttered again, "*Niños.*"

"Piccola, what did that *inflecto* code do?" Guillermo asked.

"I thought *inflecto* meant 'warp'. I imagined it would help give us warp speed or something like that to outrun the storm."

"I think the only warp it gave us was a time warp. That's why when we came out of that storm it was daylight, and the waters were calm."

"And why we couldn't get an Internet signal," Tony added.

"And why men were fighting with swords in the pub we were just thrown out of," Luca trembled.

"And why Jean Fleury—the real Jean Fleury—is trying to kill us," Enzo reminded them.

"I think that's mainly because Tony stole his treasure map," Piccola whispered to Guillermo.

"I don't understand what you're all excited about. People have always fought with swords. And Jean Fleury's always tried to kill everyone in his path. He's nothing but a pillaging pirate. But he'll pay for what he did to my ship. We'll meet again, and when we do we'll dance the forbidden dance. The dance of—"

The kids all looked at each other and then back at the mad man.

"Uh, Juan? Maybe take it down a notch or two?" Piccola advised.

"Yes, if that means 'calm down' then let's all calm down with all the crazy talk." He took a series of deep breaths. "By the way, I'd still like to meet the man who constructed this ship. She looks like the work of Poseidon himself." He ran his hand against the smooth rail approvingly. "Say, I'm going to finish up the hull and find me the bar on this thing." He headed down the galley steps.

"*Madonna mia*! How are we ever going to get back?" Mario trembled.

Piccola fidgeted with her stack of *inflecto* papers, deep in thought. "For every action there is an equal and opposite reaction," she finally said, unsure of herself.

"That's an Albert Einstein quote," Tony said, sure of himself.

"Isaac Newton," Piccola corrected. "If that time machine worked one way, it must work the other way too."

"Oh, and that's from all your professional experience working with time machines?" Enzo asked as he mounted his portrait on the wall.

For a few seconds Guillermo, Piccola, Luca and Tony lost their train of thought, taken aback by the unexplained portrait of big-chinned Enzo.

Finally Guillermo refocused and lowered his voice to make sure Juan Cruz wouldn't hear, "At least we know that treasure map really is real, and the treasure's still likely to be there. If we can get our hands on it before we time warp back—"

"*If* we can time warp back at all," Mario interrupted him.

"Well, I got us here, so count on me to start finding our way back to the present," Piccola said. She lowered her voice. "Let's just find that treasure first."

Guillermo placed one hand on the wheel and looked the crew up and down. "Full steam ahead! I mean, full sail."

"Where to, captain?" Tony asked as Juan made his way back up the galley steps.

"Good question."

"Africa!" Juan bellowed as he delighted in a deep breath of salty air.

—Chapter 7—

The Great, Great, Great, Great, GREAT Escape...

It was dark on the *Grande Infante* as she pushed across the Strait of Gibraltar, gently rocking up and down on the calm waters. The moon had slid behind the clouds and Guillermo lay sound asleep, his head nested comfortably between two prongs of the ship's wheel. Luca, Enzo, Tony and Mario slumbered deeply on the nearby benches. For pillows they used stacks of papers they'd collected from down in the cabin. Juan Cruz produced a symphony of jungle sounds with every snoring breath from the forecastle deck.

Two hours of excitedly recounting the night's adventures and two days without sleep had taken its toll on the young crew. Only Piccola sat awake, inquisitively rummaging through the piles of yellow envelopes she'd discovered in the room with the bicycles. Her candle eventually ran out of wax and she rested her head back on the bench. When she next opened her eyes the sun was high above and they were close to land.

"Wake up! Guillermo, wake up," she implored, shaking her brother.

"Huh?" His head sprang up from the wheel, which had left a red streak across his face. "Wow, guys, wake up! I think we've drifted across the whole Strait." He swung the rudder around.

"That must be Morocco," Tony said, pointing to the coastline off their portside. "Or whatever Morocco was in 1497."

"I've never been to Africa before," Mario said while briefly—but unsuccessfully—trying out a small stretching routine to greet the new day. "Actually, I've never been anywhere before."

"Me neither," Enzo and Luca said in unison.

"Did a rhino board the ship while I was asleep?" Mario asked.

"That's Juan snoring," Piccola said. "He kept waking me up."

"I should wake him up." Guillermo headed over toward Juan. "He said he wanted to get out on the other side. And this is the other side."

Guillermo nudged Juan who inhaled deeply and emitted another jungle sound. Guillermo tried again. "Juan, I think we've reached Africa."

Juan leapt up, "It would take a dozen eggs to make that horse gallop!" He got his bearings and scanned the coastline before turning back to Guillermo. "Did I talk in my sleep again?"

Everyone nodded.

"Well, never mind that. This is the place. If you get me in a little closer I'll swim up onto that beach," he said, pointing toward an empty stretch of sand while walking over to the rest of the crew.

"Will you ever be able to go back home?" Piccola asked, relieved that Juan's frame blocked out the sun beating down on her.

"Sure, I'll do a little gambling here and then go back and pay off the police. That's how things are done here." He put his catcher's-mitt-sized hands on both their shoulders. "You are braver than you know."

"You were brave first," Piccola reminded him.

Juan extended his hand for Guillermo to shake. "We are friends," he said before saluting the whole crew and then diving into the water from the top deck. Moments later he surfaced, coughing up water and holding his chest in pain. The kids recoiled, hoping he was OK. Juan struggled to speak for a few seconds but then sheepishly looked up, "You know, your ship could really use a seadog for disembarkation purposes." He started to swim toward the shore but then stopped and peered up one last time. "*Amigos,* may the sea always treat you like sailors!" They watched him paddle in like a wounded sea cow.

The sun's rays fired down on the deck as the crew regrouped at the helm. It was blisteringly hot and the air was stagnant but the current of the Strait carried the ship westward, toward the open Atlantic. The paler turquoises of the Mediterranean mixed with the darker blues of the ocean, and the winds slowly picked up.

Guillermo surveyed the horizon through his telescope. There were no storms or pirates or any other threats in sight. The African coastline was dotted with stubby olive trees, pointed cypresses and towering palms. Their different shades of green contrasted starkly with the red hue of the soil. Three melodious seagulls flew low behind the stern, conversing in cheerful notes. It was the first time in days that none of the crew felt endangered or on the run. Guillermo stretched his arms and legs and straightened out the captain's uniform he'd borrowed from the wardrobe downstairs. "Tony, are you sure you can get us all the way to the Canary Islands? They must be a thousand miles from here."

"My father let me navigate his boat all the way to Marsala and back once. And I never got lost. I just plotted the course on my iPad and followed the line."

"Marsala's only an hour from Pizzolungo, straight down the coast," Luca said. "Anyone can navigate there from Pizzolungo, you just have to follow the shoreline."

"That's true," Enzo confirmed. "In gym class Marco Catalina told me he went there and back, and he's so dimwitted that he's still trying to learn the colors."

"In Marco's defense, some of those colors are complicated," Mario said. "A lot of them look really similar. Take red and cinnamon, for example. Or orange and peach. Or—"

Everyone eyed him angrily.

"We're back in time, there is no Internet, and your iPad isn't going to be helpful." Guillermo looked at Tony squarely, "And the Canaries are half an ocean away."

Tony sighed, "Maybe you're right. All I know is that we need to go south, and then keep going south. But I've never tried anything like this before. I'm only twelve."

"How are we on food and drink?" Guillermo asked Mario.

"We have enough pasta for at least ten days, and sauce for about half that time. No shortage of H_2O."

"Unless you eat it all, Six-to-Four," Tony snickered at Mario.

"And if we're out here longer, there's always bacon," Luca said, eyeing Romeo.

Mario picked up Romeo and embraced him. "We'll pretend we didn't hear either of those comments."

Piccola poked her head up from the time machine that got them there, where she was searching for any clue that might get them back. "Why do you call Mario Six-to-Four?"

"Never mind," Mario said. "Captain, how long do you think this wind will be at our backs?" he continued, trying to change the subject.

"You don't know why Mario's called Six-to-Four?" Enzo asked Piccola, who shook her head, while Mario's complexion started to resemble a tomato. "Mario beat Carlo Guadagnolo, a 36-year-old barista, in the Pizzolungo annual ziti eating competition," Enzo continued trying to stifle his laugh.

Mario sunk down to the floor.

"He beat him *six* bowls to *four!*"

Piccola was puzzled as to why that should be so funny to everybody.

Luca took over the story, "He had already won, five bowls to four. He ate the sixth bowl because he was still hungry." Luca, Enzo and Tony all doubled over laughing. If Mario could have turned into water and dripped into the sea he would have happily done so.

"Well, I think it's pretty cool that Mario won first prize in a competition against someone three times his age. How many first place trophies do you guys have in your room?"

Luca, Enzo and Tony quieted down.

"That's what I thought," she continued. "Good for you Mario."

Mario sat up a little prouder. And fell in love a little deeper.

"All right guys, story time's over," the captain said. "Luca, I think you should prepare some of the cannons ahead of time, in case we run into any more danger. And Enzo, you should get back on guard duty. From the top yard of the mainmast we'll be able to spot danger, and land, much quicker."

"I guess this time I don't have to ask you what I can do," Piccola said as she stuck her head back under the time machine. The top chamber of the hourglass was no longer full, nor was the bottom empty. She watched as one grain of sand slid through the glass neck and fell into the collection of sand gathering below.

Guillermo noticed Piccola's mood darkening as she studied the hourglass. "What is it?" he asked.

"Not sure."

"Well, get back to it then."

That afternoon Mario emerged from the kitchen and the crew reunited on the deck. The pasta with sauce proved sufficient for lunch and dinner while sailing south. The sun had baked the ship's wooden frame so thoroughly that the scent of roasted pine held heavy in the air. At last the sun gave way to the evening sky. It was as if someone had turned off a giant heater.

Tony lay back on the deck. "I've never seen so many stars. You can see the entire Milky Way." He thought for a second. "And this is all he used, just the stars."

"Who are you talking about?" Luca asked.

"Prince Henry. The Navigator. He had a school in Lisbon in the 1400s where he taught people how to explore the world, and how to navigate using the stars. Back then there was no light pollution from the cities, and no TV or Internet to distract people, so they had plenty of time to study the stars. If I could go back in time, Prince Henry would be the first person I would want to meet."

Piccola smirked at him. Finally the light bulb went on above his head. "*Oh Dio mio,*" he said jumping to his feet, "what year are we in again?"

"1497," everyone yelled.

Tony slouched back down. "The Prince died in 1460."

"I wonder what was happening around here in 1497? I mean, what *is* happening around here... now," Enzo mused.

"Well," Luca said, "in 1492 Columbus sailed the ocean blue."

"True," Guillermo nodded.

"From history class I think I remember something about an Inquisition around that time. But I'm not sure what everyone was inquiring about," Enzo added.

"Hey guys," Guillermo asked, "do you remember that old painting in my house? The one above the living room sofa?"

Piccola and Luca indicated their familiarity with the painting. Enzo, Tony and Mario shook their heads.

"Well there's this old painting there of a sea captain. My father told me his name was Lorenzo Infante, our relative from like 500 years ago, which would mean from around this time. I don't know too much about him, except he was a courageous hero who mastered the ocean at a young age. But one story I do know is pretty crazy." Guillermo lay back and gazed at the stars. "It's a little scary, so maybe I shouldn't even tell you guys."

Those words of course made it impossible for him *not* to tell the story.

"All right, all right, I'll tell you what my father told me."

"I've never heard this story before," Piccola said.

"That's because you were too small."

"Tell it, tell it," Mario pleaded.

"So apparently this Lorenzo Infante, my great, great, great, great, great grandfather, or whatever he was, was a nobleman and the best sea captain in all of Florence. And the

Governor asked him for a big favor, which nobody was to know about. He asked him to secretly travel on a small boat to somewhere in the Adriatic Sea to spy on their rivals, the Venetians. It was the middle of winter, and extremely cold. He was all alone one night when the temperature dropped so quickly that he thought he would freeze to death."

"Freezing to death sounds better than boiling to death," Mario proclaimed, still perspiring.

"Lorenzo had already started preparing for the worst," Guillermo continued. "And then his little boat bumped into something far bigger. At first he thought it was land. It was so foggy that it was hard to tell. But then he realized it was a much bigger ship he had banged up against. He waited for a few minutes to hear who was on board but he didn't hear a sound. So eventually he climbed onto the ship to look for a warmer place to stay for the night. He didn't see a single soul. It was completely dark as he tiptoed across the main deck, shivering.

And then a timid voice from the darkness whispered, 'You're... alone?'

Lorenzo spun around, his heart pounding. A frail, old man had lit a candle and was observing him.

At first Lorenzo thought the man must be a Venetian, a Venetian who would kill him for trying to spy on them. But from the man's voice it seemed that *he* was even more frightened than Lorenzo.

The man told Lorenzo that his whole crew had gone missing. And he had only been the ship's cleaner, and didn't know how to maneuver the vessel himself to get back home.

Lorenzo asked the man where he thought his crew might have gone. All the cleaner could say was that everyone had disappeared some days before, and from time to time he heard banging and rattling chains coming from the depths of the hull, always at night. But he always waited for daybreak

93

to investigate and there was never anyone there. Just then the cleaner hushed Lorenzo and told him to listen. Both men heard a faint rattling from the hull."

"I don't think I like this story anymore," Mario interrupted.

"So Lorenzo, the brave warrior that he was, convinced the cleaner to show him to the ship's hull right then. The cleaner led the way down the stairs, his single candle illuminating the way. It got warmer and warmer as they descended the long staircase. And then just as they reached the bottom the candle went out."

"Oh no," Piccola covered her mouth.

"Lorenzo asked the man to re-light the candle but he didn't answer. For a few seconds all was silent. Then Lorenzo heard the man reversing up the stairs. As he ascended he started laughing. Not an ordinary laugh. A deep, evil laugh.

The cleaner yelled into the darkness that there was nothing to fear and that Lorenzo was all alone, not with any army.

Laughter echoed through the dark hull. Then Lorenzo heard a door slam and he knew he'd been locked down in the dungeon of the ship, with no light, no windows, little air and an unknown number of people who he doubted were going to be very hospitable. He drew his sword but didn't know where to swing it because it was so dark."

"Please say he doesn't die. I don't want him to die," Mario whimpered.

"Quiet down, Six-to-Four," Luca said, putting his hand over Mario's mouth to muzzle him.

"Just then a candle was lit," Guillermo continued. "And then another. Soon forty small flames burned. And then the room was light enough for Lorenzo to see the entire Venetian naval crew. They had tricked him into coming onto their ship and had surrounded him deep in the hull.

They told Lorenzo they had been waiting to ambush what they thought would be a hundred Florentine soldiers. They couldn't understand why the Governor of Florence had sent one man out alone. Then the Venetian boss ordered his deputy to kill Lorenzo.

But Lorenzo reacted fast and swung his sword at the Venetian closest to him. He jumped over a table and ran to the far end of the hull with everyone slowly following. The Venetians knew he had nowhere to run, and nowhere to hide. But what they didn't know, what they couldn't have known, was that Lorenzo had a special tool on him that allowed him to escape."

"What kind of tool? Like a weapon or something?" Luca asked, keeping his hand firmly pressed up against Mario's mouth.

"No, my father said it was a round piece of metal powered by heavy-duty springs. If you undid a latch the springs would rocket forward. He used it to literally punch a hole right through the wooden boards of the ship. He split the hull planks apart right in front of the Venetians' eyes and as water began to gush into the ship it further ruptured the hole. Lorenzo eventually swam to safety through the hole before the ship sank, with most of the Venetians on board."

"I saw Popeye do something like that once with his bare fist," Tony noted.

"Legend has it that a very special friend of Lorenzo's made that tool for him," Guillermo continued. "When he got back to Florence he suffered from pneumonia for weeks because of the frigid water but he became a hero for having sunk the biggest ship in the Venetian fleet. That's why the Governor commissioned the painting of him that now hangs in our living room."

"Sounds made up," Enzo said.

Piccola flicked Enzo's ear, "If my father told it then it must be true."

Everyone leaned back and let their imaginations wander. Later that evening Guillermo pulled himself to his wearied feet, grabbed a lantern and headed down to the library to lug out and snuggle up with 'Magister Mari'. He read voraciously, trying to apply everything in the tome to the reality of the magnificent vessel he was championing. His only wonderful distraction being the waves that bumped up against the *Grande Infante's* side. Nobody up on deck spoke again that night. The star-laden sky provided the best nightlight anyone had ever slept with.

At daybreak Guillermo found Tony on the forecastle deck anxiously staring at the treasure map. He put an arm on his shoulder. A few seconds passed before Tony spoke, "This is really tough. I don't know what all these numbers mean on the map. They must be coordinates of some kind. If I could get on the Internet I'd solve this in no time. But all we have to go on are guesses. And the ocean's a pretty big place. I was thinking, maybe we should turn back."

Guillermo turned over the suggestion in his mind. Then suddenly something caught his eye on the horizon and he grabbed his telescope. A group of tall ships were just visible way out in the distance. "Or we could just ask for directions."

—Chapter 8—

Superstition and a Spider Named Liza

The *Grande Infante* cautiously approached a flotilla of four caravel ships. Luca, Tony, Mario and Piccola stood at the ready next to the cannons, prepared to fire at the first sign of danger. Enzo vigilantly monitored the situation from high up on the mainmast. Guillermo steered.

The ships were small in comparison to the *Grande Infante*. None was longer than 100 feet in length, and no more than a third of that across. Their foremasts and mizzenmasts rose only a little higher than schoolyard flagpoles, and their mainmasts were far shorter than the humblest mast on the *Grande Infante*.

The decks of the four ships were loaded with about 50 sailors each. Most of the men sported thick stubble and they all wore black berets and gold embroidered red vests. Many had polished swords clasped to their belts. The flagship caravel nudged past the other vessels and pulled up right under the nose of the *Grande Infante*. The ship was called the *São Gabriel*.

"Greetings from the crew of the *Grande Infante*," Enzo screamed down from the mast. "We have some questions but first we'd like to know if you are pirates."

The men on the ship conversed among themselves before responding. "*Bom dia a todos!* No young sailor, we are not pirates. We are on a mission to find a new trade route to Asia."

"*Allora*, that's a relief," Enzo yelled. "OK, let me inform my crew."

Enzo hollered down to Guillermo that it was safe to engage and then climbed down from the mast. Guillermo relayed the message to the crew at the cannons. The kids convened on the main deck and stared down at the seamen two stories below on their small ships. The sailors continued to speak intensely among themselves.

"Would you be able to help us with some directions?" Guillermo called down, interrupting them. "We'd like to sail to the Canary Islands from here and we need help navigating because they seem really far away."

A portly man with a trimmed beard and a long cloak pushed his way through the crowd on the deck of the *São Gabriel* and gazed up at Guillermo. "Son, I'd like to speak to the captain of your vessel. Are you sailing with charters from the King of Spain or the King of Portugal?"

"He *is* the captain," Piccola shouted down, pointing to Guillermo.

"We're not sailing on anyone's behalf. We're just on a trip by ourselves and then we're heading home. But first we need some help with directions," Guillermo replied.

The men below again conversed among themselves.

"Permission to board, young lad?" the portly, bearded sailor called up. "Just me and my boatswain?"

The kids looked at each other hesitantly.

"I don't know," Luca said. "What if they're just pretending to be nice to board us but once they do they'll throw us into the sea and sail off with our ship?"

Guillermo contrasted the tone of the man's voice who was requesting permission to board with that of Gascon's when they first met. Nobody on the *São Gabriel* seemed to possess any of the antagonisms or hidden agendas that the pirates did, Guillermo assessed. He hoped his intuition was right. "Permission granted, but no swords," he called down.

The crew of the *São Gabriel* chuckled at the instructions being given to them by a troop of pre-teens. "Throw us down the sea dog," the boatswain ordered.

"We have to get one of those," Mario said to Guillermo.

Luca lowered a rope to the men, "This is all we have."

The two middle-aged men grimaced and then took off their vests and began climbing up.

"Maybe we shouldn't tell anyone we're from the future," Piccola quickly advised. "Let's just get some directions and be on our way." Everyone agreed.

"Ahoy young sailor, I'm Captain Vasco da Gama and this is my boatswain Pero de Alenquer. We sail on royal orders from the King of Portugal. Now… who are you?"

Tony nearly lost his balance as his crewmates all observed each other with mouths ajar.

"Are you really Vasco da Gama? I mean, like, the real Vasco da Gama?" Guillermo struggled to even say the words.

"Why, have you met other sailors with the same name?" Da Gama was surprised by the question. So surprised in fact, he performed the sign of the holy cross and spit into the sea after a few words to the Man Upstairs. "It's unlucky to have the same name as a stranger."

"Captain da Gama is a very superstitious man," Alenquer told the kids.

"We meant," Tony interjected, "*the* da Gama, ya know, who discovered the first sea routes from Europe to India?"

Alenquer and da Gama seemed confused. "Well let's not jump to any conclusions. We just set sail from Lisbon yesterday and we aren't sure what we'll end up finding. We have a long, long voyage ahead."

Tony turned to his friends and whispered "That's right, it's 1497, and da Gama's just leaving on his first exploration. He doesn't even know what he's going to find." He rubbed his hands together excitedly, "But we do."

"Vasco, if I may," Tony began.

"That's *Captain* da Gama," Alenquer interjected firmly.

Luca punched Tony's arm. "You *idiota*, show some respect."

"S*cusa, scusa*. Captain da Gama, it's a real pleasure to meet you," Tony tried again. "I did a report about you at school last year." He thought for a second. "I mean, I'm planning on writing a report about you if you end up finding the sea route to India... or something like that."

Da Gama didn't appear exceedingly interested in school reports and proved that fact by opening his mouth wide and yawning into Tony's face. As big a fan as Tony was, he was less a fan of da Gama's breath and backed away accordingly. "I would like to understand what kind of ship this is, and where the real captain is. You all seem a bit too small to be in command of such a Herculean vessel."

"That's what *everyone* keeps saying," Mario butted in.

"It's a long story," Guillermo explained, "but we *are* in command of the ship, and we just need to figure out how to get to the Canary Islands. We are meant to pick something up there and then we are going straight home to Italy."

Da Gama squinted in order to see all the way down to the stern of the *Grande Infante*. "Right, to Florence. I've heard great things about Florence."

"No, not Florence." Guillermo and da Gama uttered the name *'Florence'* at the same time. "We're from Pizzolungo. In Sicily."

The kids all watched da Gama in silence for what seemed like an eternity. They looked at each other nervously as da Gama's face began to turn purple.

"You said a word at the same time as him," Alenquer explained. "He can't talk until you say his name."

"Why isn't he breathing?" Piccola asked, her own face starting to redden with anxiety.

"I told you. He's very superstitious."

"Vasco da Gama!" all the kids yelled at once.

Da Gama inhaled as much oxygen as he could swallow and steadied himself. "It was your flag I was referring to," he said, pointing to the flag flying off the stern as his complexion returned to its original color. The flag was white with a large red symbol in the middle— sort of a cross between a flower and a sword. "I held court with the Governor of Florence once when he visited Lisbon. Dreadfully boring man, but sending a fleet of kids out into the ocean like this certainly makes him a bit more interesting." He turned back to the kids who tried their best to follow the conversation.

"We just want to travel from here to the Canary Islands," Guillermo said, "and if you can tell us how to get there, that would really be helpful."

"Well young sailor, there are over a dozen islands in that archipelago. And I'm not in the business of doling out navigation advice for free. These days there are a lot of people who would pay a lot of bullion to get their hands on this sort of information. I'm sailing with direct orders from His Majesty King Manuel, and we are not to share our maps with anyone, not even—"

"Captain," Guillermo said, "sorry to interrupt, but you've got this all wrong."

Da Gama straightened his posture and reached for the small dagger on his belt. He removed it and stepped toward Guillermo.

Quickly realizing that da Gama wasn't used to being interrupted, much less spoken back to, Guillermo began retreating, afraid for his life: "I mean, Captain, we haven't made our request very clear. We don't want to see your maps, we have our own. I'm sorry!"

"This will only take a moment," da Gama said as he came swiftly at Guillermo with his knife. Guillermo covered his face with his hands as da Gama proceeded past him to the side of the ship where he bent down and carefully maneuvered his weapon.

"Alenquer, my jar," da Gama ordered while rising to his feet. Alenquer, apparently with a jar always at the ready, rushed over to da Gama who turned around with a spider on his knife and carefully slipped it into the jar. He closed the air-slitted lid with his free hand. "Good luck to find a spider on another man's ship. I shall name her Liza."

"People are so weird in the 1400s," Mario whispered to Piccola.

"Believe me, not much has changed in that department," she replied, eyeing the chubby chef.

Guillermo collected himself again. "We just want to know how we can sail from point A, here, to point B, there, without getting lost." He paused briefly. "Hold on, why don't we bring you our map from down below."

The rest of the crew gasped. Piccola was about to protest the suggestion but Guillermo looked at her strictly.

"Tony, come get the map with me," he grabbed Tony's arm and ushered him toward the cabin stairs. "We'll be right back."

Da Gama bit his lip and elevated his cheeks. He was as visibly excited about getting his hands on Guillermo's map as the other kids were horrified about it.

"Wanna meet Romeo, my pet pig?" Mario asked da Gama and Alenquer, practicing the concept of 'small talk' that his mother had been teaching him.

"It's bad luck to have a pig on a ship. Even I know that," Alenquer said as Mario furrowed his brow with worry.

Down below deck Guillermo spoke quickly. "Da Gama's not going to help us out using his map and we obviously can't show him our treasure map because he could steal it."

Tony was relieved to hear those words.

"And we can't bring him down to the map room because then he'll see all the other things we have on board and, as Luca suggested, he might try and steal our whole ship, like Fleury wanted to."

"So what are you suggesting?"

"Well, if we match the location on the treasure map to the map on your iPad then we can just show him the iPad map, which doesn't indicate any treasure. Do you still have any battery life in that thing?"

"Sure, it's connected to the mini solar charger."

"Can you bring up a map without being online?"

"Ah, yeah," Tony said, implying by his tone that Guillermo needed to brush up on his application basics. "The maps are all preloaded and cached. But we won't be able to zoom in much while we're offline. And it won't indicate where we are now."

"That's fine, we just need to navigate to the general area. Once we're there we can try and figure out those exact coordinates on the map."

Tony looked Guillermo in the eyes, "Don't you think da Gama is going to ask what this iPad is?"

"I'll handle that."

Guillermo and Tony pulled out the treasure map and examined the shape of the island nearest to the depiction of the gold bars. They compared it to the map on Tony's iPad.

"Tenerife," they both said at the exact same time. Guillermo imagined how freaked out da Gama would be by his and Tony's overlapping words.

Tony returned the treasure map to his back pocket. "I hope this is a good idea. Maps back in that time period… I mean, in this time period, were heavily guarded secrets. They held the key to a country's riches."

Mario was halfway through explaining the recipe for Chicken Milanese to the Portuguese explorers when Guillermo and Tony returned to the deck.

"Are you kids trying to get yourselves killed?" da Gama yelled as his eyebrows nearly collided with his hairline. "Always enter the main deck right foot first."

Guillermo and Tony ignored da Gama's advice on cabin footwork. "Captain da Gama, we can use our map and you can show us how to navigate to the island of Tenerife." Guillermo showed da Gama the iPad. The screen displayed the map of the world. The kids held their breath.

Da Gama and Alenquer stared at the machine, completely perplexed. They looked at each other, then back at the screen, then back at each other.

"What is this… strange instrument?" da Gama asked.

"It's a map of the whole planet," Guillermo explained. "The Governor of Florence gave it to us. He told us he was the only person in the world who had it." Guillermo thought for a second. "One of his, um, top confidants, a Signore

104

Lorenzo Infante, secretly prepared it for him. I know the Governor admires your seafaring credentials Captain da Gama so I'm sure he wouldn't mind if we let you see it… in the event, of course, that we are able to inform him that you helped us navigate to Tenerife."

Da Gama steadied himself against the rail of the deck. "A map of the whole planet you say?" He put his arm around Guillermo, his eyes transfixed on the map. "If this is what you say it is then it's worth an absolute fortune, the sum of the entire Portuguese treasury."

"Even more," Alenquer suggested.

Da Gama grabbed his spider jar. "You're already bringing me luck, Liza. Now we can ensure we find our way to India by sea," da Gama added, running his finger southwest from Portugal, around the bulge of West Africa, then downwards through the southern Atlantic and around the Cape of Good Hope. From the southernmost tip of Africa he traced his finger up the coast of East Africa, past the islands of Zanzibar and Madagascar, and finally across the Indian Ocean to India. "If this map is correct then our presumptions were imperfect; we can save weeks if we cross the Indian Ocean here," he said, pointing to the screen.

Alenquer nodded in astonishment.

"The map is correct," Guillermo assured him.

"Young man, I don't know who you are or how you and your friends ended up on a ship working for my friend the Governor of Florence. And I don't know how this square map box came into being." He touched the iPad. "But today the Good Lord is obviously shining down on my voyage and the welfare of the Portuguese Crown. It is destiny that our paths have crossed. And your request is our command. You wish to travel to Tenerife? We shall make sure you get there." Da Gama stared at the heavens and quietly murmured,

"*Obrigado, Obrigado.*" Then he spit twice for good luck, narrowly missing Luca who jumped out of the line of fire.

"Captain," Alenquer interrupted, "Shall I summon the Chief Navigator?"

"*Si,*" da Gama nodded, "and send for the Master Artist, too."

Moments later two men hurried up the rope. The first was João de Coimbra, who clenched a bulging bag in his teeth as he hoisted himself on board. He was plump and had beady eyes and elevated, thin eyebrows. After coming aboard, right foot first of course, he spoke privately with da Gama and then looked over at the kids.

Tony leaned in close to Guillermo, "They don't even realize that they can shift the map around if they want."

Guillermo hushed him, "I think they're getting more than they could ever dream of."

The second man up the rope was Javier Nuñes, a tall and slender man with pointy boots and a ruffled shirt. His soft hands seemed far more practiced at swinging a paintbrush than a sword. He removed a canvas strapped to his back and extracted a set of paints and brushes from his carry pouch.

"Copy it," da Gama instructed Nuñes, pointing to the iPad screen. "For our eyes only. The last thing we need is for the Spanish Crown to get wind of this, put a hex on us, and start funding expeditions to the remaining unknown territories." He pointed at the North American landmass.

Nuñes carefully observed the map and shook his head in disbelief. "With this we'll change the world." He rolled up his sleeves, "India will be ours."

"I've never seen him help a foreign party before," de Coimbra told the kids, "but if the Captain asks me to train someone in high-seas navigation then train them in high seas navigation I shall." He removed two devices from his bag and laid them side-by-side on the deck next to the helm. "It's time for a master class on the mariner's astrolabe and the cross-staff."

Luca looked at Tony, "You're our navigator, don't you already know how to use these kinds of things?"

"Um, no, I've always used GPS."

That evening after bidding farewell to one of the most famous—and superstitious—explorers in the history of seafaring, and with the western coast of Morocco far off to their portside, Guillermo held the *Grande Infante's* rudder as steady as he could. The sea was calm and the air was thick. He could taste the salt on his lips from the breeze.

Luca grasped Tony's feet to keep him planted in one place. "I can't get a good reading," Tony called down. He clutched the brass astrolabe, trying not to move. But even the smallest swells made it difficult to accurately line up the Pole Star with the horizon to get a latitudinal reading. He held it by its ring at the top, leaving it hanging at a vertical plane. He tried his hardest to get a reading off the outer degree scale.

"Mario," Luca yelled, "Come hold me steady."

Mario wrapped his beefy arms around Luca tightly. "Any better now?" Mario called up to Tony.

"A little, but I'm still rocking too much."

Enzo and Piccola ran over to help.

"Ouch!" Luca yelled.

"Sorry," Enzo said as he retracted his chin from Luca's shoulder blade.

"*Bella*, you smell like a freshly-picked tulip," Mario said as Piccola crushed up against him in the huddle.

"And *you* smell like a giant head of garlic, so stop talking," Piccola retorted.

"Got it," Tony yelled loud enough for the captain to hear. "We're at 34 degrees north, so we still have six degrees to go before turning west, according to de Coimbra."

"*Va bene!*" Guillermo said. "We'll get another reading tomorrow using the sun."

"And we can match that up to the numbers on the cross-staff," Tony said. "It was nice of da Gama to leave us with his spare instruments."

Guillermo strolled over to the crew exuding happiness. "We did well today. I think we'll find that treasure. And hopefully soon, because I'm ready to go home."

Everyone looked at Piccola. "I'm working on it," she said with a hint of trepidation in her voice.

"Wait, shhh!" Enzo said nervously, his spine straightening as he spoke. Everyone quieted down. Enzo cupped his right ear to amplify his hearing. The breeze came from the north, and it carried with it a few barely audible but unmistakably human sounds.

"Da Gama?" Tony asked.

"Da Gama's ships went ahead to the south today," Guillermo responded, swallowing slowly.

"So who else is out there?" Luca whispered.

—Chapter 9—

So Nice to See You Again

The first rays of pale yellow light began to sneak across the eastern sky. Even though the crew knew they were upwind of the other vessel, they had stayed silent all night, communicating only in whispers and hand gestures. Enzo had volunteered to stand guard on the mizzenmast, as he had the keenest eyesight. And besides, no one else had volunteered. If he listened really carefully, he was able to make out a sound or two every once in a while. A laugh or a good spirited hoot. Nothing more than a few people out at sea having a good time, he concluded.

Just before daybreak Enzo descended from the mast and woke Guillermo up. The captain groggily opened his eyes and appealed for a five-minute snooze. Piccola flicked her brother's ear to jolt him awake. He threw on his captain's uniform and shuffled over to the side railing to greet the new day. He extended his telescope and looked out, observing the sapphire-blue water sparkling in the early-morning sun. He followed it across the horizon when all of a sudden he froze and almost dropped the scope. At the other end of the lens was a man on a ship, hand cupped over his forehead to block the sun, squinting straight at *him*. Guillermo and the other man stared at each other briefly.

"Fleury!" Guillermo yelled.

"*Ze* sailors of Pizzolungo!" Fleury sputtered out with a hoarse, early-morning voice. "So nice to see you again," he snarled between clenched teeth. "Gascon, deploy the crew!"

Gascon rushed hammock to hammock poking his men awake with the handle of his sword. The disturbed crew stumbled into early-morning action, tightening the ropes on their square-rigged cog sails and tacking starboard, straight at the *Grande Infante*.

"I'm gonna rip that silver right outta his teeth," Gascon mumbled.

Over on the *Grande Infante* Tony checked his back pocket, "They must be after the map."

"They're a ways out," Luca said hurriedly. "Why don't we feed them a volley of iron for breakfast? The cannons are at the ready captain."

"I'm not sure. If we turn broadside to aim the cannons it'll slow us down, and they might catch up."

"If we sink them, they'll never catch up." Luca's eyes were bulging, "Let em' swim with the sharks!"

"*Andiamo!* Sink them!" Enzo yelled.

"Iron for breakfast!" Mario roared.

Guillermo sought Piccola's advice but she was non-committal.

"*Va bene,* engage the enemy," Guillermo gave the order to fire as he steered the ship to the left. "Enzo, get back up on the mizzenmast, we need to come around sharply; Luca, Tony, Mario, Piccola: prepare to fire from portside." The boys on the cannon brigade hopped on their bikes and pedaled toward the cabin stairs. Piccola ran behind them.

Down below Piccola lit three cannon fuses, one after the other.

"We'll cut through their ship like butter," Mario said.

The brigade braced themselves for the backfire. BOOM, BOOM, BOOM! The *Grande Infante* was thrust backwards by the power of the thunderous explosions that shook and rattled the entire ship. Despite Piccola's firm grip on a wooden beam, she ended up in the corridor on her back once again. The breeze cleared the smoke quickly and the crew examined the situation. The sea where the cannonballs had entered was frothing wildly, sending wave after wave of white water radiating in every direction. But none of the shots had landed even close to their intended target. The *Black Bass* was unharmed and still charging.

"It's like trying to score a goal from two fields away," Tony said glumly.

"Let's try again," Luca shouted, "we still have three more cannons fully loaded."

Piccola hobbled over to the cannons and lit the fuses. She dashed back out into the corridor, embracing the inevitable. BOOM, BOOM, BOOM! The smoke cleared and the kids peered out from the gun ports. This time the cannonballs had landed even farther from their target.

Fleury ran up and down his forecastle deck waving his hat and barking orders to his crew. Then he stopped and pointed his sword at the *Grande Infante*. "Those little snappers have the nerve to send *me* a warning? Full speed ahead!"

Beside the cannons on the *Grande Infante* Luca struggled to swallow, "Fleury probably thinks we sent him a warning."

Tony and Mario nodded fearfully.

"Let's move on to plan B," Luca continued.

"What's plan B?" Mario asked, using the sleeve of his uniform to mop off his sweat.

"Plan B is called 'ask the captain what to do'."

The crew raced for the helm.

Fleury's ship pushed to within a mile of the *Grande Infante*. "Prepare *ze* boarding party. And bring out *ze land dog*," Fleury winked at Gascon. Gascon winked back accidentally with an eye spasm and hurried below deck. He returned a minute later with two other pirates; they carried a long wooden ladder on their shoulders.

"We finished building this just in time, *patron*," one of the pirates said to the boatswain.

Gascon was too excited to contain himself, "I'm gonna shred their organs with my blade."

On the *Grande Infante* Guillermo put down his telescope, "*Oh Dio mio*," he said aloud as the cannon brigade ran toward him. "Terrible news. They're coming in fast. And now they have a ladder to board us."

"Do you think they would really hurt us?" Mario asked. "I mean, we really haven't done anything wrong…"

"Except for stealing their treasure map," Piccola recalled.

"And shooting a lot of cannonballs at them," Enzo added.

Guillermo thought for a second and then lowered his voice, "Remember in the 2nd grade when we used to play castles and knights?"

Luca looked at him uneasily.

Minutes later the *Black Bass* pulled up alongside the *Grande Infante*. "You didn't *sink* you would outrun us did you, you little snappers?" Fleury called out.

Gascon ran his sword one final time across a sharpening stone.

"Yep, he's definitely gonna cut us," Mario cried as he and Romeo scurried down the cabin stairs.

Fleury and Gascon shared a confused glance, unable to make out a single sight or sound up on the *Grande Infante's* deck. "They must be hidin'," Gascon said.

Three pirates angled the *land dog* from the *Black Bass* up to the main deck of the *Grande Infante*. Fleury gave the command to ascend.

"Not yet," Guillermo whispered to his troops, peeking out from a slit in the wood of the deck railing. He looked over to the galley steps. Mario quietly surfaced from down below and flashed the captain a thumbs up sign.

Five, then six, then seven pirates started making their way up the ladder.

"Now!" Guillermo commanded.

Mario emerged from the galley and steadily crossed the deck. "You missed our breakfast so here's lunch," he screamed as he emptied a huge pot overboard. "Pasta with no sauce... oh, and hold the pasta! *Bon appétit!*"

The pot full of scalding water cascaded onto the men climbing up the ladder. They tumbled downwards into cooler waters, hollering in pain.

The crew huddled together and hoisted a 42-pound cannonball up onto the railing of the top deck. Guillermo and Fleury locked eyes. Fleury took in the disarray of his men. He grimaced back at Guillermo.

"Bombs away," Guillermo ordered. The kids pushed the cannonball over the rail. It plummeted thirty feet down, slicing through the air and crashing straight through the deck of the *Black Bass*. The iron ball smashed downwards and out through the hull, sending a geyser of seawater shooting up into the lower bowels of the ship.

"Well, that's another way to do it I suppose," one pirate said to another.

"Full sail ahead!" Guillermo commanded with swashbuckling enthusiasm. The crew bolted for the sails.

Fleury watched as his ship took on water from the gaping hole left by the cannonball while the *Grande Infante* picked up wind and got smaller and smaller in the distance.

Gascon approached his boss. He was so frazzled that he spoke without a single twitch of the eye and so scared to say the wrong thing that he spoke barely above a whisper. "I've got the men patching up the hull now. She should be ready to sail by tomorrow."

"Just make sure *ze* wood is good," Fleury said, almost under his breath.

"Sir?"

"*Zose* kids will walk *ze* plank. Every one of *zem*!"

—Chapter 10—

The Compass

The crew of the *Grande Infante* slurped pasta from the ceramic bowl. The salty breeze that pushed up onto the deck tickled the back of Guillermo's throat. Enzo swore he could discern a faint scent of jasmine in the air, indicating they might be getting close to land.

"Guys we have a serious problem," Mario announced. "We're running dangerously low on spaghetti and we're already out of fettuccini and linguini. This was the last of the sauce."

"A couple days ago you said we had enough pasta for ten days, and sauce for five," Luca said.

"Well, you know at night I get really hungry."

"Six-to-Four!" everybody said at once. Even Mario chuckled.

"We'll restock when we get to the Canary Islands," Guillermo promised.

"We'd better. You know a ship sails on the stomachs of its crew," Mario lectured. "If we ever get our hands on that treasure I'm going to buy myself the biggest kitchen in the world with the hugest supply of pasta ever! And saffron. *Lots* of saffron."

"Saffron is good," Guillermo agreed. The others also nodded their appreciation of saffron.

"*Allora, y*ou know how at home it's usually our mothers cooking?" Mario asked. "But in the famous restaurants and on cooking shows it's usually men behind the stove. I'm going to be one of those men. The kitchen at the restaurant where my father works is so small you can barely beat an egg without banging your elbow into someone's arm. One day we'll cook together in *my* big kitchen."

"If we get the treasure then I'll be able to go to one of the world's best maritime universities when I'm older and I'll become a professional navigator," Tony said. His eyes met Guillermo and Piccola's. "I mean, if there is anything left after we replace your father's ship."

"If there is a treasure, we should all be able to get whatever we want," Guillermo said.

Piccola remained quiet throughout the meal

"What is it?" Guillermo asked.

"Mama must be so worried by now."

"I know, all of our parents must be."

The crew continued to eat in silence until Enzo shot up excitedly, "Land!"

Everyone rushed starboard to get a glimpse.

"That must be the Canaries!" Tony said pointing to the collection of islands out in the distance and cross-checking them against the treasure map. "De Coimbra told us it would take two days if the Easterly winds cooperated, and I guess the Easterlies have cooperated."

The sails of the *Grande Infante* remained plump as the winds propelled the ship toward the islands.

"We should head due west to hit Tenerife," Tony instructed.

The captain cut the rudder to the right and the ship pushed across the crystal clear water. Enzo climbed up the foremast to stand lookout.

Tenerife was green along its coast but as its interior rose in elevation it turned rocky and arid. An enormous, snow-covered volcanic mountain rose in the interior. The mouth of a harbor came into sight and Guillermo steered toward it.

"Someday, I'll take Piccola here for our honeymoon," Mario whispered to Luca.

Luca shook his head in disbelief, "When will you realize she doesn't like you?"

Mario puffed out his chest, "I won't rest until she's mine."

"You rest after a nap."

As the *Grande Infante* approached the island's harbor Enzo hollered down from the mast, "Ships! Portside."

To the west, three ships had come around a hilly peninsula that jutted into the sea. They too were making their way into the Tenerife harbor.

Guillermo could see that Fleury's ship wasn't among the small fleet. He knew that it would have been impossible for Fleury to have beaten them to Tenerife, given the damage they had inflicted on the *Black Bass* and the sail size differentials between the two ships, but still... he knew Fleury was somewhere out there, and that he would not rest until he caught up with them.

"Start lowering the sails," Guillermo called up to Enzo while dispatching Tony and Mario to the other masts to bring down the sheets. "We should stay out in the open water until we're sure it's safe."

"Should I prepare a defensive position?" Luca asked, his heartbeat accelerating.

"Do it, and take Piccola to help." He quickly recalled a diagram he'd reviewed in 'Magister Mari'. "If we need to

117

fire, aim for their bows or sterns; they're the weakest parts of a ship."

Luca and Piccola rushed down into the cabin to restock and aim the cannons. Guillermo motioned for Enzo to stay up on the mast. He wanted to turn the ship broadside to better position the cannons in case their unexpected company proved to be trouble. And he wanted Enzo watching vigilantly from high above. They all waited with knotted stomachs as the ships approached.

"Hallelujah!" someone from the flagship cheerfully roared, "*Viva España, Viva Castile!*"

The sailors on all the ships exploded in gleeful celebration as they floated past the towering *Grande Infante*.

"Glorious Europe at last!" one yelled, looking up at Guillermo.

Guillermo watched the hundred or so sailors rushing about their decks preparing to dock. They were completely unaware that two children had cannons pointed right at them. They seemed too busy rejoicing to even care. Some of their arms were locked around each other and they formed a circle and danced, singing up to the heavens. A few waved to the kids but most were so excited to be arriving in Tenerife that they barely even noticed them.

"My brother once went on something called a 'booze cruise'," Luca said to Piccola. "Maybe that's what this is." She wasn't sure.

The ships—a 75-foot carrack and two smaller caravels—were even smaller than da Gama's, and appeared to have weathered a lot more time at sea. The carrack had three masts that supported five sails: three square cogs and two lateen mizzens. Off the bowsprit was a small spritsail. The caravels hung single lateens off their mizzens and just two square cogs up front.

Luca and Piccola ascended to the deck and Enzo came down from the mast. Twelve eyes met in confusion. "It's hard to say who those sailors are but they're definitely not pirates," Enzo said.

Everyone agreed.

"Tony," Guillermo suggested, "why don't you copy onto a piece of paper the treasure location coordinates listed on the map and then we can ask these sailors how to get there."

Tony grabbed a piece of paper and Piccola handed him the fountain pen.

"Captain, they might ask us why we want to go to that *exact* location," Tony said. "And I don't think the truth would serve us very well."

"We could tell them we're just going fishing there," Mario paused, "At that *exact* location. *"*

"Or that we're conducting oceanic research," Luca said, looking at the youthful crew.

"How about we say we were sailing with our parents but they fell off at that exact place, and now we want to go find them," Enzo offered.

"And we were able to write down these advanced coordinates to locate them but now we don't know what they mean?" Piccola asked, rolling her eyes.

"We'll think of something," Guillermo assured them.

With just a light breeze blowing, the *Grande Infante* had lost most of its forward momentum shortly after the crew had lowered the sails. Guillermo steered into port with none of the chaos that had faced him while docking in Gibraltar. When Luca released the anchor it pulled the ship to a final stop with little fanfare. The three smaller ships looked like toys next to the monstrous vessel from Pizzolungo.

At the port, the recently arrived sailors were spilling out of a small inn, still dancing and singing. One of them was kissing the ground repeatedly.

The crew of the *Grande Infante* poked its way into the crowd. "*Oye,* kids, have a drink," one of the sailors yelled.

Mario leapt up, "I'll have a Coke please."

The sailors didn't seem to understand Mario and turned away to continue celebrating whatever it was they were celebrating.

"How about a chocolate milk?" Mario tried again.

"*Scusa,*" Guillermo tapped one of the sailors, "could you please point me in the direction of your chief navigator?"

The sailor stopped dancing and looked at Guillermo evenly. His skin was sunburned and wrinkled and his beard sent whiskers wandering in every direction. He smelled salty and his teeth looked like a rotten ear of corn but that didn't discourage him from sporting a wide grin.

"If you're referring to Benjamin Blanco then I have bad news. We buried him at sea in the Indies a month ago. He was a fine sailor… up until that point."

Guillermo stumbled for words and stumbled backwards to add distance between himself and the stinky sailor.

"Then can you show us who your captain is?" Piccola asked.

"The Captain's inside tryin' to forget about the month of rough seas we just endured on our way back home. I don't think he's going to want to be disturbed right now but don't let me stop you from tryin'." He grinned.

The smiling sailor's oral cavity let off so foul a smell that Piccola couldn't bear another second. She pushed Guillermo in the direction of the inn. Everyone followed.

"By the way," the salty sailor called out, "what's a crew so small doing with—" His voice was drowned out by the singing sailors. Two gleeful men tripped off the pier and fell into the water, laughing the whole way down.

The kids pushed their way inside. The inn was overflowing with rugged sailors who, like their shipmates on the dock, seemed to seldom run a razor over their face, or a bar of soap over their body. Servers ran about trying to keep up with the thirsty sailors. The kids listened in as the crew members closest to them recounted the horrors they'd just experienced at sea. The Tenerife dock men hung mesmerized on their every word. One sailor whispered about a mutiny that had been planned against the captain some weeks ago after everyone on board went days without a shred of food. Some of the men had resorted to sucking on their boots for strength. And a bout of scurvy had killed off the navigator and twelve others.

"*Oh Dio mio*," Mario whispered, "and I thought we had it rough out at sea with no sauce for a few days."

Standing at a table on the far side of the inn was an extremely tall man dressed differently from everyone else. Despite the heat he donned a cloak with long velvet sheets draped over his shoulders. A black triangular hat hid most of his bushy hair and accentuated his pale skin. His curious eyes were oversized even for his round face. There was a crowd surrounding him, listening to him speak. Guillermo found the man's voice surprisingly nasal and high pitched for someone of his height; but he had such an air of self-assurance that it was unthinkable anyone would question, let alone challenge him. The towering man radiated leadership and Guillermo motioned for his crew to follow him as he snaked his way up front to listen to the man speak.

"The natives we encountered in the Indies walked around less than half clothed, like savages. And most are sick with disease," he said in a voice that reminded Guillermo of a Mickey Mouse cartoon.

"The Royals will reward you plenty for bringing civilization to their shores," a dockworker called out.

The man in the black hat stopped. He put two fingers to his chin and rubbed softly. He seemed to enjoy the feel of his rough skin. "Five years ago the Monarchy offered me ten percent of the take from the new lands I so bravely went on to discover. But, dear friends, hazard a guess as to why His and Her Majesty ever offered me such a deal?"

Nobody hazarded a guess.

The man snapped his fingers and a crewman brought him his fancy hand mirror. He fixed himself while he spoke. "Not because they liked me. Not because they thought I was in command of my faculties. And most certainly not because they valued my estimation of the distance to the Indies. No, none of these reasons. They offered me ten percent because they thought I would never find anything out at sea. And if I did, they thought I would never be able to return from so far." The man sneered as the audience prodded him to go on with the story. He put down his mirror, satisfied with his appearance.

"The Royals, their Excellencies, simply did not want me to try my luck with another sovereign state," he continued. "*Amigos*, that was three voyages ago. And thousands of leagues of sea behind me. And since then I've gone on to discover more lands than King Ferdinand and Queen Isabella know what to do with. And ten percent of it is my due." The man slammed his fist on the table to emphasize his last point. The crowd instantly settled down, unsure of how to respond. After a few seconds the man cracked his knuckles before looking up and smiling pleasantly at his onlookers.

The crowd roared approvingly and someone offered up a toast to the man.

Guillermo and his crew tried to make sense of the bizarre scene they'd stumbled upon. "*Scuza*, sir?" Guillermo said, poking the tall man on his hip.

The man whipped around and took in the group of children standing there in their outsized sailing uniforms.

"Are you the captain of this fleet?" Guillermo inquired.

"Hello young sailors," the man said in a cartoonish voice while he snapped for a crewman to grab him his fiber-tipped pen. "I am the captain, but why don't you call me Chris. Who shall I make this out to?" The Captain started to sign his autograph for the confused kids.

Just then a sailor came in holding three squawking chickens. "Captain Columbus, dinner will be ready soon."

The crew of the *Grande Infante* locked eyes as they all mouthed the same words while trying to contain their excitement. "Chris-to-pher Col-um-bus?!"

Guillermo leaned in, "Um, Mr. Columb… Chris, I'm Captain Guillermo Infante. I think this is the most exciting moment of my life. I mean, to speak with the man who discovered America."

"Well, I appreciate the kind words, er… captain? But you must have me confused with someone else. Another sailor, perhaps. I've never come across a place by the name of America."

"But aren't you Christopher Columbus," Tony asked, "the Genoese explorer who in 1492 sailed the ocean blue?"

"Indeed, I did sail across the Ocean Sea in 1492. And a grand voyage it was—made possible by the grace of the mighty heavens. But, young lads, that voyage was to find a western route to Asia. I discovered and named dozens of islands in the Indies but this was my third voyage and I'm still seeking a route to mainland Asia. 'America' is not a place-name I'm familiar with. Now run along little ones, my dinner's on its way and I shall eat in peace."

"Hold on a second," Tony said, motioning for the kids to huddle a few feet away from Columbus. "I see what's going on here. Columbus never knew that he'd found a new continent. He died in 1506 still thinking he'd discovered a western route to Asia. The Americas were named after another explorer, Amerigo Vespucci, because he proved that Columbus had been wrong all along."

"Well, should we tell him the truth now?" Enzo asked.

"Are you crazy?" Piccola looked into Enzo's eyes, "If we tell him that he's been completely wrong about everything he's ever done he might get really angry."

"And to tell you the truth, he kind of seems like a jerk," Mario added.

"It's a shame he'll never know what an amazing thing he really did find," Guillermo said.

The kids re-approached Columbus. Guillermo made sure his uniform and hat were on straight before he spoke. "Chris, sorry to interrupt you again, and right before dinner at that. Never mind what I said before about America, I mixed things up. I meant Asia. But that aside, we really need your help."

"Where's my chicken?" Columbus yelled to no one. "And it's *Captain Columbus*." He was starting to get cranky.

Piccola sidled up with a panicked look on her face. "Captain Columbus, we're in a lot of trouble, sir. We're lost, no doubt because we're a young and inexperienced crew, and my brother, our captain, only wishes he could hold a candle to a captain of your caliber and esteem. If you could just give us a moment of your time I know that would prove more valuable than a whole year under our simple captain's leadership."

The kids all waited to see if Columbus bought the piled on flattery while Guillermo scowled at Piccola for the insults.

"Make it fast," Columbus finally replied, his vanity taking over.

Tony handed Columbus the piece of paper where he had written down the numbers on the map next to the treasure location. "Can you please tell us what location this is and how we can get there?"

"I can," Columbus said. "But first I require to know what brings you and your friends here to Tenerife." He turned to Guillermo, "And what are you the captain of?"

"Our ship, the *Grande Infante*, is docked just next to yours. Before you ask, I really am the captain and this really is my crew. And we've managed to sail here all the way from Pizzolungo. All by ourselves. So despite what my sister said, I think I've done a pretty good job. Not to mention the pirates we had to outrun along the way."

"Pirates?" Columbus sat up straight and cracked his knuckles forcefully. "When and where did you encounter these pirates?"

"There's a guy named Fleury who's been chasing us for days. He's probably not far behind us. We dropped a cannonball on his ship to slow him down."

"Jean Fleury?" The inn quieted down and everyone looked at Columbus. "Is that devil Gascon with him?"

"Yes."

"And he said he wants to bleed us," Mario chimed in.

"And I don't doubt he would," Columbus said.

Guillermo shivered, "Fleury told us he once used someone's arm bone to stir his stew."

Columbus paused and his face turned dark. "That arm belonged to my best rear oarsman. He was a good man... with a family." Columbus stared at Guillermo. "And you say Fleury's heading this way?"

"Definitely."

"That's extremely valuable information young sailor. Without this knowledge there's no telling what might have happened to my crew and my cargo."

Columbus stood up and projected his squeaky voice. "*Hombres*, prepare the ships! We are setting sail to the west immediately! I'm not taking any chances with our cargo from

125

the Indies." He rubbed his stomach, "And bring me my chicken!"

The room erupted into a frenzy as the mob of sailors ran for the ships.

"Wait, wait," Guillermo yelled. "Please tell us where this location is."

Tony once again showed the piece of paper with the coordinates to Columbus, who was busy barking orders to his men. He glanced at the paper and reached for his magnetic compass. "Lads, I'm not sure what you're in search of, but whatever it is, it's right here." He put away the compass.

"Huh?" Tony asked. "What do you mean 'right here'?"

"I mean, these coordinates are for this harbor and its surroundings. You are already here. And all the way from Pizzo—?"

"Pizzolungo," Tony helped.

"The Little Sailors of Pizzolungo," Columbus repeated with a smile.

"Are you sure, Captain Columbus?" Piccola asked. "This is really, really important to us. We're trying to buy my father a new ship."

Columbus knelt down next to Piccola. "*Niña*, I've just navigated across the Ocean Sea and back for the third time and I've explored lands that no European boot has ever touched. If I tell you you've found your destination then trust me, you've found your destination." He pinched her cheek. "And it's Chris."

Guillermo flicked Piccola's ear, "And which captain got you here?"

Columbus then turned to Guillermo. "Young captain, I wish to give you something." Columbus reached into his pocket. "Have this compass of mine. I'm thankful that you warned me about Fleury, and your seafaring grit has reminded me of what I was like at your age. Although I'm much more handsome, we both possess the spirit of the adventurer running through our veins. Through determination and perseverance maybe one day you'll find you've become an inspiration to others and you'll be remembered for it. Just like me." Columbus turned and swaggered confidently out of the inn.

Guillermo gazed at the weighty, bronze compass. It was larger than his palm and shinier than anything he'd ever seen. On the back was a small engraving that said '*To the One and Only CC, Admiral of the Ocean Sea. With best wishes, F&I*'. It reminded him of a compass his father had once shown him.

"Thanks Chris," Guillermo yelled.

Everyone bid farewell to Columbus as the sailors hurried out to sea.

Guillermo gripped his new compass tight as he took in his crew members, who were eager to make their exit as well. "Let's go find that treasure."

—Chapter 11—

Tenerife

The crew of the *Grande Infante* sat on the pier in Tenerife examining the treasure map. A warm breeze carried with it the scents of summer wildflowers from the hills, and the fish in the harbor poked their heads out of the water to get a closer look at the crew from Pizzolungo. Columbus's fleet had just slipped out of sight over the horizon, leaving behind it a wake of ironed out, placid sea.

"If there had been a shipwreck in the harbor we'd have already seen it, given how clear the water is," Enzo said.

"And others would have already gotten to it," Tony added.

"I told you we should have just gone home," Mario said.

Piccola rubbed her chin with her forefingers. "Papa always tells us that in order to solve the most vexing problems you need to think outside the box."

"What box?" Mario wondered.

"Yeah, what does that mean?" Enzo asked.

"It just means that maybe we need to search for the treasure in places we wouldn't expect to find it," Guillermo explained.

128

"My cousin Vito in New York once told me about an exam he had to take to become a detective," Luca said. "It had one question, and if you passed it then you would get an interview. Very few people passed the exam though."

"What was the question?" Tony asked.

"Rearrange all the letters in the words 'New Door' to make one word."

"Sounds like a dumb question for a detective's exam," Mario quipped.

"That doesn't sound very hard, but I'd need a pen and paper to work it out," Tony said.

Luca shook his head. "No you wouldn't. You could spend hours trying to make it one word but there's not a single word in the dictionary that can be formulated using all those letters."

"Then I repeat, it's a dumb question for a detective's exam," Mario stressed.

"But it's not," Luca insisted. "Because I already gave you the answer when I asked you the question. The answer was so easy that nobody recognized it. That's why they give the question to people who want to be detectives, to see if they can figure out questions that, as Piccola would say, require out-of-the-box thinking."

"So what's the answer?" Enzo asked.

"One word," Piccola said, raising her chin and folding her arms proudly.

"Yeah, but which word?" Enzo asked.

"Congratulations Piccola!" Luca said, impressed by her problem-solving prowess. "The answer is literally *one word*. I asked you to make one word with the letters in new door. Just shift them around to spell 'one word' and you're all done."

"I don't get it," Mario said.

Piccola rolled her eyes.

129

"Maybe the treasure's on land," Guillermo suggested.

Everyone scanned the surroundings. Hugging the nearby shore was a cluster of houses, each resembling the white-painted, red-roofed homes of Gibraltar. In between them were stone walkways narrow enough to prevent the sun's rays from blazing down onto the pedestrians. Beyond the houses were dirt paths leading up into the hills, where somebody had planted orange, olive and almond groves. The color of the soil was deep red, almost clay-like. The unique, sweet smell emanating from the fig trees danced about in the broiling air.

"We can explore the area with our bikes," Luca suggested. "That way we can cover more ground."

The kids ran to the ship and lowered five bicycles down by rope, one at a time. The crew rode off the pier and past the houses, pedaling harder and harder as the slope veered upwards and the wax covered wheels struggled to grip the loose earth. Piccola brought up the rear on foot. Finally everyone dismounted; they'd reached the top of a small ridge overlooking the village. Piccola caught up with the boys and caught her breath. The bicycles had raised a huge dust cloud as their wheels churned over the dry path. Piccola's hair was coated in fine, red dirt. A breeze charmed the sweat on the back of Guillermo's neck and gave him the shivers.

"What should we be looking for captain?" Enzo asked. "Treasure chests?"

"I'm not really sure. I guess anything out of the ordinary. Maybe some freshly dug up soil or something like that."

"To me everything here looks out of the ordinary," Luca commented, as he pointed back down the path from which they'd arrived. "Especially those townspeople staring at us."

"I think everyone's staring at these bicycles as if they've never seen one before," Tony said.

Piccola concurred, "They probably haven't."

"If anyone in Pizzolungo saw us on these old bikes they'd mock us," Enzo said. "But I think the villagers are staring at us because they've never seen anything so futuristic."

Luca looked at the crew, "The strangest thing is that even though our ship is also supposed to be from 1497 it's so much bigger and more modern than all the other ships. And it has all these machines that are far more modern as well. I can't figure it out."

"It is all a bit strange. But so is a growing, time traveling ship," Guillermo said.

Just then two couples from the village trudged up the hill and approached the kids. One of the men stepped forward. He was tall, with a thin oval face and small eyes. It was impossible to tell whether he was forty or sixty years old. The sun had baked his skin thoroughly, and the sunlight reflected off his balding head.

"*Chicos*, my name is Pablo Rodriguez Vasquez Jimincz Benitez Fernandez del Rey, but you may call me Pablo Rodriguez Vasquez del Rey for short." He motioned to his three companions, who stood attentively at his side but didn't say anything, "We're curious what brings you here to Tenerife on these..." he pointed to the bicycles, "rolling horses?"

"We're just riding around..." Guillermo answered.

"Yeah, my mother said I need to work on my thighs and abs," Mario added.

The villagers conversed among themselves.

"*Perdoname chicos*, we didn't understand a word of what you have said. Maybe it is your accents or maybe it is that you are not from these parts." He leaned in closer to the kids. "We have never seen a ship like yours, nor a crew without adults. And we have most certainly never seen rolling horses. *Honestamente*, your presence scares the villagers."

"Oh, there's nothing to be scared of sir. It's a long story as to why we are on a big ship without our parents, and we are trying to get back to them. And these aren't rolling horses, they're—"

"*Chicos,* I know they are not horses. But I have never seen such a contraption…"

Pablo Rodriquez Vasquez del Rey's three companions shook their heads to indicate they'd never seen a rolling horse before either.

"If you push on the pedals with your feet then you can get around faster than if you were walking," Guillermo explained.

"If you say so then you say so. We just came up here to let you know that some of the locals question why you're here. We live far from mainland Spain, and people here are superstitious, and suspicious of strangers. Recently we had droughts followed by floods. And floods followed by droughts. There was a pirate attack and a shipwreck. The people are on edge."

The kids traded unsettled looks as the three other villagers confirmed what Pablo Rodriquez Vasquez del Rey had recounted.

"So they see you *chicos* riding around on your rolling horses and it makes them nervous. *Me comprendes?*"

"*Si Signore,* we understand. And no problem, we'll put the bicycles… I mean, rolling horses, back on our ship. And we'll be leaving soon," Guillermo assured them. "But can we ask you one question? You mentioned a pirate attack and a shipwreck. What happened?"

Pablo Rodriguez Vasquez del Rey looked at the woman to his side, who nodded for him to proceed.

"*Chicos,* this is not a story I enjoy telling, but if you ask, it is my obligation to tell. Some weeks ago pirates raided us. We did not have much to give them. A few bushels of wheat, three hogs and a basket of fish, that's all. We aren't rich, as you can see. In any case, the pirates must have been hungry as they did not seem to care how meager our offerings were." He paused, seemingly uncomfortable with what he was about to say next. "That night the pirates moored just outside the harbor walls and we were terrified that they would come back in the morning and demand more, as all we had left were our homes and our lives. Then we heard yelling and screaming from the ship. A terrible, violent fight had broken out amongst the pirates. Over what we will never know, but it went on for nearly an hour."

"*Oh Dio mio,* what happened?" Guillermo asked.

"At daybreak we all went to the harbor to see what had transpired. We saw a man stagger up onto the deck—bruised and in bad shape. He spat in our direction, pulled up the anchor and sailed away."

"Only one man survived the fight?" Luca asked.

"Apparently. But he didn't get very far. Someone must have scuttled the ship during the fight, because it started taking on water as it sailed out. The heavens were dropping their tears on us that morning and we lost sight of the vessel soon after. But later that day the same injured pirate was spotted crawling back onto our island."

The townspeople nodded to corroborate the story. One of the ladies finally spoke, "*Es la verdad.* The truth."

Pablo Rodriquez Vasquez del Ray continued, "All the men in the village went to track down that last pirate. We searched the island for days, but never saw him again. Only a very elusive man could swim to shore wounded and evade our week-long search."

"He's still here?" Mario gasped. "I mean, on Tenerife?"

"I doubt it, *chico.* Soon after, a hunter on the other side of the island was found killed. Next to his body was evidence that someone had built a boat from downed trees. The pirate probably took his chances on the high seas rather than confront us alone. Which was a smart decision on his part."

"Do you think that the pirate who escaped knew where his ship had sunk?" Tony asked, biting his lower lip.

"*Chicos,* if anyone in the world knows where that ship went down it would be him. All we know is that he sailed into the rough waters on the western side of the island," Pablo Rodriguez Vasquez del Rey said, pointing over the hill behind the houses.

"Did anyone try to locate the sunken ship?" Luca asked hesitantly.

"Some of the *jovenes,* the young men, had a swim around, but no one found anything. Even if they had, you'd need to be a fish to get down there."

"*D'accordo,*" Luca said, his wide eyes and jittery enthusiasm revealing his burgeoning excitement. "We better be on our way." He locked eyes with Guillermo, "Captain, we should go. We've bothered these good people long enough."

Guillermo observed the solemn and shaken villagers. "We're sorry for any trouble we've caused."

"No trouble," one of the other male villagers replied, testing out his voice for the first time. "Get back to your parents safely. They must be worried about you."

"Wait, can I ask one more question?" Tony called out to the townspeople. "I'm Tony, the navigator, and something has been puzzling me. Our map has depictions of big dogs next to these islands. Since they are called the Canary Islands, why doesn't the map show birds?"

Pablo Rodriguez Vasquez del Rey winked at him. "The islands take their name from the Latin word for dogs: *Canariae.* The birds are named after the islands."

"I see," Tony said as Luca grabbed his arm and pulled him toward his bike.

"Latin's a lot more useful than I suspected," Mario said. "I might give up on my Hungarian lessons when we get home."

"Are you kidding?" Enzo asked. "*Hungary* is your middle name!"

Everyone sighed at the awful joke, turned their bikes around and pedaled back toward the ship with a newfound sense of urgency. Piccola ran behind them, stopping every few seconds to cough up dust.

"Captain!" Luca said excitedly as they arrived in front of their ship, "remember those sketches of instruments we found below deck? One of them was for a dual periscope, which can be used to look above and below the water. Maybe the actual periscope exists in the room filled with machines. And we know for sure that we have two old diving suits."

Excitement radiated across everyone's face. Guillermo scratched his head as his mind speedily began hatching a plan. "It's getting dark already, but first thing in the morning, we'll begin the search, hopefully before Fleury gets here. Tonight we'll look for the periscope." He thought for a second and then examined his crew. "Does anyone know anything about scuba diving?"

Silence.

Guillermo sighed.

"Well a few days ago none of us knew how to sail to the Canary Islands either," Piccola noted. "We'll figure it out."

"By thinking out of the boxes?" Mario asked.

"Yes Mario, by thinking out of the boxes."

"Speaking of boxes, I'm going to open a box of linguini right now. After Columbus left, I picked up a few pounds of pasta, a chicken and some vegetables with Tony's last coin."

Tony checked his pocket. Indeed, other than a ball of lint and a few grains of sand it was empty. He eyed Mario angrily.

Moments later Luca—machine blueprints in hand—led the crew past the rows of cannons and artillery and stopped in front of the cubbies stuffed with contraptions. Each was labeled with numerical notations and impossible-to-read Latin script. The room smelled like a mixture of polished metal and damp paper. Musty, but almost pleasantly so.

Luca ruffled through the blueprints and finally pointed to the periscope design. "This one."

"Yeah, that must be it," Guillermo confirmed.

"So we're looking for a long pipe with bent extensions at the top and bottom, like the letter "S" but with a very long mid section," Luca explained.

The crew surveyed the cubbies. "This might be it," Enzo said. "It's huge."

Luca bent down and examined the equipment. "Captain you were right, we'll need good sunlight overhead for this to work."

"Wait, what was that?" Enzo asked. "Did you hear that?"

"I didn't hear anything," Guillermo said.

"Me neither," Piccola said, still wiping dust from her eyes.

"I heard something," Enzo insisted.

"It's probably just Mario's stomach," Tony offered.

"Let's get this periscope up on the deck and figure out how to use it," Guillermo said.

The kids each grabbed a corner of the device and pushed it out into the hallway and over to the stairs heading up to the main deck. They finally managed to lug the periscope up onto the deck. Once fully extended the main tube measured over fifty feet long. Inside the bent ends were mirrors angled at 45 degrees to enable vision around corners. The ends were covered with round, clear glass.

"Whoever invented this ship was a genius," Piccola said, staring down the deck. "Look at this," she stepped forward and touched a large hinge built into the railing. "Since we got on board I've been wondering what this hinge is for. Now I see the periscope has the opposite hinge. It must get attached here so that we can move it up and down easily to look under the water." Piccola walked back and pointed to the inverted hinge on the periscope.

"She might be right captain," Luca said.

"Yeah, maybe she is. I was just about to point out the same thing. The, um… hinges are a dead giveaway."

Piccola glanced at Guillermo to let him know that his fib didn't go unnoticed.

Twenty minutes later the periscope was in place, one end resting just below the surface of the water while the other end reached the railing of the top deck. Guillermo peered into the long tube but it was already too dark to see anything.

"Let's eat," Tony suggested.

"That's my line," Mario protested before heading down to the kitchen to get started on dinner. As usual, he lit the stack of firewood in the stone pit and refilled the cauldron hanging above the fire with fresh water from the ceramic jars. The smoke exited through a brick chimney that released its fumes toward the stern of the ship. From a distance a modern onlooker might perceive the vessel to be a steam ship whenever Mario was stoking the flames down below.

The crew of the *Grande Infante* feasted on a simplified Chicken Milanese and Mario's first steamed broccoli rabe, drenched in oil. Luca was so famished that he outwrestled Mario to lick the bowl of chicken skins clean.

"Hey, do you think the pirate who escaped from Tenerife was one of the guys on Fleury's ship?" Tony asked.

"Either that or Fleury already stole it from that guy," Luca said. "How else would he have gotten the map?"

"All I know is that we better find that ship before Fleury finds us," Guillermo said. "We can be sure that even without the map he'll remember the general area to sail to."

"Wait, there's that sound again," Enzo yelled. "And I felt the ship rock a bit."

"I definitely heard something this time," Luca said.

"What sound?" Mario wondered aloud.

Enzo leaned upwards and straightened his neck to optimize his hearing. His chin nearly poked Mario's head.

"Yeah, I heard something this time too," Guillermo said.

Mario whipped his head around in every direction, nearly dislocating his back. "You don't think it's Fleury do you?"

"No ships have come in or out of this area since Columbus left," Piccola assured them. "I think you're letting your imaginations run wild. I didn't hear a thing."

Mario relaxed his shoulders.

"Well, I'm exhausted. We should rotate sentry duty, just to be sure," Guillermo said.

Minutes later Enzo climbed the foremast to stand guard. Nobody had a better sense of hearing and, of course, no one else had volunteered.

The rest of the boys began preparing for bed. Piccola reopened her envelope filled with the parchments she'd collected from around the ship. "It was these blueprints that led me to find the *inflecto* machine in the first place but I've been studying them for days now and I can't find any other clues as to how to get us back home—to the present. I'm almost ready to give up."

"*Bella, y*ou can't give up, I know you'll get us home," Mario said.

"You got us here. And I don't want to stay in 1497," Tony emphasized. "They don't even have Internet."

"What if there isn't a way back? What if we have to spend the rest of our lives being chased by smelly pirates, without television, and... without parents?"

"Don't say that," Guillermo pleaded. "Don't even think it. We *will* get back. There's always an answer. We just have to find it."

"Have you tried thinking out of a box?" Mario asked innocently.

Piccola glowered at him. "First of all, it's thinking out of *the* box, not *a* box. And yes, Mario, I've been trying to think out of *the* box this whole time."

"Well if all you've been doing is thinking out of the box, why don't you try thinking *in* the box?"

Luca and Tony tried not to giggle.

"Mario, stop being an idiot," Guillermo said.

"Wait. Wait a second. Think *in* a box." Piccola grabbed a candle and hurried over to the helm, with everyone following her.

The boys looked at Mario curiously. Realizing he might have said something useful he grinned at Romeo. "I know things, Romeo." Romeo snorted his retort and waddled off.

Piccola planted her candle beneath the wheel console and scrutinized the time machine box. She slowly re-read the text engraved beneath the dials which she had originally turned to initiate their time travel.

From you to me, and me to you,
Just this one time, you may pass through.
My greatest masterpiece at hand,
Created specially for the Grande.
Dial the numerals left to right,
And Inflecto shall guide your flight.
But be so warned before you fly,
You're offered only this one try.

Inverse to Reverse.

She cleared her throat. "The 'inverse to reverse' part must mean something."

"What does 'inverse' mean exactly?" Guillermo asked.

"I think it's the opposite," Luca said.

"The opposite of what?" Mario asked.

"No, it just means 'the opposite,'" Tony said.

"Maybe here 'reverse' means something like to go back, to go home," Piccola suggested.

"I hope so. We can try and put this ship in reverse if you think it'll help," Mario offered.

"To reverse, then, must require the inverse, or opposite, of something. But what is that something?" Piccola pondered aloud.

"It could be the inverse of something in that riddle," Tony put forward.

"Or a million other things," Guillermo said.

"Well, it says we only get one try, so we better be sure," Luca reminded everyone.

Tony bent down for a closer look. "What about this hourglass?"

"The top chamber was filled with sand when I first noticed it during the storm," Piccola explained. "Then after we dropped Juan Cruz off in Morocco I saw that about a quarter of the sand had fallen to the bottom. Now it's almost half empty."

"I'd like to think of the hourglass as half full," Mario proclaimed.

"That's just a time keeper," Piccola said.

"Must be," Tony agreed.

"Or a countdown," Guillermo countered.

"A countdown to what?" Tony asked.

"Maybe until we go back to the present or something?" Luca suggested.

"Or maybe that's the time we have *left* until we're stuck back in time," Guillermo suggested.

Tony sat down and cupped his face in his hands. His voice was muffled when he spoke. "So we have to inverse something that we *haven't* identified in order to *possibly* go back in time. And we might need to do that *before we run out of time*. Or we could be stuck in the past forever. I have to be honest, I'm really starting to get nervous."

Piccola looked at the hourglass and tugged on Guillermo's uniform, "We might be half way away from never seeing Mama and Papa again."

"Hey, there's that sound again," Luca called out.

"Times ten!" Guillermo yelled, grabbing the deck rail to hold onto.

The sound had been brief but deafening. And this time it was accompanied by a trembling of the ship's frame. Romeo fell right off his feet, squealing. Piccola grabbed hold of her brother.

"That sounded like the time that freight train passing Pizzolungo lost its wheel and skidded along the rails," Luca said.

"Guys!" Enzo screamed from his lookout post on the mainmast. "I don't know what's going on but I think the mast pole just dropped. I think it's a little shorter now."

Tony turned to Guillermo, "Captain, how can a mast pole get shorter?"

"Maybe the ship is breaking apart," Luca interrupted.

Guillermo leaned over the rail and gazed out at the darkening sea. "Or shrinking."

—Chapter 12—

The Trujillo

"**N**o sign of Fleury," Enzo said at first daylight after descending from the foremast.

"*Va bene*," Guillermo said, "but unless we actually sank his ship when we dropped that cannonball, then I doubt we're out of danger."

"I could barely sleep last night," Tony grumbled.

Mario rubbed the crust from his eyelids, "Me neither, I kept waiting for the ship to shrink more."

"Maybe we're just scaring ourselves," Luca said. "I didn't hear anything the whole night."

Enzo headed over to the periscope and looked into the tube. The sun's rays had lit up the sea. "*Oh Dio mio!* There's tons of fish down there." Everyone crowded around to peek into the periscope except Luca, who kept a respectable distance from the railing.

"Come here you chicken, there are no sharks," Enzo said.

"I'm fine where I am."

"Luca, that movie *Jaws* you're always freaking out about took place in America, not around here," Tony pointed out.

"Like I said, I'm fine where I am."

Mario could barely stand still, "Did you find the treasure yet?"

"We're still docked, numbskull," Enzo moaned.

Guillermo stepped back from the railing and projected his voice. "Mates, man your stations. We're setting sail for the western side of the island."

Luca managed the anchor pulley while the others headed for the masts to say good morning to the sheets. A small crowd of Tenerife locals gathered to wave goodbye to the ship's crew.

"They seemed like good-hearted people," Luca said once the crew reunited back on deck.

Guillermo knelt down beneath the wheel. Piccola was already sprawled out on the floor examining the time machine box. "Did you figure out what we need to 'inverse to reverse' or what that sand timer is for?" he asked.

"We just woke up ten minutes ago," she replied testily.

Guillermo steered the ship out of the harbor and cut the wheel to the right. With the sudden change of direction, though, the sails came up against a headwind strong enough to flip the sails around. An enormous whoosh of air blew across the masts and slowed the vessel to a halt. Luca hustled over to the captain to help him hold the wheel in place against the tremendous pressure of the wind as the ship started to be pushed backwards. The rest of the crew headed back toward the helm for further instruction.

"*Madonna mia*," Enzo griped. "It must be a draft off the mountain or something."

The feeling of being pushed backwards helplessly, with no motor to turn to, completely unnerved the crew. Everyone instinctually grasped for something sturdy to hold on to, a response driven by the gut not the brain. There was no danger of crashing into anything. Yet.

"We're never going to be able to sail into that wind," Mario lamented.

"Everyone!" the captain shouted while clasping the wheel tightly. "To move forward we need to angle the lateen sails at 22 degrees to the wind. The pressure of the sails at that angle will be balanced by the keel and it'll take us forward."

Guillermo indicated for Luca to maintain his grip on the wheel as he dropped to the ground and flipped through the pages of 'Magister Mari', which he'd brought up from the library. Meanwhile everyone wondered what 22 degrees looked like exactly, and whether the captain had hit his head that morning.

Guillermo hoisted the enormous book onto the ship's wheel console and showed everyone the diagram indicating the 22-degree scenario.

The crew huddled around the captain to study the diagram as the ship's stern continued to act as its bow.

"Return to the masts!" Guillermo ordered, "Get those sheets as close as you can to 22 degrees against the source of the wind, like it shows here. Once we get out of this vector the winds will die down."

Piccola listened proudly to how her brother delivered his crisp and confident commands, like a real captain would (she assumed). She began to believe more than ever in their prospects at sea. What really worried her was the time machine conundrum—her personal responsibility.

As the headwinds blasted the *Grande Infante*, Luca and Tony scaled the foremast and Piccola and Enzo headed up the mainmast. Mario chugged up the mizzenmast. Slowly they all managed to maneuver the pulley systems so that the sheets were positioned as the captain had instructed. Guillermo guided them from the helm until the sails were aligned. Sure enough the physics worked just as the diagram had suggested. Everyone up on the masts gazed down proudly at their commander.

The *Grande Infante* fought through the wind as it traced the island's coastline southwards. Finally the land's rocky terrain sloped downwards and faded into the sea. Guillermo waited to pass a rock breaker before again rotating the wheel all the way to the right and pulling the ship parallel to Tenerife's western coast. As he did the winds died down substantially and no longer came at the ship head on. He motioned for the sail brigade to even out their angles. True to the word of Pablo Rodriguez Vasquez del Rey, the unprotected sea on the western side of the island was far choppier than on the eastern coast. It was difficult to see beneath the surface because of the waves.

The sail masters descended to the deck, ready to search for treasure.

"Tony, man the periscope. Let's see if we can find ourselves a shipwreck," Guillermo instructed.

Tony maneuvered the lens into position and rotated the hinge clockwise to scan the bottom of the sea. "Just more fish," he said, "and an octopus."

Mario ran over and elbowed Tony out of the way to get a peek into the periscope. "I love octopus. If we had fishing nets I could cook us up the best *Polpi alla Marinara* ever."

Tony nudged Mario aside, "We're looking for gold today, not grub."

Just then the ship jolted up and down powerfully, accompanied by a piercing sound that penetrated deep into everyone's ears. A handful of splinters from the floorboards popped up and the periscope lens banged against Tony's eye, flinging him off his feet.

"I think the ship really is starting to shrink," Enzo fretted.

"Seems so," Tony uttered, pulling himself up from the deck while nursing his eye.

145

Guillermo examined the floorboards, "Yeah, those sounds are the different parts of the ship compressing."

"You think it'll eventually shrink back to the size it was when we found it?" Mario asked with trepidation while gazing out at the massive vessel, "because it would be pretty hard for the six of us to fit on that model ship."

"Your belt wouldn't fit on the model ship," Enzo said.

"*Allora*," the captain stood up, "even if it is shrinking it's doing so pretty slowly. So if we start heading home soon then we should be OK. Right?"

Nobody felt qualified to calculate a theory on the shrinkage rate so everyone half-heartedly nodded.

"Captain, there's also the problem that we're still stuck in 1497," Tony said. "There's that sign in Pizzolungo's main square that says 'Founded in 1571'. If we make it back home without fixing our time travel dilemma, we'll return to a hill of rocks and grass, but no people."

Tony took another look through the periscope. Everyone held their breath waiting for his reaction. He looked back at the group and shook his head. "Nothing."

"I tried inversing the different parts of the rhyme this morning," Piccola said, "but so far I haven't found any clues."

"What kind of clues are you looking for?" Enzo asked.

"I thought maybe there would be a code, like a backwards written sign."

"Like a palindrome," Mario interjected.

"A what-a-drome?" Guillermo asked.

"Ya know, a palindrome. When something reads the same way backwards and forwards. My favorite one is 'Amore Roma' because I know if I ever went to Rome I'd fall in love, too. But I also like the name 'Bob' because it's nearly impossible to misspell, even if you're dyslexic."

Luca shook his head at Mario, "It's amazing how you can know nothing most of the time and then know something like this."

Mario turned, "Thanks?"

Guillermo went back to the helm and edged the ship away from the coast. "Let's head out deeper."

Tony turned the periscope as the ship veered southwards, bobbing up and down on the swells. Luca got the nerve to join him, then quickly lost it again. "Even if we do find that sunken ship I don't want to get in this water and swim with all those fishes."

"It's always like that," Piccola said, "the biggest guys are always the most afraid of the smallest things."

Luca looked down at her small frame, "Don't you have some palindromes to work on?"

Piccola begrudgingly retreated back to the time machine box.

"Hey guys, I think I see something," Tony called out. He pressed his face against the periscope lens and squinted. "There's something down there, that's for sure."

"Let me take a look," Guillermo said. He squeezed one eye tightly and opened the other as wide as he could to try and make out the murky image on the bottom of the sea. "*Allora,* it's something man-made but I can't tell what. Enzo, have a look."

Enzo took hold of the periscope and peered through. "The '*Trujillo*'."

"Huh?" Guillermo and Tony asked together.

"It's the *Trujillo*. That's the name written on the stern of that ship down there," he said matter-of-factly.

"It's probably the ship from the treasure map," Tony said, glancing at the map in his hand.

The kids looked at each other in astonished delight. Everyone started exchanging high fives. Mario grabbed

147

Piccola in euphoric delight. "You're squeezing me too tightly," she cried out.

"Sorry *bella*, I got a little carried away." He loosened up. "We're gonna be rich. I mean, after we get your father a new ship."

As he angled in closer toward the *Trujillo,* Guillermo instructed the crew to bring down the sails and lower the anchor. Once they returned to the deck Enzo grabbed the periscope to get a second look. "It looks like a caravel ship that's partly buried by sand and reef. It's probably about twenty feet down."

"Twenty feet is a lot," Luca said. "The deepest part of the Pizzolungo Public Pool is eight feet and I only touched it once and nearly ran out of breath on my way up."

"I tried to get down to the six feet marker but my ears popped from the pressure," Tony said.

Guillermo cut off the discussion on the depths of the Pizzolungo Public Pool with a wave of his hand. "Let's head down below to get the diving equipment."

Soon the crew surfaced onto the deck lugging up the two clunky dive-bell suits. Luca and Mario laid the suits out on the floorboards and wiped the sweat off their faces.

Luca stepped forward, "Now let's be clear, I'm not volunteering for this, but I've been studying these suits for days and I don't think it will be too difficult to use them. There are no air tanks or anything else mechanical, like with modern equipment. These really long tubes are basically extended snorkels. They bring the fresh air from the surface down into the helmet."

"I'll volunteer," Enzo said.

"Me too, I've always wanted to try scuba diving," Piccola said.

"If there is a treasure down there it will be heavy," Guillermo noted, "so Mario should go instead of Piccola."

"No way," Mario exclaimed. "I'll *eat* an octopus but I won't swim with one."

Piccola turned to Guillermo, "First of all, things are *much* lighter under water than on land. And second of all, there might be small spaces to crawl into and..." she pointed at Mario, "he may not fit."

Mario agreed, "I'm not good at small spaces."

"Can I go?" Piccola asked.

"Well, I thought Luca should go because he's the strongest." Luca started turning white with fear. "But since he's also the biggest wimp when it comes to the water, I guess you can go. But you have to be *really* careful; we're counting on you to find our way back home."

Piccola shot Guillermo a nasty look.

"And um, you know, because you're my sister too."

Everyone helped Enzo and Piccola into their dive-bell helmets. It took Enzo a bit more time to adjust the helmet to accommodate his chin.

"You look like chipmunks in motorcycle helmets," Tony said.

"Or spacemen from Mars," Mario offered.

Piccola opened the round, glass window in the middle of the helmet and stuck her tongue out at both of them.

Luca looped a weight belt around each of their waists and tightened the leather straps on the bottom of their copper helmets so that the waterproof material fit snugly around Enzo and Piccola's necks. "Let's test the breathing apparatus," he said.

Each helmet connected to two breathing tubes made of hollowed-out bamboo sticks fastened together by pigskin leather. Metal springs between the pigskin connectors allowed the tubes to bend and ensured they wouldn't collapse from the water pressure. The tubes eventually connected up to a floating air chamber made of cork that let air pass in and out of the system. The chamber then connected up to the ship.

"Now remember," Guillermo stood in front of the two divers, "if you need to come up fast just pull three times on the tube and we'll yank you up."

"Three times," Enzo confirmed.

Enzo and Piccola flashed the thumbs up sign and Luca finished attaching a rope from their waists to the pulley system. "Let's lower them down."

Guillermo, Luca, Mario and Tony lowered the divers into the water. Once wet, Enzo and Piccola signaled all was OK to proceed.

"Good luck!" Guillermo yelled from high up on the top deck, but the divers' copper helmets were already below the surface and out of sight.

"I hope they survive," Mario said to no one in particular.

Everyone shot him a harsh look.

"Did I say that out loud?"

The divers descended slowly, holding hands. Schools of tropical fish glided through the forest of corals and reeds. They all seemed determined to get a glimpse of Piccola and Enzo, the newest and strangest-looking creatures in their neighborhood. The closer the divers got to the *Trujillo* the more fish there were and Piccola realized that the shipwreck had serendipitously offered all the ocean dwellers a comfortable home. For the rest of the way down she thought about her own home back in Pizzolungo, and how much she didn't want to have to move away. She hoped the fish didn't mind that she wanted to take something away from their home in order for her to keep hers.

The *Trujillo* rested on its portside and was draped eloquently in fine silt. As the divers neared the bottom they could see there were two holes cut out of the hull's midsection. The scuttled panels confirmed for Enzo that it must be the ship that Pablo Rodriguez Vasquez del Rey had described. And if it wasn't, it would be some coincidence.

Enzo and Piccola finally planted themselves on the seabed, just next to the ship. Their feet stirred up a small cloud of dust from the bottom causing an octopus to slither away fearfully. Enzo motioned toward the stern of the wreck from where there was a simple place to enter the ship's cabin. He clasped Piccola's little hand and the two proceeded ahead, eventually reaching the wooden swing door leading to the hull.

"Arrrgh!" Enzo screamed, loud enough for Piccola to hear through both of their helmets. He kicked up so much dust retreating backwards that the daylight turned instantly into night. The divers hurriedly swam back past the stern to where they had originally landed.

Realizing that they could hear each other through their helmets, albeit with a rattling echo, Piccola screamed, "Shark?"

"No, a skeleton!"

Piccola looked at her diving companion curiously. "What do you think happens to dead pirates?" she yelled back matter-of-factly. "They become skeletons, just like everyone else."

Enzo caught his breath and wondered what to make of Piccola's bravery. "You knew there'd be dead pirates down here and you didn't tell me?"

"The man in Tenerife told us all the pirates went down with the ship except one. I assumed you also knew that we'd be meeting the rest of the crew today."

"The skeleton crew," Enzo said ominously. "And why are they skeletons anyway? The ship went down less than a month ago."

"I'm sure you noticed how big and well fed the fish are around here…"

Enzo swallowed hard, shook his head and grabbed Piccola's hand again, this time much tighter. "You go first."

Piccola led the way past the first of the deceased pirates. All that remained of him was a stack of bones and a shredded uniform. Small fish swam peacefully in and out of his rib cage and eye sockets. Enzo exerted every effort to avoid touching the former buccaneer. Piccola shook her head in bewilderment, "They're dead. They can't hurt you."

I'm swimming with the strangest girl on the planet, Enzo thought to himself.

The open door allowed enough light into the sideways hull for the divers to count eight more skeletons. Each time the tides moved the skeletons swayed along with them, and each time the skeletons swayed along with the tides Enzo spun around in panicked circles to make sure he was safely out of their range. The air tubes attached to his helmet started getting increasingly twisted.

Piccola swam over to one of the pirates and eyed the dagger lodged between two of his ribs. He sported a full mouth's worth of gold teeth. She motioned for Enzo to catch up, "Should we try and take this gold?" she asked, humoring herself.

Enzo could barely even look at the skeleton. His young face was already developing stretch marks from grimacing for so long. "Are you completely out of your mind?"

"Fine, let's keep going."

Piccola noticed that Enzo was so preoccupied trying to avoid brushing up against any bones that he'd forgotten the purpose of their mission altogether. She pushed his arm forcefully, flinging him past her toward the deeper and darker corner of the hull. "I like it down here, I can easily toss you around."

"Just wait until we're back on board."

Then suddenly both Enzo and Piccola froze. She squeezed down on his hand so tightly that he thought he might lose a finger. A few feet in front of them two enormous glowing green eyes met their four.

"Don't make a sound," Enzo yelled.

"Stop talking," Piccola mouthed.

The green eyes held steady. Enzo caught sight of Piccola's frightened face through the glass window in her helmet. Finally she's afraid of *something*, he thought. That consolation made him feel slightly better until he realized that if *she* was afraid, he should be *very* afraid. Just then the eyes darted out toward the divers but quickly pulled back into the darkness. *Mamma mia*, that fish is enormous, Piccola thought. Enzo imagined Piccola and himself both fitting inside its slimy stomach. He reached to pull three times on his oxygen cord but Piccola intercepted his hand after just one tug.

"We're not going up till we've found the treasure!"

"I'd rather go home treasure-less than be eaten by… that," he pointed at the green bulging eyes.

Up on the *Grande Infante*, Luca turned to the gang. "I just felt a strong tug on the line."

"How many pulls?" Guillermo asked.

"Just one."

"They probably just got it caught on something," Tony said. "They know to pull three times if there's danger."

"Well, Enzo and Piccola aren't very strong. Maybe their three pulls only equals one that you can feel," Mario said.

Everyone looked on apprehensively.

Down below, the green eyes started toward the divers again. Enzo and Piccola held each other tightly, trying to avoid becoming fish food. The fish swam up to the glass windows of their helmets and locked eyes with them. It opened its mouth wide, revealing a set of disproportionately gigantic lips and sharp teeth. And then it bit down, hard, on Piccola's helmet. Enzo's heart was pumping so hard his chest started to hurt. The sound of teeth scraping against the metal helmet reminded Piccola of the crazy sounds the *Grande Infante* had started making. Both she and Enzo desperately wanted to tug on their cords three times but were equally afraid to get their hands anywhere near the monster's mouth.

"It's a giant grouper!" Piccola hollered as the fish continued to bite and toy with the outside of her helmet.

Enzo looked directly into the grouper's eyes, extended his chin and took a deep breath. "You better swim away or it's going to be sushi for dinner on the *Grande Infante* tonight!"

The fish held steady for another few seconds before taking one more futile nibble. Copper didn't seem to be the taste he was searching for though, and he finally turned and pushed himself out past the swing door, back toward the bright sea and, perhaps, a better tasting snack.

"That was close," Piccola exhaled, still shivering. "Sushi?"

"I don't know. I heard if you yell at a bear it runs away."

Enzo lowered himself to the floorboards to catch his breath. "Ouch!" he moaned as something sharp pressed up against his bottom. He spun around to find the silt being thrown off a large oak chest studded with precious stones. Piccola swam in for a closer look and for a moment the two stood speechless.

"We found it," Enzo said, his heartbeat speeding up again.

Piccola threw her arms above her head, "*Bravissimo!*"

154

The divers embraced again, this time out of pure joy, not utter fear. Enzo threw open the lid and the two divers hovered above to survey their riches.

"It's… empty." Piccola could barely say the words.

Enzo fell to his knees and threw his arms into the chest to see if he could feel anything. Two small clownfish shuffled out of the box, leaving nothing else inside. Piccola felt her throat start to swell with disappointment.

Back on the ship, Guillermo was getting increasingly worried. "Let me take another look," he muttered to Tony. He pressed his eye against the periscope lens and could just make out the oxygen lines curving away into the interior of the ship.

Tony looked the captain up and down, "I've never seen you bite your nails before."

"I saw an enormous fish swim out of there a little while ago."

With the sun hovering directly above the *Grande Infante* there was nowhere to hide from its direct rays. Sweat dripped onto the deck from everyone's faces, but not only because of the heat.

On the seabed, Enzo shouted to Piccola, "Hold on, the man in Tenerife told us how the pirates had fought each other all night. Maybe the treasure ended up scattered about in the process."

Piccola looked up, a morsel of hope injected into her perspective. "Let's look around. I just hope there are no more toothy beasts."

The divers descended deeper into the hull. "There's so much silt we'll need to feel our way through," Enzo yelled, dragging his hands across the floor of the ship. "Hey, I got something." He wiped off a rectangular object and triumphantly held up a gold bar for Piccola to see.

"We did it!" she shouted emphatically. Although her cheeks and lips had started turning blue from being under water for so long the excitement of finding the treasure sent a burst of adrenaline into her system and her face returned to its natural rosy color. She ran her fingers down the smooth bullion; it was as if she were already touching her father's new ship.

Enzo swam over and deposited the bar into the treasure chest. He and Piccola went back to work dredging the area for more gold.

"I've got another one," Piccola called out soon after.

"Me too!"

Ten minutes later the treasure chest was filled with gold bars.

"I think we've got enough," Piccola yelled. "Let's get out of here, grab the right side of the chest."

The divers went to lift the crate but couldn't get it to even budge.

"Way too heavy," Enzo cried. "I thought you said everything was light under water."

"I said *lighter,* not light."

"I don't think even Luca and Mario could lift this crate. We'll have to carry them up one-by-one."

"That'll take us forever," Piccola protested. "And we don't know how close Fleury is, or how long before our ship becomes too small for us to sail on."

"Well what do you suggest?"

Piccola put her thinking cap on.

Back on board the ship the crew took turns looking through and pacing around the periscope.

"Let's pull her up," Mario begged. "I mean, pull *them* up."

"Give them another minute, and then we haul them up," Luca countered.

"Yeah, one more minute, that's all I can take." Guillermo sat down, "I'm getting nauseous."

Tony lay on his back, too tense to follow the developments.

From inside the *Trujillo* Piccola flashed three fingers to Enzo, then two, then one. "Now!" she commanded. Both divers swallowed the biggest breath they possibly could and quickly untied the oxygen tubes from their helmets. Moments later they yanked three times on the cords.

"That's the sign," Luca bellowed. "Reel em in!"

Luca, Mario, Guillermo and Tony sprang into action. They pulled their hearts out, hand over hand.

"*Oh Dio mio*, they're heavy," Mario shrieked. "I thought Piccola said everything was light under water."

Luca's muscles bulged and Guillermo's hat flew off his head. Tony's bony arms nearly fractured. The wheels of the pulley systems churned spastically, emitting a harsh rattle. Finally the treasure chest broke through the crested surface of the sea, Piccola and Enzo's oxygen tubes retied onto the handles.

"Huh?" Guillermo wondered.

A mix of glee and terror instantly blended across everyone's faces.

"Oh no," Guillermo cringed as tears began pooling around his eyelids. Everyone gasped in panicked shock, trying hard not to imagine the worst as they heaved the chest up the side of the ship and onto the deck.

But seconds later Enzo and Piccola shot up from the depths gasping for air.

The glee and terror were instantly replaced by colossal shrieks of joy. Everyone on board hugged each other with raw emotion.

"You did it!" Mario screamed with delight.

Guillermo flung down two ropes from the pulley lines for Piccola and Enzo. After attaching them to the waist buckles of their dive suits, Luca pulled up Enzo while Mario heaved Piccola up onto the deck. The exhausted but exhilarated divers fell over in their clunky suits. The crew was rambunctious as they stripped the dive gear off and threw open the treasure chest. Their eruptive cheers could have been heard all the way in Pizzolungo (had Pizzolungo existed in 1497).

Luca lifted up a gold bar from the chest. "We're rich!"

"We actually pulled it off," Enzo shouted.

Guillermo helped Piccola off the floorboards with a big grin, "Not bad for a little twerp."

"Quit it with the compliments, Guillermo, or I'll get a swelled head."

Guillermo stared up at the open sky, almost hitting the cloud above with his grin. His chest muscles finally relaxed and his pulse evened out. "We did it," he said softly. For the first time on the voyage he allowed himself to imagine what the *Coraggio II* might look like.

Suddenly the ship made an awful groan. And then without any further warning it started repositioning itself as bundles of wooden splinters shot up into the air. The shaking ripped the dual periscope off its hinge and it plummeted down into the water and toward the *Trujillo*.

"Guys, I think we better get out of here," Guillermo suggested, jumping back to his feet. "We've got the treasure, let's sail." He ran over to the hourglass and observed a few more grains of sand falling from the top chamber to the bottom and felt another rumble, both from the ship and from his nervous stomach. "I think this really *is* a timer," he shouted. "If I'm right, then when this sand runs out, this boat will have returned to its original size."

"Are you sure, captain?" Mario asked.

"I'm just connecting the dots. All we know is that the ship is starting to shrink, and there's less and less sand in the top chamber."

Piccola scratched her chin. "If it shrinks back to its original size then the time warp machine will be too small to use."

Luca pondered this. "There's only one thing to do. We have to figure out the riddle to get back to the present, and figure it out fast."

"Meanwhile, let's head in the direction of home," Guillermo commanded. Without wasting a second he and the rest of the crew started pulling up the anchor and preparing the *Grande Infante* to travel.

The crew members assumed their usual positions on board and the ship began to inch forward.

"There's just one quick stop we need to make before we go," Guillermo said, turning the wheel eastwards.

—Chapter 13—

Battle Lines

Pablo Rodriguez Vasquez del Rey nearly fell over when he first read the note. He put his arm around his wife and called out for all the townspeople to gather at the end of the dock, from where the *Grande Infante* had just hurried back out to sea. When everyone had assembled he unfolded the paper and read it aloud:

Dear nice people of Tenerife Island,

We didn't mean to scare you yesterday, and we feel bad that the pirates stole your food. We found something of value while we were swimming and we wanted to leave you a gift because you were very nice and had to suffer through difficult times. Also, since you were interested in our ~~bicycles~~ rolling horses you can have all six of them too. We realized a moving ship is no place for a steady ride. We hope Tenerife will be a rich and happy place one day, and that you never have to meet any pirates ever again.

Your friends,

Guillermo, Piccola, Luca, Tony, Enzo, Mario (and Romeo)

Joyful tears streaked down from Pablo Rodriguez Vasquez del Rey's wife's face as she passed around two heavy gold bars. The townspeople were speechless.

With the Moroccan coast off to their right this time, the crew of the *Grande Infante* found it easy to navigate northwards. Tony knew they'd eventually spot the break in the coastline separating Africa from Europe and until then there'd be no need for any significant navigational adjustments. He put away the cross-staff and the astrolabe and borrowed the captain's telescope to survey the sea up ahead. "We're all alone out here, I wonder if we really sank Fleury's ship or if he just gave up."

"I don't know," Luca said, "he doesn't really strike me as the 'giving up' type."

Piccola bent down next to the time machine and tried to focus on solving their biggest conundrum. "What I wouldn't give for access to a Wikipedia page," she grumbled to herself.

"What would you even research on Wikipedia?" Luca asked. "Riddle clues to help your ship travel to the future?"

Up on the mainmast, as exhausted as he was, Enzo kept lookout for unwelcomed vessels on the sun-drenched horizon.

For the next few hours Luca, Tony and Mario manned the sails while the captain held the wheel steady and daydreamed about his father's reaction to his seafaring accomplishments, not to mention the family's newfound riches. Only once did the ship experience one of its shrinking fits, just before dusk. That served as a gathering bell for the crew. Everyone congregated at the base of the mizzenmast.

Enzo lifted the top of the treasure chest and gazed down at all the gold. The sunlight waltzed about the surface of the shiny bars. "Can you imagine how stunned everyone back home will be? I bet we'll be on the front page of the Pizzolungo Post."

"Well, let's just hope the gold bars don't start shrinking like everything else," Mario said. "I was in the kitchen last time the ship was downsizing and the pot I was holding got smaller too."

"Take a look at your shirt," Tony said, pointing to Mario's slightly exposed belly.

"All of our uniforms have shrunk," Luca confirmed.

"And the sails have become easier to pull from side to side," Enzo added.

"Everything that was on this ship grew proportionally, so everything should shrink proportionally," Piccola suggested. "I mean, imagine if the ship shrank but not the things on it. Eventually the cannons, tools, and even the plates would be bigger than the ship itself."

"How about the treasure chest of gold?" Guillermo asked.

"Or my portrait?" Enzo wondered, glancing up at his visage adorning the wall.

"I wouldn't mind that thing getting smaller," Tony scoffed.

"What about Romeo?" Mario asked.

"Maybe those things will all be OK, because they didn't come with the original model ship," Piccola said.

Enzo re-examined the size of the canvas. "Yeah, I check on my portrait every day and it hasn't gotten any smaller."

"Neither has your chin," Tony smirked.

Luca picked Romeo up and inspected him, "If anything, he's gotten *bigger*."

"There's a strong tailwind," Tony observed, "and if it keeps up we may be able to round Gibraltar and turn toward home tomorrow."

Luca looked up at the sails flapping in the breeze, "As long as the sheets stay big enough to keep digesting the wind."

All of a sudden the ship began to jerk, spasm and crank again. The wooden planks, beams and masts contracted significantly, inwards and downwards. Splinters flew in all directions as everyone shielded their eyes from the onslaught. Through his fingers Enzo observed the masts getting shorter and the sails getting tauter. One of the benches pushed into the treasure chest and knocked Mario over. Everyone held on tight until the tremors stopped and the ship stabilized.

"I'm glad I wasn't in the middle of making dinner," Mario said as he pulled himself out from under Enzo and Tony, who had fallen on top of him, "We would've had a lot of mopping up to do. Come to think of it, we better stuff our bellies before the pots are too small to cook with." He swallowed hard and hurried off to check on the kitchen.

"We've got to make it back to Pizzolungo before this ship fits in a cereal bowl," Luca remarked.

Throughout the blustery evening the crew plowed north at good speeds. The ship continued to shrink, and the more it shrank the faster it shrank—but less violently, and with far less sound or drama. It was as if it were settling into a shrinking rhythm, fast enough to be perceptible if you paid attention but slow enough to overlook otherwise.

Before dinner Piccola called a meeting to update everyone on her riddle research. Mario crossed his fingers on both hands. Enzo rubbed his palms together in anticipation. Guillermo balanced his internal unease with an outwardly stoic face.

Piccola pointed to a large piece of brown paper resting on an easel she found lying on its side in a utility room below deck. On it she had written the riddle, the four password clues and 'Inverse to Reverse'.

"Inverse to reverse," she repeated. "This must be the key somehow. I've ruled out inversed codes in the text on the time machine. There are no palindromes in any language I know.

"Including Latin?" Tony asked.

"Including Latin. I even tried inversing the letters in the words 'inverse to reverse' but believe me, there's nothing."

The rest of the crew sat motionless, begging for even a scrap of hopeful news.

"But then I took one key word from each sentence of the riddle... 'Inflecto', 'Masterpiece', 'Grande', 'Numerals', 'Inverse' and, of course, 'Reverse', and I was able to come up with anagrams for each of them. When I rearranged the letters in 'Inflecto' the only thing I found of any meaning is the term 'of licet', which means 'lawful'. For 'Masterpiece,' I came up with 'Escape Timer'; 'Grande' becomes 'Danger'; 'Numerals' can spell out 'Man's Rule'; 'Inverse' can be transformed into 'Serve In'; 'Reverse' can become 'Severer'."

"Where does she come up with this stuff?" Tony asked Guillermo.

The rest of the group stared blankly, waiting for Piccola to continue unraveling the mystery. Finally Luca spoke up, "So how does any of this help us?"

Piccola drew a long breath. "I have no idea." She stared at her five shipmates with desperate eyes. Her cool and confident demeanor that everyone had known throughout the trip was no longer cool or confident.

"Just relax," Guillermo gently said to Piccola, "the answer will come to you." He took his hand off her shoulder and with urgency in his voice addressed the crew, "We are running out of time. We all need to pitch in to try to solve this riddle."

Everyone emphatically agreed. But each sailor was secretly hoping someone else had any idea of *how* to help.

Once the sun clocked out, Mario cooked up his signature pot of steaming hot pasta with sauce. And though the pot was smaller than before, no one mentioned it. The crew ate quietly, each sailor trying—but more often pretending—to inverse or reverse things in their minds. No breakthrough ideas materialized over dinner, though. With appeased bellies but restless minds, the crew drifted along until they eventually drifted to sleep.

Toward daybreak on the second day of the northward voyage, the side of the deck shrank sufficiently to rub against Enzo's foot, jarring him awake. It was still too dark—even for Enzo—to survey the ship's newest dimensions, but he felt around to make sure the treasure chest hadn't gotten any smaller. Satisfied, he made his way across the deck and scaled the mainmast to await first light and the magenta sunrises he had come to expect along the journey.

The height of the mainmast seemed decidedly shorter than the day before, Enzo reckoned. From atop, he extended the telescope and looked out to the east where a light morning mist was beginning to creep in over the sea. Way up ahead he could make out what looked to be a hillside of flickering torches. He adjusted the scope to bring himself up to maximum vision. The lights weren't moving left to right or up and down, so he deduced that they weren't coming from a ship. "Must be land," he said to himself excitedly. Not long after, more and more flames came into view and, as the horizon continued to turn toward the sun, the enormous dark shadow of the Rock of Gibraltar became apparent. Enzo turned around to climb down the mast and alert the crew, but instead froze.

"*Madonna mia!*" he mouthed to himself as he squinted into the distance, assuring himself it was neither a glare nor a mirage nor his eyes playing some wicked trick on him. "Captaaaain!"

Guillermo and the crew shot upright, flipping their heads from side to side seeking the origin of Enzo's panicked voice. As soon as Enzo reached the bottom of the mast, Guillermo grabbed the telescope and zoomed in on Fleury's devilish grin. He was standing with Gascon at the bowsprit of the *Black Bass*, which was heading right at them.

Guillermo straightened out his captain's hat. It finally fit now that it had shrunk so significantly along with the ship. "All right, we've been through this before and we'll defeat these pirates again. They're coming in fast and have momentum. There isn't time to turn our sails to outrun them."

"And I think their sails are bigger than ours now," Luca added.

Everyone regarded the sails and let the implication of that statement sink in.

"We have to stand our ground," Guillermo called out. "We are going to need all hands on deck like never before."

"Captain, we should hide the gold below deck, in case they get on board," Tony exclaimed.

The crew dumped the contents of the treasure chest down the cabin staircase, sending the gold bars tumbling into the corridor below. Enzo flew down the stairs and started stashing away the treasure in a storage room by the landing while everyone else ran for the cannons.

"One thing's certain," Guillermo yelled while leading the troops, "they won't shoot at us."

"How can you be so sure?" Luca asked.

"Because they know we have their map, and possibly their treasure. Either way, if they sink us, they get nothing."

Guillermo, Luca, Tony, Mario and Piccola flew around the corner of the machine room. And since the cannonballs had shrunk by half Luca and Mario were able to load them without any help. Guillermo wondered if their firepower would have any power once fired.

On board the pirate ship, Gascon approached Fleury as they angled in on their prey, "Cap'n, did they switch ships or somethin'?"

Fleury rubbed his fingers across the rim of his hat. "Same name. Same flag. Same ship." He paused, "Different size?!"

Gascon rocked his head back and forth, "Bizarre..."

"*Très, très bizarre* indeed."

Fleury pointed to the bicycles they'd snatched from the locals in Tenerife. "And what about *zose*?"

Gascon's scraggy face tightened up. "Those used to be... bigger... too."

Fleury picked up the two gold bars and confirmed that their size hadn't changed. "As long as *ze* shiny stuff stays plump and juicy *zen* all's good."

Gascon ran off to get into position.

Guillermo and his crew peered out the gun ports waiting for the pirates to draw nearer. Their intense concentration was only punctured by Romeo who, having picked up the scent of home, tried to reach out to his old friends at the bazaar with a salvo of boisterous oinks.

"I think their ship is even bigger than ours now," Guillermo lamented.

"That means they can board us at will," Luca said.

Mario could barely speak, "They won't even need a sea dog."

Gascon dashed out onto the bowsprit and raised his sword high to indicate a full and final charge.

"All right, let's make these shots count," Guillermo ordered. "Aim for the bow. Fire!" He clutched his captain's ring and hoped for the best.

Luca and Piccola lit the cannon fuses and everyone wrapped their arms around the ship's beams to cushion against the backfire.

The three projectiles flung out of the cannon bores but compared to the awesome power of the weaponry at its largest, the backfire was minimal. For once Piccola wasn't ejected out into the corridor. The iron balls briefly arched through the sky before plunking into the sea in front of their intended target. The sea accepted them with barely a muffled hiccup.

Luca slouched down and held his head in his hands, "They're too small."

In Gibraltar the locals hurried out onto the docks to cast their eyes on the early morning naval battle shaping up outside the harbor. Juan Cruz, who had just returned from Africa, scaled the harbor master's control platform to get a better look. The increasingly dense mist made it difficult to see but a clearing in the sky briefly gave him a clear line of sight. "Fleury," he said with merry disgust, before spitting on the ground. "Come to dance the forbidden dance, have you?" He focused in on the other ship. "And my little friends... again." His pupils flashed wide as he went in for another look. "What's that smaller ship they're on now?" Juan frantically scanned the piers and then took off running.

"Fire again," Guillermo commanded from in front of the gunports on the *Grande Infante*.

Luca jumped back to action and he, Mario and Tony each lowered the cannonballs into the bores. The kids watched in sublime expectation as one of the shots gained promising velocity and height. It arched handsomely and homed in on the bow of the pirate ship.

"*Mamma mia,*" Luca shouted. "That one might hit them!'"

"Take cover!" Fleury screeched as if a guillotine's blade were set free above him.

The pirates hit the deck and held onto whatever they could to brace for impact.

"Here we go!" Luca exclaimed.

The cannonball smashed directly into the bow of the *Black Bass*. Gascon slipped from the bowsprit and landed hard on his groin; Fleury banged his head on the jib while trying to take cover. Their hope of getting their hands on the *Trujillo* treasure appeared to be sinking, along with their ship. The sound of the impact carried all the way back to the *Black Bass* as everyone held their breath until the smoke cleared. But the cannonball had ricocheted off the bow planks and tumbled into the sea below. An awkward moment of confusion gave way to instant misery for the kids and joyous celebration for the pirates.

"What'cha reckon they're using for ammunition, snowballs?" Gascon asked dryly.

"Fire the cannons, mates!" one of the pirates yelled before being backhanded by Fleury. The loose-lipped pirate fell to his knees.

"Hold your fire," Fleury commanded as he picked up the pirate by his collar. "You *imbécile*. You sink *zat* boat, you sink my gold."

The pirate stumbled backwards, trembling. "Sorry, Captain."

"*Zat's* two mistakes. Who told you to shout orders on my vessel?" Fleury's eyes narrowed as he matched a step forward for every step backward the petrified pirate took. Gascon relieved the tension by rushing over, "What are your orders, Captain?"

"Full ahead," Fleury said as he put his arm around the shuddering pirate.

"We all make mistakes, sailor," Fleury said with a grin. "Just be glad you're my chum."

The pirate offered a toothless and relieved smile as Fleury walked away.

"Gascon, march *zis* man off *ze* plank."

The pirate's knees buckled as he slouched to the deck. "I thought you said I was your chum?!"

"You are my chum, sailor. Gascon, feed him to *ze* fish. Let *zem* chew on *ze* little brains he has."

"Full retreat," Guillermo bellowed from behind the cannons of the *Grande Infante*. "It's our last option. Man the sails!"

The crew dashed up the cabin stairs. Luca and Tony hurled themselves up onto the mizzenmast, while Enzo climbed the mainmast and Mario lumbered up the foremast. Piccola followed Guillermo to the helm. He cut the rudder hard as the crew swung the sheets to the right.

"I guess this is the end of the adventure," Piccola said glumly.

Guillermo put his arm around her as he managed the wheel with his other, "I guess so."

On land, Juan thundered toward the outermost docking station, his every leap calling into question the constitution of the pier. He hastily approached a middle-aged, bearded man garbed in a captain's uniform. "Captain, I've never seen you around here before, but I beg you to take me out there," he pointed toward the scene of the battle, "Right away! Some friends of mine are in terrible danger."

The bearded captain tried to make swift sense of the situation. "I just arrived in Gibraltar and my crew's all up on the mainland having some time off from the sea."

"Captain, I only need your help. But immediately. There are children out there who need assistance. They're in great danger."

"Children?"

Juan nodded, "Please."

Meanwhile, Fleury's ship sped to within ten yards of the *Grande Infante*. He gave the order with wicked merriment, "Ram 'em!"

Guillermo begged the *Grande Infante* to turn quicker but it was hopeless. He eyed Fleury and Gascon as they got closer and closer. "Hold on!" he hollered to his crew.

The *Black Bass* smashed into the *Grande Infante's* starboard side at full speed. It banged into its outer hull, and pushed the ship almost completely over onto its other side. Guillermo gripped the wheel and Piccola wrapped her arms around his legs. For a moment it seemed as if the steering console would be ripped right off the mainframe of the ship. Nearly everything on the top deck—pots, plates, the empty treasure chest, the map, the golden key, even Romeo—plummeted into the sea. Enzo's portrait swung from side to side but clung onto its nail. The flag at the rear of the ship came loose and fell onto the back corner of the deck.

Screams of distress echoed from all directions. The *Black Bass* slowly slid back off the *Grande Infante's* side and Guillermo and Piccola's bodies thumped down onto the wet deck. They pulled themselves to their feet and scanned the sails frantically in search of the crew.

"Down here captain," Mario bellowed. Guillermo and Piccola rushed to the railing and spotted Mario, Luca, Enzo, Tony and Romeo all treading water in between the swells.

The pirates brushed themselves off and Fleury's men shifted their sails with aplomb. A minute later they tacked back and forth in a triangular pattern and headed right for the helpless swimmers.

"They're going to run us over!" Mario called out.

"Get me out of this water," Luca pleaded, scanning the surface for signs of aquatic danger.

Fleury hung the rudder to the right and the pirates dropped sail and threw in their anchor.

"Fish 'em out!" Gascon ordered as he pushed his men off the ship. He flashed his golden teeth down to Enzo as he pulled the blade of his sword against a sharpening stone. The sound of the metal grating against the stone echoed across the surface of the water. Enzo felt his stomach nearly pop out of his mouth as he tried to avoid imagining what it would feel like to have his flesh pierced by sharp metal.

A group of pirates surrounded Mario, Luca, Enzo and Tony in the water. They dragged them—as well as Romeo, who clung to Mario—effortlessly by their uniforms back toward the *Black Bass* and forced them up the sea dog.

Guillermo and Piccola looked on aghast from the deck of the *Grande Infante*, which had already begun listing to its side. The two ships had floated a little ways apart.

Gascon put his sword around Enzo's neck. The scent of the heated exchange between the blade and its sharpening stone drifted into Enzo's nostrils. He closed his eyes firmly.

Fleury projected his voice so that Guillermo could hear him across the way, "Now… *Petit Capitaine*, let's see how fearless you are without your big ship and your little crew. *Ze* man who brought me *zat* beautiful map went through a lot of trouble getting it to me. And to make sure its whereabouts remained hidden I rewarded him with a dagger through his heart. Imagine what I am prepared to do to you to get *ze* gold *zat* map led to!" Fleury spit onto the deck before continuing. "But I'll offer you a deal. Bring me *ze* gold right now, and I won't cut your friends into *leetle* pieces and feed *zem* to *ze* sharks."

Mario couldn't hold his composure any longer and Luca turned whiter than a ghost's tooth at the mention of the sharks. Tony bit down on his lip trying to hold back tears while Enzo determined never to open his eyes ever again. He didn't want his last sight to be of Gascon.

Guillermo sighed at Piccola. "We have no choice."

"We didn't get the treasure," Piccola yelled back to Fleury. "We tried but it was deep under the water. You'd have to be a fish to get it."

"Your friends on Tenerife would beg to differ." Fleury cleared his throat, "And believe me, *zey* did beg." He extracted a folded piece of paper from his pocket and put his finger on the sentence he was looking for. "Tell me if *zis* sounds familiar *ma petite*." He read aloud: "We found something of value while we were swimming and we wanted to leave you a gift because you were very nice and had to suffer through difficult times." He threw the paper into the sea and stroked the gold bar next to him before spitting another spray of mucous down onto his deck. Even his pirate shipmates appeared disturbed by his behavior.

Piccola stared harshly at Fleury. "Those nice people from Tenerife? You're an animal!"

"Now you're starting to get it *ma petite*. And you are my prey!" Fleury pushed his hat above his eyebrow line. "Last chance to come over here in one piece," he said sharply.

A strong gust of wind pushed the *Grande Infante* backwards, adding some additional space between the two ships.

"You're not going anywhere you maggots. Not while I have your friends on *ze* chopping block."

"OK, we're coming over," Guillermo called out, defeated and petrified. He looked at Piccola, who was shaking. "You go down below and hide wherever you can."

"Not a chance," she replied in her bravest voice.

"Fleury you snake in the grass!" Juan Cruz's voice piped up. He screamed from the tip of the ship's bowsprit on which he had hitched a ride, "Remember me?"

The four hostages couldn't believe their eyes, and their luck. "Admiral!" they yelled in Juan's direction.

Gascon looked at Fleury sideways, "Cruz? Where'd he come from?"

Fleury stuck his head over the side of the ship. "Look mates, it's *ze* Admiral," he said mockingly. "Admiral, allow me to show you the same kindness we did last time we met. When I sank your ship." He pointed to his men, "Fire the cannons!"

From their positions on the two different ships the crew of the *Grande Infante* watched as a cannonball sliced through the air and smashed straight into the ship carrying Juan Cruz. Juan and the bearded captain were both thrown from their feet as their vessel lost its momentum almost instantly and started taking on water.

"Thanks a lot," the bearded man said, glaring at Juan.

"Epic fail," Juan replied to his incredulous shipmate. "We tried."

"Did you really have to yell at them before we were in position?"

"It's been a while since I've battled at sea."

On the *Black Bass,* Mario, Luca, Enzo and Tony slouched back while over on the *Grande Infante* Guillermo and Piccola released their hopeful embrace.

"This one's for good measure," Gascon said maliciously, his eye twitching like a sailor sending Morse code across the sea. He relit the fuse and dispatched a second burst of iron toward Juan and the bearded captain. The cannonball tore the deck of the sinking ship to shreds. Juan leaped to safety just in time off the bow. The bearded captain dove over the portside rail and disappeared under the water.

Five wet pirates hurled themselves back into the sea and caught up to Juan Cruz. It took all of them to subdue him and two of them almost drowned in the process.

Guillermo and Piccola watched as their last hope, the sinking ship with two cannonballs lodged in its stomach, started to slide under. The water rose over its mid section and twirled its frame around. As the stern slowly came into view Guillermo noticed the ship bore the exact same red and white Florentine flag that his own ship had flown. The fog started to roll in more densely but just before the sinking ship succumbed to the sea's grasp Guillermo and Piccola caught sight of its name: the *Infante.*

—Chapter 14—

Blood in the Water

Fleury pointed his sword at Gascon, "Have *ze* men raise *ze* anchor and prepare a boarding party. It's time to take our due."

The fog thickened and pushed out across the sea's surface as the currents began adding more and more distance between the *Grande Infante* and the anchored pirate ship.

Fleury walked in front of his line of hostages, all of whom now had their hands tied behind their backs. His boots creaked with each step. "Looks like your spineless shipmates are trying to abandon you. *Zere's* nothing like a loyal crew," he smirked.

Enzo thought back to when Fleury had marched one of his own crew members off the plank. Had he known Fleury had thrown another shipmate overboard moments before he may very well have fainted.

Juan Cruz struggled to break free of his ropes and it took three husky pirates to hold him down. Gascon shoved his sword up against Juan's neck and pulled just enough to draw a few beads of blood, "Give me a reason to cut deeper Cruz. But know this... I'm only keepin' you alive for now 'cause

177

the Captain wants to take his time with you after we get the loot and off the kids." Juan settled down and tried to look away from the small pool of blood collecting on the deck.

"Gascon, *zat's* not how we treat guests." Fleury leaned over to his old acquaintance. "We're in the company of greatness. *Ze* Great Admiral Cruz. *Ze* Great Admiral with his ships so nice, we had to sink *zem* twice." The pirates seemed to find enjoyable their captain's penchant for poetic verse.

Mario, Luca, Enzo and Tony shivered from the wind hitting against their drenched bodies and, moreover, from the sheer sense of helplessness they were all feeling. The chatter of Mario's teeth was so loud that Enzo wondered whether they'd eventually shatter into pieces. He imagined what it would feel like to have your teeth break apart. Not worse, he figured, then being ripped open by a steel sword. A flood of thoughts and no thoughts simultaneously occupied everyone's clouded minds.

Guillermo and Piccola faced each other by the helm of the *Grande Infante*. They could faintly hear the commotion on Fleury's ship but the blanket of fog completely obstructed their view. Guillermo started pacing in small circles. Piccola reached out and anxiously fingered the hourglass. "Only a third left."

"That's the least of our worries now."

Piccola slumped down. "I guess we should just give them the treasure and hope they'll let us all go."

"If they get their hands on the gold they'll kill all of us right away, just like they do to everyone who crosses their path. I'm sure they're only keeping the others alive until they confirm the treasure's here on the ship, and that we didn't hide it somewhere else. "

178

"Then our only option is to figure out a plan to free our crew without giving Fleury the treasure," Piccola said, trying to sound brave. "But since they're already planning to board us as we speak that's pretty much impossible."

"*Andiamo*, let's go downstairs to see if we can come up with any ideas, or find some weapons to help us."

They started toward the cabin stairs but then heard a faint noise and darted back behind the steering console.

"*Attenzione*," a voice whispered. "Anyone here?"

The siblings poked their heads around the helm and saw a dripping wet man with a beard crouched down on the deck. He had a broad torso and brawny shoulders wide enough to eat dinner on. His rugged build stood in stark contrast, though, to the calm features on his square-shaped face. Despite the ruinous circumstances he didn't appear stressed or frazzled to Guillermo.

"I think that's the guy who was with Juan Cruz on the ship that Fleury sank," Piccola said.

"He sure looks familiar," Guillermo uttered.

"Over here," Piccola whispered back.

The bearded captain sloshed over to the kids. "Where's your crew?"

"The pirates on the other ship kidnapped all of them," Guillermo said.

"*Allora*, I mean, your crew. The adults."

"It's just us. We're trying to get home to our parents. But now Fleury has our friends and he's probably going to kill them. And us. And you too if you don't jump ship."

"He destroyed my ship too," the bearded man said in disgust. "He'll pay for that. He will wish our sea lanes had never crossed today."

"Can you help us get our friends back from Fleury's ship?" Piccola asked.

"Why'd he want them in the first place?"

"Because we have—"

"Because he wants to steal our ship," Guillermo interrupted.

"He does have that reputation," the man confirmed. "If I'd known it was Fleury out here I'd have never let that giant bonehead in the harbor convince me to sail into this mess unprepared. I would have assembled my crew and sailed at them hard charging!"

"All we want is to get our friends back and to go home to Pizzolungo," Piccola said.

"Where's Pizzolungo?"

"Sicily."

"Sicily, huh?" He looked up but couldn't even see the top of the mainmast through the fog. He looked down at Piccola, her little knees knocking back and forth, trying to hold steady but hardly succeeding.

"We've got to save our friends."

"I'll come up with a plan. I always do."

"Why was your ship called the *Infante*?" Guillermo asked.

"I wanted to ask you the same thing. The coincidences I stumble upon as I make my rounds never cease to astonish me. Two ships called the *Infante* in the same place..."

"Ours is called the *Grande Infante*," Piccola noted.

"Even though it's a slightly smaller ship," the man said, chuckling. Anyway, my name's Lorenzo. Lorenzo Infante. My ship was named after me."

Guillermo and Piccola stepped back in total disbelief. Guillermo immediately realized why the man looked so familiar: he'd seen his face every day of his life on the wall above his living room sofa.

"Is it true," Guillermo couldn't resist, "that you once defeated an entire Venetian squadron by sinking their ship from the inside out?"

"I'm impressed," Lorenzo said. "Since Gutenberg rolled out his printing press word travels fast. That incident on the Venetian ship happened less than a year ago. It's typical though how these stories always get embellished as they're told and retold. I did sink a Venetian ship, but a squadron they weren't. Just six men in fact. They tried to ambush me in their hull but I broke free and yes, I sank them."

The Infante siblings looked at each other and shrugged their shoulders.

"I think it's time to get to work wouldn't you say?" Lorenzo asked.

"Work on what?" Piccola asked.

Just then the sounds from Fleury's ship started getting nearer. It was impossible to see anything though; the fog hung off the ship like dense swirls of cotton candy. "On the plan to save your crew, and teach Fleury a lesson. The first thing to do is move this ship to another location while we determine how to retrieve your friends... and my new buffoon of a shipmate."

"But we must hurry," Piccola insisted. "There's no telling how much longer Fleury will let them live."

"He can't kill them," Guillermo said, "until he sets his eyes on our... ship."

"Maybe he'll also keep them alive to make sure we don't fire our cannons at them again," added Piccola.

"I don't think Fleury is too worried about that," Guillermo bemoaned.

"If your friends are safe until Fleury finds this ship then that buys us some time," Lorenzo said, wringing out his wet shirt. "What are your names?"

"I'm Guillermo and this is my sister Piccola."

"I can see why she's called that," Lorenzo said playfully. "Now Guillermo, while I tune up the sails, I need you to steer us away from the sounds coming from Fleury's ship. Do you know how to steer?"

"I think I can figure it out."

Lorenzo pulled on the sail ropes like a master puppeteer pulling his characters' strings. Guillermo held the wheel tight and the *Grande Infante* shoved off into the fog, away from Fleury. As it sliced across the sea the noises from the pirate ship began to peter out.

"Shouldn't we call him great, great, great, great, great grandpapa, or something like that?" Piccola asked.

"I don't think that's a good idea. Nobody in a million years would believe our story. I'm not even sure I believe our story. Telling him or anyone else who we are and when we're from will just make them think we're crazy."

"Yeah, I guess you're right. It's worked for us so far," Piccola admitted as she and Guillermo crept out toward the mainmast to watch Lorenzo in action. Suddenly, she stopped short causing Guillermo to walk right into her.

Guillermo shoved her lightly, "What's your problem?"

"I just had a terrible thought."

"What?"

"Juan never would have asked Lorenzo for help if he didn't see our ship from the harbor. So Lorenzo wouldn't be here right now if we hadn't traveled back in time. He's not *supposed* to be here," she said gravely. "If something happens to him during this rescue mission, we may never be born."

Guillermo gulped and tried to wrap his mind around that fact. "I remember Papa saying he died young. Let's just hope it's not today." Guillermo tried his best to get the thought out of his mind. "Now come on, we have friends to save."

Lorenzo came down from the mainmast and walked over to the kids. "Let's plan our attack."

Lorenzo instilled great trust and confidence in the siblings, even though they knew that the likelihood of three people—one adult and two kids—defeating a boatload of armed pirates with hostages was infinitesimal at best.

"Captain Lorenzo," Guillermo asked, "do you think our ship will hold up much longer? Fleury rammed us pretty hard and since then we've been listing starboard."

"Before I boarded I swam around the ship and inspected the damage. This is some vessel. She has two parallel hulls and while your external wall is compromised, there's a second line of protection that keeps the water from seeping into the main body." He stretched his neck from side to side. "When I get back to Florence I will suggest that henceforth all ships are constructed like this. Who built her?"

"It is a pretty amazing ship," Guillermo agreed, "but we don't know who built it. It was sent to my house one day... but that's a long story. You should come downstairs with us so we can show you all the tools and weapons we have on board."

The Infantes hustled down to the machine room. The corridors had shrunk considerably and Lorenzo had to keep his torso bent to avoid bonking his head on the ceiling. They entered the room and Lorenzo nearly fell over in amazement. He passed the cannons, cannonballs, gunpowder bags, dive suits and other creations. Then he bent down and started rummaging through the countless tools and weapons in the cubbies. He rolled up his sleeves, "I thought there was only one person who crafts things like these," he muttered to himself.

A wooden and metal item in one of the cubbies captured his attention and he extracted it with care and astonishment.

"*Amicos*, for every action in this world there's an equal and opposite reaction. And I believe I have our reaction."

"That's a Newton theory," Piccola exclaimed.

"No dear, there's nothing new about this theory. It's as old as Adam and Eve themselves."

Guillermo and Piccola shrugged. "So what do we have to do?"

"To begin with we need to get as close as we can to Fleury's ship before this fog breaks. And we need to be upwind of him. In any battle at sea you want to be upwind of your adversary."

Over on the *Black Bass* Fleury pushed Gascon against the wall and cupped his hand around the boatswain's narrow throat.

"Calm down boss, we'll find 'em," Gascon pleaded. "There's just two of 'em left, and one of 'em's that teaspoon-sized girl. We're sure to bump into 'em sooner or later."

"See to it *zat* it's sooner!"

Gascon's eye twitched as if a hundred ants were storming about inside its socket. Fleury could see the veins across the boatswain's retina palpitating. He released him just so *he* could look away.

Gascon pulled himself up and marched across the deck rubbing his throat. "Keep yer' eyes n' ears open," he commanded to the crew. On his way back to the stern he nearly tripped over Luca's foot. He whipped around and kicked Luca's legs, hard. Luca flung back onto his tied up hands. His wrists bent and twisted painfully and the back of his head banged up against the deck.

Luca lay on his back dizzy from the impact. His vision came in and out and he wondered whether he had a concussion. The echo of his heartbeat sounded like a bass drum and he assumed the rest of his panicked crew could hear it as well. Everyone remained paralyzed with fear as Gascon walked away seething and picked up his sword before eyeing the hostages menacingly once again.

Finally Luca tightened his stomach muscles and pulled himself back to a sitting position. As he did so he felt something sharp behind him. Using his tied-up hands he probed around for whatever had poked him. Eventually he touched a pointed rusty nail sticking out of the deck. He controlled his breathing and made sure nobody was watching him. Then he slowly lowered his hands onto the nail and started to massage the rope against the iron tip. He prayed the whole time that Gascon wouldn't notice anything suspicious.

After what felt like ages the rope gave way. Luca's wrists ached from Gascon's assault and his courtship with the sharp nail, but his hands were free. Tony sat to his right and impatiently awaited his turn. He gently slid in closer while Luca shifted slightly to the side. Tony began to carve away at his rope. Afterwards it was Mario's turn, and Luca and Tony squirmed back slightly in the other direction. At one point Romeo woke up from a slumber, sensing that Mario was twitching. He let out a shrill oink, which briefly attracted the glassy-eyed interest of the pirates sitting by the stern. When they finally looked away Mario slid the ropes off his hands.

Enzo sat farthest from the nail. "What about me?" he whispered.

Fleury was alone at the helm cursing to himself under his breath. He heard Enzo whispering and flipped his head around, directing a penetrating glare at the boys.

Luca shook his head at Enzo, "No way," he mouthed, "too dangerous." Then he motioned to Tony and Mario to hold steady for the time being until they figured out a way to get Enzo and, if possible, Juan Cruz untied.

From across the deck Fleury got Gascon's attention. The boatswain shook his head; still no sign of the *Grande Infante*.

As the morning hours ticked away the sun's rays strengthened and started to slowly beat back the fog. Eventually Fleury's patience ran out. He leapt up and barreled down toward the crowd. The pirates seemed almost as scared of their mercurial boss as the hostages were.

"If that's how it's gonna be, then this is how it's gonna be," Fleury thundered. Enzo was closest to him and he shook him to his feet.

Luca, Tony, Mario and Juan recoiled in terror as Fleury marched Enzo, screaming and with his hands still tied behind his back, toward the plank. Enzo struggled to look back but Fleury gripped his neck tightly. Luca looked over the side of the ship and saw his worst nightmare—a fin jutting above the surface. He gasped and quickly turned his head back.

Guillermo stood at the bow of the *Grande Infante* trying to glimpse the water through the fog-filled air. He went to feel for his captain's ring but realized it wasn't on his finger. "I can't believe I lost it," he muttered aloud in disgust. He thought back to the words his father had told him when he handed him the ring on his birthday the year before. The big Captain had looked him square in the eye and said he was proud to be the father of Pizzolungo's greatest future captain. Guillermo wondered where he'd lost the ring. If he could never get home he at least wanted to have it as a memory of his father and the life he had back in Pizzolungo before everything changed. He slouched down on the deck and, against all his wishes and willpower, cried.

Lorenzo approached from the stern, "What's the matter boy?"

"Nothing." The tear he tried to hide betrayed him though, and Lorenzo took notice. He sat down next to Guillermo.

"The story you heard, about me defeating the Venetians... Even though it was only six men and not a squadron, you don't think I was scared?"

Guillermo didn't respond.

"It was cold and dark that night and I was shaking, but not from the cold. And not from the dark. I boarded that ship and was led down into its belly. When the Venetians sprang up from the shadows and surrounded me I knew my odds of surviving were small. No man can face death and say they aren't scared. It's OK to be afraid, Guillermo."

"I'm supposed to be brave. I'm the captain of this ship and I'm scared like a little baby."

Lorenzo looked him in the eye, "Bravery isn't about not being afraid. Bravery is about being afraid of something and doing it anyway. That's what makes a hero."

Guillermo let that sink in. Eventually he rejoined Lorenzo and Piccola to prepare for the rescue mission as the sun finally whittled away most of the remaining fog.

"There it is!" Gascon said icily, pointing to the *Grande Infante* off to the *Bass's* portside.

The pirates prepared their raiding party by readying their weapons, ropes, and ladders.

Meanwhile the three Infantes climbed silently off their stern and submerged their heads under the water.

On the *Bass*, Juan Cruz wrestled fruitlessly with his shackles. His neck had stopped bleeding and the blood on the deck had dried into narrow rivulets. He gave up and turned to the kids. They covertly showed him that they'd gotten their hands untied. "You kids get prepared to jump overboard," he whispered, "I'll do my best to distract 'em."

Luca whispered back, "Overboard, are you crazy? There are sharks in there."

"Once Fleury gets control of your ship we're all done for. Believe me, you'd rather swim with a shark than tangle with a sword."

"No *you'd* rather swim with a shark. I'm just fine here. If you want to go back in the water you're on your own!"

Tony jumped into the conversation, "Luca, there's no other way off this ship. We're going to have to get wet again. And most shark species don't bite anyway, especially in this part of the world."

Juan's voice was coarse, "He's right about that. And as for me, I wouldn't get a fish's thrust from the ship with my hands still tied. But don't worry about that, I've gotten myself out of far worse situations. And if I go down, I'm taking Fleury with me."

Luca's face sank as Juan Cruz's fate became more apparent. Tony turned to Luca and Mario, "As soon as they board the *Grande Infante* we need to jump off the other side of this ship and try to swim to Gibraltar."

"That's *really* far," Mario protested. "And we've got to try and help Piccola and the captain."

"If they were smart they would've already swam to shore," Tony murmured.

Beneath the swells Guillermo and Piccola's breaths were short and shallow through their dive suit snorkels. An extra air pipe that Lorenzo had fashioned with excess tubing diverted some of Guillermo's air into Lorenzo's mouthpiece. Lorenzo swam without a helmet.

From just below the surface it was easy for the Infantes to observe the distance between the hulls of the two ships decreasing. Finally Lorenzo flashed Guillermo the sign.

Guillermo tugged the rope in his hand. It pulled taught all the way up through the water, over the *Grande Infante's* deck and into the weapons room. The rope eventually whisked a lit candle onto its side, igniting the cannon fuses. Even from beneath the sea the Infantes could hear the blasts. Rather than iron, though, they each fired the ten bags of gunpowder that Lorenzo had stuffed into their bores.

Then Lorenzo yanked the rope in his hand. It too ran up through the water, over the deck and up to the catapult system they'd brought up from the machine room. In it, a kitchen cocktail of flour, sea salt, crushed pepper and tomatoes launched toward Fleury's deck.

Lorenzo motioned to the kids to ascend directly beneath Fleury's hull.

On board, Fleury and Gascon barked overlapping and contradictory orders to their men as panic and mayhem overran their deck. Thick smoke and raining spices turned the air above the ship into a blizzard of mild toxins. Crushed pepper and smoke lodged deep into everyone's eyes and noses as salt, flour and tomato pulp began blanketing everything.

The disoriented pirates stumbled about, producing a cacophony of coughs and sneezes.

In between gagging coughs, Juan, Luca, Tony and Mario wondered what in the world was going on. A tomato splashed across Mario's forehead and dripped down his face. "Mmm, peppery."

Just then one of the sneezing pirates stepped backwards onto Romeo's foot. The piglet spun around and dug his teeth into the back of the pirate's ankle. The man dropped his sword and clutched his wound.

Da Gama might know a lot about sailing but he doesn't know jack about pig luck, Mario thought to himself.

Luca sprang up and shoved the pirate overboard. As he fell into the sea Luca grabbed his sword and darted up behind Juan Cruz. "Juan, spread your hands as wide as possible!" Luca positioned the blade right above the rope and chopped down on it. Juan threw the ropes to the ground and Luca pressed the sword into his hands.

"Get behind me lads," Juan ordered.

Under water, Lorenzo felt the slippery outer boards of the pirate ship's hull with Guillermo and Piccola at his side. The green algae hanging off the boat swayed back and forth with the undersea current. He stroked his hands across the boards until he found the sweet spot he'd been seeking. He motioned for Guillermo and Piccola to swim clear and then unfastened the tool hanging from his belt. It was a round piece of reinforced wood with heavy-duty coil springs that pulled back a plate of solid iron. Lorenzo released the lever and the springs torpedoed the metal plate into the ship boards with tremendous force, splintering them into pieces. Dust and debris littered the area as water and fragmented wood exchanged places.

Once the visibility increased, Lorenzo motioned for Guillermo and Piccola to follow him up through the hole they'd just created and into the hull of the pirate ship, which was already flooding with water.

"This tool's been good to me," Lorenzo boasted. "Same effect going in or going out."

Guillermo and Piccola threw off their diving helmets as Lorenzo led the way up the cabin stairs toward the deck.

The impact of Lorenzo's tool and the gush of water entering the hull tossed the *Black Bass* from side to side. The Infantes saw that half of the pirates had fallen overboard. Amidst the chaos, they grasped for floating debris to hold onto as they struggled to re-board the ship to help their crewmates. Two shark fins began circling around them.

Lorenzo picked up a sword that one of the pirates had dropped and reconvened with Juan Cruz. "You take the boatswain, I'm on Fleury," Lorenzo said as he started off down the ship.

Juan stopped him in his tracks with one hand. "*I'm* on Fleury."

Guillermo and Piccola ran toward Juan. "Juan, where's our crew?"

Juan pointed toward the sea and yelled back, "I think some of them tumbled over a minute ago. There was an eruption from underneath and everyone fell in different directions."

It was hard to stand on the tilting forecastle deck, not least because it was coated with a mixture of seawater and spicy tomato sauce. Lorenzo caught up to Gascon at the bow and leapt at him. Gascon swung his sword around but Lorenzo ducked and then struck him in the gut with a well-placed knee. Gascon doubled over, trying to find his breath. Lorenzo finished him off with an uppercut to the chin. As Gascon flew backwards a pair of his gold teeth rolled out onto the floor. Two pirates crept over to wrestle over the fallen gold as Lorenzo made his way back toward the main deck.

Guillermo and Piccola spotted Luca and Tony struggling with the swells near the ship.

"Help! Get me out of here," Luca implored as he hastily treaded water.

"Swim toward the *Grande Infante*, it's just over there," Guillermo yelled.

"I can't. I can't," Luca screeched.

Tony thrust through the water while Mario sought refuge by cowering up on the *Black Bass's* mizzenmast. As Tony pulled himself up onto the stern of the *Grande Infante* he spun around and nearly fell over.

"*Oh Dio mio*, Luca, don't look back. Trust me."

"Is it a shark?" Luca screamed.

"Just swim *amico*, as fast as you can."

"I can't!" he cried, as a long and sleek shark began circling him. Luca fell silent and involuntarily brought his water treading down to a bare minimum.

From the pirate ship Guillermo and Piccola watched through spread fingers as the shark sniffed out Luca. Mario had to turn away. Tony stretched out his arm but wasn't even close to reaching Luca. The shark circled Luca repeatedly, even brushing up against his skin twice. But it didn't attack. It seemed driven more by curiosity than by hunger. Luca cautiously doggy paddled toward the *Grande Infante* until Tony grabbed his hand and helped him aboard. Everyone watching took their first breath in over a minute.

"Maybe you're right Tony, maybe sharks aren't so bad after all," Luca said sheepishly, half-smiling.

"No, they are. I was totally lying before about them not biting. This one must have recently eaten or something." Luca swung his feet out of the water.

On the *Bass* Juan pursued Fleury near the stern. He lunged at him but the ship's weight shifted and sent them both tumbling off their feet. Fleury swiped his sword at the Admiral, who rolled away swiftly for a man of his stature. The sharp blade stuck stubbornly into the wood and Juan landed a punch to the ribs with his ogre-sized fist. Fleury fell to the floor and rolled out of the way.

"I've been looking forward to this dance for a long time, Fleury," Juan said towering over the pirate boss.

Fleury leapt to his feet and used his speed and agility to dash around Juan. He ran down the portside and flung Guillermo to the ground before swiping Piccola off her feet. With his free hand he whipped out his dagger. "Anyone moves and you'll be putting coins over her eyes," he called out with bloody murder in his eyes. Juan and Lorenzo rushed over but kept their distance to avoid testing Fleury's limits. The French pirate caught his breath and spit a mix of blood and phlegm onto the deck. "So here's what's going to happen next, you sneaky snappers: me and *ma petite* here are going to swim out to your ship all by ourselves." Every time Fleury moved, Piccola could feel the point of the dagger jutting into her skin. She kept her eyes closed, too petrified to even try and fight back or break free. "If anyone tries *anysing* stupid while we swim away, *zen ze* sharks will be smelling blood in *ze* water."

Fleury carried Piccola backwards, dragging the heels of her feet along the deck boards. "I'm going to sail off in your ship, with *my* treasure. If everyone does what *zey're* supposed to, *zen* I'll *sink* about releasing her somewhere along *ze* way. Maybe." He pressed the blade tighter against Piccola's neck.

Guillermo watched his sister in the gnarled and blackened hands of the madman. He took a breath and inched closer, terrified. His chest was tight and his throat was so dry he could barely get the first sentence out, "You're a coward."

Fleury turned to Guillermo, literally foaming at the mouth. "What did you say, snapper?"

"I said you're a coward. I've beaten you at every turn. I stole your treasure and I'm about to sink your ship. And what do you do, you threaten my eleven-year-old little sister?" Guillermo was hoping the short, terrified gulps he was taking between sentences weren't registering to Fleury. "What kind of a pirate are you?"

"I'd watch your tongue if I were you," Fleury said pointing his dagger at Guillermo. "Or you can watch it dangling from my necklace."

"Tough talk from the pirate who got beat by a twelve year old." His fear was making him light headed, but he continued. "And you better believe that I will make sure the story gets out. Wherever you go from now on, you're going to be known as 'Fleury, the pirate who got beat by a twelve year old'."

"Your sister I was going to take hostage. You, I will kill where you stand!" Fleury shouted, increasingly distracted.

"Ahoy you *scorpione!*" The shout came hurling down from the sail beam of the mizzenmast, along with a screaming Mario. Fleury, Guillermo, Piccola, Lorenzo and Juan all looked up at the same time.

Guillermo seized the opportunity, "Piccola!" he shouted as she pushed the knife out of Fleury's hand and got out of the way just as Mario crashed down right onto Fleury's head, knocking him to the ground. Fleury's skull banged violently against the wooden deck and his eyes rolled back in their sockets.

Lorenzo grabbed Fleury's dagger and slipped it into his own sheath with pride. Juan rushed over and checked Fleury's breathing.

"Is he alive?" Guillermo asked, to which Juan slowly shook his head, "No."

"He was smart enough to deny me the pleasure," Juan continued, standing over the sprawled out pirate, fists clenched.

Lorenzo put a hand on Guillermo's shoulder. "Not bad, young man."

"Oh Mario!" Piccola screamed as she ran to him, "Are you OK?"

"I'm… not sure." He rolled over and shook his head like a wet dog as everyone crowded around him.

Piccola leaned over and kissed him on the cheek. If Mario blushed any brighter his skin would have caught fire.

"I think I'm OK, *bella*."

"Thank God," Piccola said as she started away.

"Um, owwww… wait, my, um, neck. And my back…"

Piccola turned back and put her arm around Mario, helping him up. Mario turned his face so she wouldn't catch his grin.

The remaining pirates in the water gave up trying to re-board the sinking *Black Bass and* swam toward the *Grande Infante*. But Luca and Tony were standing guard. They reminded the pirates that while the *Grande Infante's* last cannon volleys may not have sunk their ship, they'd slice through flesh like a knife through cream cheese. The spent and depleted pirates took their word for it (even though they hadn't a clue what cream cheese was) and opted to maximize their chances of survival by swimming toward the mainland instead.

Only about a quarter of the *Black Bass* remained above water. Guillermo scrambled up to the highest point and caught Tony's eye over on the *Grande Infante*, "Come pick us up."

Fleury remained lifeless as the water rose past his waist. But once it reached his mouth, his eyes began to flutter.

Juan picked up Mario and carried him to the highest part of the deck while Lorenzo helped Piccola to the top of the floating debris pile.

Luca raised the *Grande Infante's* anchor and Tony took control of the rudder. They drifted up alongside the rubble of the former pirate ship.

No one noticed Fleury getting to his feet, blood trickling from his forehead as he stabilized himself. His eyes were wild like a man possessed. "It's dying time, snapper," he hollered as he lunged toward Guillermo. But just as he got close enough Juan blocked him, and using Fleury's momentum to his advantage he pushed him straight overboard.

Juan leaned over, "That's for my ship! Say hello to the sharks for me."

Fleury churned the water spastically to stay afloat as a desperate blankness covered his face. Two nearby sharks got their first scent of blood in the water.

"Look away," Lorenzo suggested as he and Juan helped Guillermo board the *Grande Infante*.

"Wait a second," Guillermo stopped. "Where's Enzo?"

Silence befell the deck. Luca, Tony, Mario and Juan lowered their chins and stared down at the sea.

"What?" Piccola said. "Where is he?"

Finally Luca eyed the captain. He couldn't speak without choking up. "Fleury made him walk the plank early this morning."

—Chapter 15—

Catch of the Day

The *Grande Infante* lumbered toward the Gibraltar harbor as the sun crept to its highest point in the Iberian sky. Juan and Lorenzo closed down the sails on the main and mizzenmasts and Lorenzo took charge of the helm. Juan climbed up the foremast to shift the sheets into a docking position. Through his tears Guillermo observed how the two accomplished seamen brought the ship into port without relying on an anchor toss to slow them down.

That afternoon, as Juan and Lorenzo filled the pier with all the sounds of a carpenter's workshop repairing the ship, Guillermo knew that as captain he should be the one to say something meaningful about their fallen friend. But he couldn't find the right words. Or any words at all. No one could. His throat was closing up and despite the cool breeze off the sea he felt stubbornly overheated. Truth be told, all he wanted was to be alone somewhere so he could grieve for Enzo.

"If his hands hadn't been tied he might have been able to swim to shore," Luca whispered, breaking the long heavy silence.

"No way. It's too far, even if his hands had been free," Tony shook his head.

"If we ever get back to Pizzolungo how will we tell Enzo's parents?" Piccola asked.

"I'll tell them," Guillermo finally said, pushing back his emotions as best he could. "I'll tell them what a hero he was on our travels. How he was the best lookout on the ship and how he risked his life to bring up the treasure from under water." He sat down. "And how it was my fault for getting him into this mess in the first place."

"This never would have happened if I hadn't stolen Fleury's treasure map," Tony said.

"I should have risked untying Enzo when I had the chance," Luca added between heavy breaths.

Piccola put a hand on both Luca and Tony's shoulders but looked her brother in the eye. "It was nobody's fault that Fleury sent him off the plank. Nobody's fault but Fleury's, and we need to remember that."

"Poor Enzo…" Mario glanced up at his portrait, "he was just a kid."

"Well, it doesn't seem like we're ever going home anyway," Piccola mourned. "I've all but given up on the riddle. And the ship keeps getting smaller and smaller, along with the time machine."

"So we're going to stay in Gibraltar forever?" Mario bemoaned. "I miss my parents and my house. I even miss school and I never thought I'd say that."

"We'll get home," Luca said as Juan emerged from the lower deck covered in grease, filth and sweat.

"You're ready to sail," Juan said to Guillermo. "Lorenzo's just putting on the finishing touches from the dock."

"Just a minute," Guillermo said, holding up an index finger and motioning for Luca to follow him below deck.

Luca slipped on a wet step on his way down, almost losing his balance completely.

"LOL," Juan said to Piccola, who smiled and walked over to him.

"I think I'm actually going to miss you," she said looking up at the man who may as well have been standing on the roof of a building.

"Maybe we'll meet again," Juan said. "I've decided to return to the sea. I've been away for too long. I'm ready to put the past behind me."

"You and me both," Mario said.

"I suppose Pizzolungo isn't too far for a visit when you have a ship to sail on and a crew to sail with," Juan said.

Piccola almost let slip that no matter how far Juan sailed he'd probably never find them, but instead she gave him a hug. (Her arms made it half way around his upper thighs, but it was a hug all the same.)

Lorenzo returned to the deck at the same time Guillermo and Luca emerged from the cabin stairs, each carrying two bars of gold. Guillermo spoke, "We want to thank you for saving us. Fleury would have killed us all if you didn't sail to our rescue. We know that he sank both of your ships. And we want to help you buy new ones."

They handed two gold bars each to Lorenzo and Juan who inspected them in shock.

"Where did these come from?" Lorenzo asked.

"Is this real gold?" Juan questioned.

Mario took a deep breath and explained. "Tony found a treasure map on Fleury's ship and then we sailed to the Canary Islands and then we used a dual periscope to find the shipwreck and then Piccola and Enzo went scuba diving and brought the gold bars to the surface." He reloaded, "And we met a lot of nice people in the Canary Islands who called our bicycles 'rolling horses'. All that was before we lost Enzo, our ship's lookout, and our good friend." Mario pointed to Enzo's portrait.

"We're very sorry about your friend," Lorenzo said.

"He was a good man," Juan noted. "And a good sailor."

Nobody spoke for a few long seconds. Guillermo broke the empty silence by returning to business. "Juan, I think once people find out about what you did today they'll start calling you 'Admiral' again with respect."

"Now I see why those weasel pirates kept after you all this time." Juan shook his head. "You know, I usually subscribe to the notion of 'finders keepers', 'what's yours is yours' and all that but I suppose if you insist I could take a little gold off your hands. It would certainly expedite my quest for a new vessel."

"They had 'finders keepers' back then?" Mario whispered to Tony.

Guillermo turned to Lorenzo. "Lorenzo, while we're happier than you can ever imagine that you survived this ordeal,"—Piccola elbowed Guillermo who took his cue to change the subject—"we're really sorry that Fleury sank the Infante. Maybe with this gold you can get an even greater ship."

Lorenzo held the gold bars. "Son, even though I'm not a wealthy man, I'd ordinarily never accept this offering from you. But I'm far from home and I need to finance my whole crew's return journey. As such, I would accept this only if you inform me of exactly how and where I can return the value of this gold to you. I promise you I will find a way. I've always wanted to see Sicily and I've even thought about moving my family there one day."

"That's great. And you should," Guillermo said a little too eagerly. "There's no need to repay us though, you risked your life for us and we're happy to give it to you. You're a real hero and your portrait deserves to be hanging in my house."

Lorenzo looked at Guillermo sideways.

"I mean, it deserves to be hanging in someone's house… one day." Guillermo reached into his pocket. "I want to give you one more thing." He extracted the compass that Christopher Columbus had given him. "This is something very special that you can remember us by. It would be an honor if you would accept it from us for your bravery."

He handed the compass to Lorenzo who examined it. "It's beautiful. I'll treasure it as long as I live and think of you every time I look at it. My son will love it too."

"I hope he will."

"Well," Juan interjected, "Until the next time you need your lives saved, eh?"

"Good luck sailors," Lorenzo said as he and Juan made their way down the gangplank. "Find your way home safely."

"You too," Guillermo said as the crew slowly started taking their positions to sail. Juan and Lorenzo untied their docking ropes and waved farewell.

"Say," Juan looked at the kids, "was I soused up on the ale last time we met, or has this ship gotten *a lot* smaller since then?"

"The ale," Tony said quickly, biting his lip. Everyone nodded in agreement.

"May the sea always treat you like sailors!" were Juan's parting words to the crew. He put his arm on Lorenzo's shoulder and they headed off toward the nearest pub, "Lorenzo, I think this is the start of a beautiful bender."

Back out at sea the sense of urgency to sail east and solve the riddle hung heavy in the air, but nothing weighed on the crew's minds more than the dreaded thought of returning home without Enzo.

At first the *Grande Infante* struggled to pick up speed against the back current of the Gibraltar Strait. After some time Luca, Tony and Mario reconfigured the small sails in such a way that the ship edged forward and pulled free of the current. The crew gathered at the helm, where Piccola was waiting by the time machine.

"Any luck with the answer?" Guillermo asked.

"I've been thinking a lot about Occam's Razor," Piccola finally replied.

The crew, as usual, looked at her clueless.

"You're not familiar with Occam's Razor?"

Mario rubbed his cheeks, "We're not even old enough to shave."

"Occam's Razor is the scientific theory that all things being equal, the simplest solution is usually the right one."

"So what's the solution?" Guillermo asked.

"7941. The exact same numbers that got us here."

"What?" Tony asked.

"Maybe we've been over-thinking this the whole time with all these anagrams and letter inversions. Or I have anyway. After we time-traveled, the dials were reset to zero," she continued. "Which convinced me that we need to reenter the same code to go home; if it worked once it should work again. And it's so simple that we never even recognized it."

Everyone pondered Piccola's theory.

"Think about the time machine like a safe. A safe always requires the same code to open it. You don't enter a different combination each time."

"Sounds like a safe bet to me," Mario said, not realizing his unintentional wit.

"Maybe whoever designed this ship and the time machine just used their lucky number as the time travel code, like an email password," Luca said.

"It's an interesting theory," Guillermo said. "But what about the whole inverse to reverse stuff. We're not inversing anything here."

"I thought about that. But when we answered the original riddle we never inversed anything either. I think we got lost on a tangent trying to inverse things that didn't need inversing."

"All that inversing for nothing," Mario lamented.

Guillermo put his hand on Piccola's shoulder, "I knew you could do it."

Piccola turned away from the rest of the group, perhaps not as confident as she wanted to appear.

"Mates," the captain stated, "we must make a decision soon, and we've come up empty handed for the past few days. Piccola's suggestion makes sense to me. It's simple and logical. None of my passwords ever change. I think we should try it."

"Let's go home," Luca said.

Guillermo took Piccola aside. "Is this going to work? I mean, are you sure? We get one chance at this."

"I think I'm as sure as I'm ever going to be."

"What is it then? What's wrong?"

Piccola shook her head, "Something just doesn't feel right about this."

"It's that Enzo isn't coming back with us," Guillermo said.

Piccola shrugged, took a deep breath and hesitantly reached for the first dial. Everybody crouched as low as they could, oscillating back and forth between the wild excitement of going home and the deep despair of leaving behind Enzo. She rolled it to 7.

"Goodbye Enzo," Tony said to the sky.

9

"Hold onto something," Guillermo instructed.

4

Everybody held tight and closed their eyes.

"*Mira! Mira!* Look out!" Guillermo heard the cries, almost too late. The screams brought everyone to their toes. Guillermo yanked the wheel downward just in time, scraping the fishing boat next to them and turning both vessels in at awkward angles so that they ended up parallel to one another. Days ago the *Grande Infante* would have simply crushed the other boat and been on its way without even a scratch, but now Guillermo stood almost eye to eye with the seething fishermen.

"*Oye,* it was our right of way! And what's a kid doing sailing this thing? You're gonna get yourself killed," one of the fisherman scolded. "*Niños!*"

"Sorry," Guillermo hollered. "We'll shove off and be on our way."

"What is *with* you kids today?" another angry fisherman said as he spit into the water in Guillermo's direction. "First the foreign kid with the big chin floats by and interrupts our approach on a school of tuna and now an entire crew of children almost rams right into us."

"Did you say a kid with a big chin?" Luca almost fell off his feet.

"Yeah, what of it?" the man asked. "Biggest chin I've ever seen for a person of that size."

"Or any size," another fisherman added.

"*Mamma mia!*" Guillermo almost exploded with excitement. "Is he OK? I mean, is the kid with the big chin... alive?"

"He should be. We handed him off to some crabbers who were heading toward Malaga. Ruined half our day, fishing *him* out of the water instead of the tuna. We'll have to work double tomorrow."

"Where's Malaga?" Tony asked impatiently, as everyone held their breath.

"It's a short ways to the east, if the wind's blowin' from your tail. Which it is."

"This is the greatest news of all time!" Luca exclaimed as everyone hugged and ended up on the deck in a pile of joy.

"What's wrong with these child-infested waters today?" a fishermen asked aloud in disgust.

"Wait, how can we be sure it's Enzo they're talking about?" Guillermo asked as everyone got back on their feet and the euphoria died down a bit.

"It has to be him," Piccola said. "What are the odds of another foreign kid with a big chin floating around here this morning?"

"Slim," Luca said.

"None," Mario added.

"OK, I just don't want us to get our hopes up until we make sure it's him. And we make sure he's really alive."

With spirits as high as Gibraltar's famous rock, the crew put the time machine code on pause and pushed back from the fishing boat. Luca, Mario and Tony ran for the sails.

"You'll never know how happy you've made us," Guillermo yelled to the fishermen, his heart swelling like a balloon as they passed each other. He let go of the wheel and sprinted down the cabin stairs to grab a reward for the bearers of good news. "This should make up for your lost tuna," he called out as he launched the gold bar onto the fishermen's vessel. It landed heavily, too heavily in fact, as it traveled straight *through* their deck and into the water.

The fishing Captain raised a fist in the air and screamed out words that Guillermo's parents had forbid him from using back home.

One of the fishermen grabbed the Captain's shoulder, "I think that was gold."

"Gold?!"

The Captain was first in the water with his six crewmen diving in right behind him.

The crew of the *Grande Infante* set out once again to the east in search of a town called Malaga and a big-chinned castaway.

—Chapter 16—

Malaga

The *Grande Infante* had been heading east at a fair clip, shadowing the coastal beaches stretching out into the distance. But as the sails got smaller and smaller the boat sailed slower and slower.

Eventually the crew passed two wrinkled fishermen on a wooden skiff who showed off a net filled with thousands of thin, glimmering anchovies and confirmed that Malaga wasn't much further ahead.

"This boat is getting so small that I can barely fit through the galley hallway," Mario complained as he squeezed by Luca on his way upstairs. Soon we won't be able to get down to the kitchen."

"Or the machine room," Luca added. "We'll lose access to the cannons."

"You mean the ones that shoot gunpowder and useless cannonballs?" Tony scoffed.

"Well, if we need to get to the kitchen once the hallway gets smaller we can always send Piccola," Luca said. "She can squeeze through a mouse hole."

Piccola pushed her finger into Luca's chest.

"It'll be the biggest among us who will have to jump overboard first as this ship gets smaller."

Mario started laughing until he realized the ramifications of the comment.

Tony assumed Enzo's normal lookout position on the mainmast. He only had to ascend ten feet to reach the top. He recalled how high Enzo used to climb to stand lookout. Finally Tony spotted Malaga up ahead. As the town came into view another ship pulled out of the harbor and headed out toward the open sea. Soon after it changed course and swung around in the direction of the *Grande Infante*.

"*Attenzione*! That ship's heading right for us," Tony called down. "And that's a dangerous looking ship. If they mean trouble, then we're in a world of trouble." He rushed down to the deck.

"Maybe it's just a huge fishing ship," Mario guessed.

"A fishing ship stacked with all those cannons?" Luca asked. "What do you think, they shoot at the fish?"

"Maybe those pirates who swam ashore already stole a new ship and are coming to get us," Tony suggested.

"We've always managed to defend ourselves somehow. We'll do the same now if we have to," Guillermo said unconvincingly as he scanned his vessel's unimpressive size.

The crew waited on deck to find out who had taken an interest in them. The incoming ship was almost as big as the *Grande Infante* used to be. Its frame was painted red and yellow, and its cannons pointed out from three levels of gun decks. There were hundreds of finely dressed crew members in elegant and colorful outfits. The ship plowed right past them before it hung a sharp turn and came up behind their stern.

"These guys seem all right," Tony said. "Definitely not pirates, and definitely not poor. I don't think they could want much from us."

The incoming vessel dropped sail and a tall, cleanly-shaven man with a wide plumed hat signaled for the kids to tie up to their ship. He raised his voice so they could hear him so far below. "*Hola amigos!* What luck we have! You're the crew of the *Grande Infante* and we were just setting out to sea to look for you... although we were under the impression that your ship would be considerably larger, given its name and what we've heard about it."

"Huh?" Luca asked.

"We're here to look for our friend," Guillermo shouted, holding up Enzo's portrait. "Have you seen this boy?"

"Sure," the man with the plumed hat chuckled, "that's Enzo the *Encredible*."

"Enzo the *Encredible*?" Tony asked aloud.

"Fishermen found him this morning in the fog. He was floating on his back with his hands bound together, and quickly losing strength. He'd already turned blue from the cold. The fishermen pulled him onto their boat and hitched him a sail to Malaga. Anyone who can survive an ordeal like that is most definitely incredible."

The crew of the *Grande Infante* celebrated confirmation of Enzo's survival.

"Your friend's recovering now. He'll need some rest, but be assured, he's in good hands."

"Very good hands," another man on the elegant ship added, the corner of his mouth spiking upwards.

"*Molto bene!* What news!" Guillermo said. "Who are you, sir, and why were you searching for *us*?"

"Enzo the *Encredible* told us that the rest of his crew was battling Jean Fleury somewhere near Gibraltar. We were sent to investigate. Fleury's been attacking Spanish ships ever since our discovery of silver and gold deposits in the Indies. But I can see that you and your crew managed to evade him."

"Evade him?" Luca laughed. "We sank Fleury's ship this morning."

"What do you mean you sank him?"

"Well," Guillermo explained, "we shot cannons and catapults at him and then broke holes in the bottom of his ship. So much water flooded in that it sank about twenty minutes later."

The finely dressed sailors began chatting among themselves. The sounds quickly turned from a soft banter to a jubilant celebration as the news spread through the crowd.

The man with the plumed hat yelled above the din, "If you really ended the Fleury threat that we've all endured for years you'll become heroes in Spain." He paused for a second. "Did you know Fleury once used someone's arm bone to—"

"We know," Guillermo interrupted.

The sailors continued celebrating the news. "Come, follow us in to Malaga" said the man with the hat.

Guillermo instructed his crew how to pull into port based on his observations of Lorenzo and Juan Cruz's technique back in Gibraltar. Luca stood ready to deploy the emergency anchor but it wasn't needed.

Once on dry land the sailors congratulated the crew of the *Grande Infante* for their victory over the detested French pirate. Two jewel-plated, horse-drawn carriages pulled up and the kids were ushered inside. The carriages sped off toward the outskirts of town. Piccola took in the scenery through the window, "I've never been in a carriage before. I feel like Cinderella."

"Well we need to get Enzo, get back out to sea, and get back to 2015 before *our* carriage turns into a pumpkin," Guillermo said.

The horses stopped and a man opened the carriage door for the visitors. A dozen men in shiny suits of armor led them down a red carpet and through a luxurious courtyard of manicured gardens. Interspersed throughout the green hedges and beds of roses were dainty canals channeling fresh, crisp water into the gardens from the nearby hills. The sailors stopped for a quick drink. Mario pulled two figs off a low-hanging tree and Piccola peeled an orange that had fallen.

Then the trumpets sounded. The red carpet wove around the end of the gardens and into a high-ceilinged room with flowing curtains and a table long enough to seat the entire village of Pizzolungo.

"*This* is where the crabbers brought Enzo?" Piccola asked in amazement.

Mario admired the silverware and china adorning the table, "Crabbers must have made a pretty good living back in the 1400s."

The crew followed the knights through the banquet room, out past another equally impressive courtyard and then finally into a room brimming with people and commotion.

The trumpeters stopped playing and a heavyset man spoke with a bold voice, "His and Her Royal Highness, the King and Queen of Spain, welcome you to their lands."

"Are they talking to us?" Luca asked.

"I guess so," Guillermo said.

"The King and Queen?" Piccola mouthed, dropping her orange.

The crowd in front of them slowly broke apart to reveal three carpeted steps, on top of which rested a pair of ornately carved wooden thrones where a middle-aged couple sat. The Royals both wore golden crowns lit up by electric-colored gems and they donned long burgundy and ivory gowns that reached down to their toes. They were flanked on either side by Spartan-like guards.

"I'm King Ferdinand, and this is my wife, Queen Isabella," the man on the throne said. Ferdinand had dark brown hair that reached his shoulders, oval eyes and lips that fell downwards, giving him a somber appearance. Isabella had frantic, wavy hair that contrasted sharply with her poised and stoic facial features. She was a supremely powerful queen, Guillermo knew, but certainly no beauty queen. Mario thought that if he were a king he'd definitely find a better-looking wife.

"All of a sudden I'm feeling slightly underdressed," Tony said as the kids checked out each other's frayed uniforms.

"Literally underdressed," Guillermo added, observing half of Luca's chest and all of Mario's belly escaping from beneath their radically shrunken fabrics.

"Until now I'd only seen kings and queens on playing cards," Luca whispered.

"The only royalty I've ever encountered is Burger King," Mario added.

"Good afternoon your Highnesses. I'm Guillermo Infante and this is my crew. We sail on the *Grande Infante*. Have you seen our friend Enzo Bonaventura?"

"Yes, *hijo*. Enzo the *Encredible* is recovering in the next room," Ferdinand said.

"I can't believe he got that nickname to stick with these guys," Tony whispered to Guillermo.

"Let's go mates," Guillermo ordered.

The sailors were about to rush over to the next room when the Queen rose to her feet. She inhaled deeply, which caused her cheeks to puff out nearly as far as her nose. The crowd waited impatiently to hear what important message she would deliver.

"Enzo the *Encredible* is most certainly a survivor, like my younger brother Alfonso. Alfonso suffered through accident after accident. He fell off our castle's ramparts while competing in an archer's competition that resulted in a fractured left clavicle. And then the next summer he almost

212

drowned in the Pisuerga River adjacent to our palace. Alfonso could swim as well as anyone in the kingdom, mind you, but there was an ungodly current that day. And neither of those incidents compare to the time a bull impaled him as he—"

King Ferdinand cut her off, "My dear, the young sailors simply want to see their friend."

"We really do, your honor," Mario said.

The Queen ignored her husband, Mario and the expressions of the other uninterested and restive, young sailors. "What I was trying to say before His Royal Highness so objectionably interrupted was that Enzo the *Encredible* is a survivor, just like my brother. And I should tell you of my first cousin Pedro who—"

"Please, Your Highness," Guillermo spoke up. "We're desperate to see how Enzo is, and we don't have much time."

The King appeared satisfied that his visitors had validated his previous interruption of his loquacious wife.

"Then *vamos*, let us escort you to see him at once," Isabella said, less cheerfully. "I should warn you, however, he's been through a great ordeal and has been sleeping like a bear on a cold winter's day. Like my eleventh niece, Beatriz, who once slept through a storm of such epic proportion… or was it Maria… Darling, which one of my nieces was the sleeper?" she asked her husband who merely shook his head and gestured for the kids to follow.

The Royal Couple and the five young sailors entered a chamber off to the right, just beyond the portico. Two knights opened the intricately carved wooden doors for everyone to pass through.

There was a bed in the corner of the room encircled by a white linen canopy. A young girl robed in a flower-embroidered gown stood vigil, trying to keep whoever lay there cool with a hand fan. The girl had red hair long enough to sweep the floor with, and a round face with pudgy cheeks. She acknowledged the children and softly nudged the person in the bed.

Enzo woke up and looked over the wooden bed sidings, "*Amicos*, you're alive!"

The crew ran up to embrace Enzo but the young girl glowered at them and forbade anyone from getting too close.

"He's weak," she said as she placed the back of her hand up against Enzo's forehead to gauge his temperature.

"I'm fine," Enzo blurted out. "I can't believe you guys are alive."

"You can't believe *we're* alive?" Luca asked. "We can't believe *you're* alive!"

"I thought Fleury would have marched you all off the plank, like he did to me. It was incredible luck that I got picked up," Enzo laughed. "The fisherman who found me thought I was a sick dolphin."

"OK, that's enough time with the patient. He needs his rest," the young girl ordered.

"Who are you, his doctor?" Mario asked sarcastically.

"I'm Catherine, Princess of Spain and prospective Queen of England."

Mario thought for a second, "Ah, OK. Guys, let's back it up. Give him some room."

Catherine turned to the crew. "Enzo the *Encredible* is a stunningly brave young man. We already told him he'll be knighted if he stays in the Kingdom of Spain, but he's informed us…" her face saddened, "that he must return to a place called Pitalingos."

"Pizzolungo," everyone corrected her.

"Indeed, that's the place. And you all must be the sailors of Pizzolungo." She stroked Enzo's arm and pushed his head back onto the bed to rest. Enzo winked at his friends, milking his condition for all it was worth.

Guillermo approached his bedside and knelt down beside him and whispered, "Piccola figured out the time machine riddle but we have to go *now* before the ship gets too small to sail."

Enzo yanked off his covers and sat up quickly, "I'm feeling much better all of a sudden."

"No Enzo! Lie back down and let me take care of you," Catherine said as she smoothed out his hair.

The Queen whispered to her husband, "I've never seen our daughter like this before." She admired Catherine momentarily before carrying on, "You children must have had it rough out at sea. As a young girl in Castile I rarely had the chance to fix my eyes on the ocean. We lived far inland and the water always frayed my nerves. Those violent waves crashing against the shore, the serpents and monsters of the depths, the thought of drowning, the—"

"They get the point, my dear, you're not crazy about the sea," the King said.

"Pray tell," she continued, "how did you end up alone at sea in the first place?"

"It was an accident," Guillermo said. "Long story, but we're just trying to get home now, to get back to our parents. Now. Like right now."

"I see," the Queen said. "The First Admiral of the Royal Ship who brought you into port today already informed us of how you sank Jean Fleury's ship. For that we owe you dearly. Which reminds me of the time back in 1491 when—"

"Queen Isabella, how did Enzo end up... *here*?" Piccola quickly interrupted.

"Oh dear," the Queen bent down to look at Piccola. "I almost missed you you're so small. How old are you?"

"I'm eleven."

"Just like my daughter." She looked at Princess Catherine tending to Enzo. "She's our sixth child and soon we'll marry her to the English Prince of Wales."

Catherine petted Enzo's arm softly and faked a smile to her mother.

Queen Isabella stood up and addressed the children: "It's just by chance that we are here to take care of Enzo the *Encredible*. We came to Malaga to commemorate the tenth anniversary of the town's re-conquest from the Moors. When news reached us about a child who survived a battle with Jean Fleury we knew, as parents, that we had to look after him. And that—"

"And that we needed to send our fleet out to thwart Fleury's presence in our waters," King Ferdinand added, partially to keep his wife from going on.

The crew thanked them both.

Queen Isabella motioned to her husband. "Why don't you give these brave young sailors a gift of some kind? In honor of their courage. What is it that you want, children? You know, when I was a child I always wanted a—"

"We just really want to go home," Piccola said, the bags under her eyes conveying her exhaustion and frustration.

Ferdinand unfastened a medallion hanging from his necklace and handed it to Piccola. The crew gathered around.

"A royal medallion, minted for the anniversary," the King said.

The front of the medallion commemorated the ten-year anniversary of Malaga's liberation from the Moors. Underneath the castle on the back was the date of mint: 1497.

"Isn't that the Disneyland castle?" Luca asked.

Ferdinand put his hand on Luca's arm, "*Marinero*, I've never heard of a castle by that name. The fortification on this medallion is located in the city of Segovia, where Queen Isabella was crowned."

"That's right," the Queen jumped in. "I had my coronation there. In case you don't know, Segovia's on the northern plains where the fields of grain cover the hills as far as the eye can—"

Mario turned to Luca, "I'll back you up on that, that's definitely the Disneyland logo. I know things about logos."

The Queen stopped talking. Neither she nor her husband could follow the conversation about a castle named Disneyland.

Piccola held the medallion in her hand endearingly. Its engraving was delicate and shiny. She flipped it between her fingers.

Ferdinand put his hand on Guillermo's shoulder. "Captain."

"King."

"Captain, Enzo the *Encredible* has told us all about you. Your story makes me want to head out to sea myself, and I would if I weren't needed here. You've ventured across the high seas with a crew of inexperienced and uncharacteristically youthful seamen. And you've sunk our most despised adversary along the way. When you're a bit older, do come sail for the crown of Spain. You and your whole crew."

"That job offer may come in handy if we can't get back to the present," Tony whispered to Guillermo.

Guillermo stood tall and proud. He wished his father could have heard the King's words first-hand. It would have been the high point of his twelve years, had the pressure of the ship-shrinking conundrum not been weighing on his mind. "Thank you, Your Highness."

Piccola interrupted, "We are very grateful that you took such good care of Enzo..." Enzo shot her a leading look, "...the *Encredible*..." Piccola continued with disdain. "But we really have to go. We have to get home, and we're in a hurry."

"I'm ready to go," Enzo shouted.

"Do stay," Catherine pleaded, again gently pushing his forehead back down onto the fluffy pillow.

"No really, Princess, we have to go. We're on a countdown."

Catherine leaned over the bed and looked sadly into Enzo's eyes. She caressed his chin. "I wish you wouldn't go."

Enzo sat up. "I know, Princess, but it would never work out between us. I'm a Pisces... and you're engaged." He climbed out of bed and joined the crew.

"It's a shame you must sail now," the King said. "The Queen and I were planning a royal feast in your honor this evening. Our way of expressing our appreciation for what you did to Fleury."

"That would have been an honor," Guillermo said.

"I do love feasts," Mario added.

The King stepped forward. "If you're ever passing our coasts again, you know you have friends here. And be careful at sea, my Royal Admiral warned me that you sail on an insufficiently sized ship."

"And getting *insufficienter* and *insufficienter* by the minute," Mario whispered to Luca.

"That's not a word," Luca whispered back.

"Thank you, Your Highness," Guillermo said.

The Queen inhaled deeply, signaling her intent to speak—for a while.

Piccola pulled her brother's arm toward the door, "Let's hurry, before she starts telling us any more stories about clavicles or coronations."

"*Gracias y adios!*" Guillermo shouted.

As the Royals waved goodbye the Queen exhaled and simply called out, "*Vaya con Dios*!" Catherine blew a kiss to Enzo who winked back.

The carriages returned the crew to the *Grande Infante* and the sailors bid farewell to the royal fleet men. The crew pushed back out to sea and Guillermo pulled the rudder to the left, due east. He stood in front of the ever-shrinking wheel. "We must hurry."

"*Oh Dio mio* did the ship get small," Enzo grumbled as he hurried to his post. "Will we make it?"

"Well, we might have if we didn't need to go and interrupt your nap at 'Buckingham Palace'," Tony said, handing him the telescope.

"Awww, I missed you too," Enzo said as Tony pushed him away laughing.

"We should have left you in Malaga."

"Are we far out enough so that people won't get affected by a giant whirlpool and blinding space light?" Mario asked. "I mean, we don't want to accidentally take some poor fisherman back with us to 2015."

"We've almost cleared the harbor," Guillermo said.

"First things first," Mario continued, "I'm getting out of this tiny uniform. It's suffocating me." Everyone switched back to their original clothes and shuffled over to the time machine where Piccola stood, flipping the medallion in her fingers, waiting for the order.

"Let's go home," Guillermo said.

Piccola crept under the wheel, opened the time machine box and looked over the dials. They remained just as she'd left them right before they'd learned of Enzo's survival: 7, 9, 4 and the final unturned dial, still set to 0.

Just then the ship made an awful noise as it buckled and shrank again. The crew gripped the railing to avoid falling overboard as Piccola hit her head on the bottom of the wheel. Splinters flew through the air, darting into faces, chests and legs. Finally things stabilized enough so that everyone could uncover their eyes and take in the ship's new diminutive dimensions.

"Hurry, Piccola," Guillermo warned.

She reached for the final dial.

"Oh no! That's new. Look at the door to the galley. It's almost too small to fit into now," Enzo moaned.

Piccola looked at the door and shook her head. "New door." She looked back down at the medallion. It was upside down in her hand and the order of the numbers below the Disney-like castle somehow caught her attention: 7941.

"Wait a minute," Piccola yelled. "We have to stop. I was wrong about the code!"

"You were wrong?" Guillermo asked, panic setting in. "Then why are you smiling?

"Because I think Enzo may have just saved us."

—Chapter 17—

Lights on the Horizon

"What's seven nine four one?" Piccola asked excitedly.

"Never heard of it," Mario said.

"It's the code you said we should use to get home," Luca shouted.

"Those were the answers to the riddle: 7 seas, 9 months, 4 corners, and 1 life," Guillermo added.

"And what else?" Piccola baited, showing the crew the numbers on the upside-down medallion.

"Huh?" each sailor muttered in unison trying to process what links might exist between the numbers on the medallion and the code for the time machine.

"Now what's the inverse of 7941?" Piccola asked before immediately answering her own question: "1497!"

"Yes! The riddle's answer was the inverse of the date we jumped to," Tony hollered.

"Oh, that's what you guys were trying to figure out? I could have told you that," Mario said.

"So we just need to enter 1497," Tony continued, "because that's the inverse of the original riddle answer.

221

Then it'll take us back home." He eagerly reached for the time machine dials.

"Wait," Piccola interceded. "This isn't so simple. I think we need to enter 5102."

"She's right," Guillermo yelled.

"The inverse of the riddle answer brought us to 1497," Piccola explained. "If we enter 1497 maybe it'll bring us to the inverse of that, the year 7941."

"*Madonna mia,*" Luca sighed, "who knows if the world even exists in seventy-nine forty-one."

"I agree with Piccola. We should inverse the number of the year we want to return to," Guillermo said.

"Exactly, that would follow the same logic that got us here. It's like the 'new door' answer from the detective test," Piccola said smiling. "I tried out that theory with the *words* from the riddle, but never the *numbers* that got us here. What I should have been doing was thinking about the numbers. And if I'm right, the answer really was staring at us the whole time. All we needed to do was inverse our own year. If we want to go to 2015, we need to enter 5102."

Guillermo glanced at the hourglass. It was so small it was hard to read, but he estimated the top chamber was roughly ten percent full. He observed the *Grande Infante*; it was the size of a small fishing boat.

"Are you sure?" Tony asked, "Shouldn't we just inverse the exact number that got us here and put 1497?" I mean, it just said 'inverse to reverse', so why not just inverse exactly what we originally used?"

"That logic speaks to me too," Luca said hesitantly as one of the deck boards pushed against his leg.

"We only get one shot at this," Enzo warned.

Piccola and Tony locked eyes. Luca stepped next to Tony and put his arm on his shoulder. Guillermo inched over to Piccola.

Enzo sighed, the pressure of the decision was enormous. Mario was shaking like a rattle.

"It's 5102," Piccola said more confidently than before. "I got us here. I'll get us back."

Everyone studied each other.

"Trust me," she said.

Tony and Luca nervously acquiesced.

Guillermo looked at Piccola in a way he never had before. He looked at her not only as a sister, but also as an equal. "Do it."

"Enzo," Piccola said, "I need your eagle eyes to help move these dials to the right numbers; they're too small for me to see."

Enzo brought his eye up to the first dial and moved it to the number 5 as the wind pushed the ship delicately to the east. Malaga was receding out of view on the coast behind them. Enzo slid the second dial over to the number 1, and then the third dial to 0.

"If this doesn't work, we'll be swimming soon," Tony warned.

Enzo rolled the last dial to the number 2.

A small, grumbling sound sputtered out of the time machine as everyone grabbed hold of whatever they could.

"Something's happening," Luca said, equally scared and excited.

Suddenly the dials spun wildly, until they all stopped abruptly at zero. The same great flash of white light that had enveloped the boat during the first time travel experience reappeared. A giant whirlpool formed at the bow and dragged the *Grande Infante* downwards, spinning faster and faster.

"Hang on!" Guillermo commanded as he gripped the little ship's wheel with every bit of strength he had.

"It's working!" Mario yelled while clinging onto the railing with one hand and onto Romeo with his other. Enzo did the same with his portrait that he'd just rolled up. Piccola almost lost her grip when a wave pummeled her from the side, causing her to drop the royal medallion into the sea. "The medallion!" she cried out.

The ship spun even more ferociously than it did on their earlier passage through the vortex, owing to the *Grande Infante's* reduced size. The glaring light made it impossible for anyone to open their eyes. The entire crew concentrated solely on holding on.

Just when Guillermo felt his grip slowly giving way, the spinning force weakened and the water's resistance slowed the *Grande Infante* to a lazy crawl. A powerful swell sped away from where the boat had been deposited. The kids gradually opened their eyes. They were in the middle of the sea and it was dark, cool and windy.

"I'm going to be sick," Mario declared as he hung his head over the side of the boat. "And I think Romeo as well."

Each face was greener than the next.

"Where are we?" Enzo struggled to ask.

"When are we?" Luca wondered.

"I hope that's home," Guillermo said as he pointed to a constellation of lights far out in the distance.

"We must have left the Middle Ages," Enzo said. "I see airplane lights up there in the sky."

"But we could be in the year 5102, right?" Mario asked. "Maybe that's an alien ship."

"Tony, have you checked your iPad?" Guillermo asked.

"I was just on my way down below to get it. If we're back home it should pick up the 4G now." Tony headed toward the cabin stairs and tried to squeeze through the door. "Hey, I can't get downstairs, the door's too small."

Just then a loud BANG went off from below and pieces of wood splintered everywhere. The crew was all knocked off their feet.

"What was that?" yelled the captain.

"Wait, gold can't be compressed, can it?" Enzo asked.

"No, don't worry about that," Luca affirmed. "Gold can't be compressed."

Guillermo and Piccola looked at each other ominously. "If gold can't be compressed," Guillermo uttered, "the floorboards and sides of the ship down below will crack as they try to downsize around it."

"Then we'll sink out here in the middle of nowhere," Piccola cried.

"Somehow we have to get down to that storage room so we can bring the gold up here to the deck!" Tony screeched.

The boys all looked at Piccola.

"But what if it closes in on her while she's down there?" Guillermo asked.

Before anyone could answer she took a deep breath, squeezed into the staircase and started crawling down the miniscule cabin stairs. "We better do this fast," she called up.

"Just hurry up," Guillermo said, biting his fingernails.

"The walls down here are snug up against the gold," Piccola yelled. She grabbed the first bar. It was heavy and the confined space made it difficult to maneuver. Eventually she managed to lug the first bar to the stairs. Luca grabbed it from her and handed it to Mario who laid it down by the helm. It took what felt like hours to transfer all the remaining bars up to the deck.

"And here's your iPad," Piccola said as she rejoined the crew.

"Another two minutes and I think you would have been stuck down there forever," Guillermo said as he stood her upright.

"We're online!" Tony exclaimed. "We must be back in the present."

"Check where we are," Guillermo said.

"*Allora*, I'm on it." Tony opened his Maps App and requested their current location.

"Soooo?" Mario begged.

Tony lifted the iPad up to his face. "It says we're in the South Pacific, just off the coast of New Zealand."

"What?!" everyone screamed.

"Oh wait," he flipped around the iPad and typed in some new coordinates. "Sorry, this was in my cache. I'll delete it. We're almost home. Those lights out there should be Pizzolungo."

Luca punched Tony in the arm and Enzo gave him a noogie. Mario tried out some excited dance moves with Romeo in his hands but the small boat almost capsized with the shifting weight. He quickly settled down.

"We did it," Piccola said wearily.

"We did it," Luca affirmed.

"We'd better move fast," Guillermo said as he cupped the wheel and set course. He leaned over to check on the hourglass but it had gotten so small it was impossible to estimate the amount of sand remaining in the top chamber. "We're still a ways out and we've barely got enough wood left to float on."

The crew huddled together on the remaining deck space in the breezy night air. Between the gold and their feet there was little space left. Luca maneuvered all the sails by himself without having to climb any masts. The winds off the water inched them toward the lights.

They sailed for some time without speaking until Tony turned to the captain, "What kind of ship will you buy for your father?"

Guillermo pondered the question as he picked up the now tiny flag from the back corner of the deck and bent down to refit it on the short flagpole. "I don't know. I guess I'll give my father the gold bars and let him decide."

"And remember, if there's any money left over we should fix up the tree house in the schoolyard," Mario said.

"After this trip, it'll be tough to go back to playing Captains and Pirates in a tree house," Enzo said.

"I can ask my father to borrow his ship when he's not using it. We can have our games on board," Guillermo offered.

"Yeah right," Piccola laughed. "Every time you ask Papa to go on his ship he tells you you're too small."

"Well, after I tell him how we sailed to the Canary Islands all by ourselves, I'm sure things will be different."

With those words the boat began buckling and shrinking violently. The masts came down further and the deck pushed in closer. The catapult system that the Infantes had brought up from the machine room rolled off the deck almost knocking Luca over the edge in the process. Everyone grasped for something to cling onto but the potency of the shrinking fit was stronger than it had been since way back in the Atlantic. Tony and Piccola were propelled into the water. Seconds later, the stack of gold bars tipped over and, strewn across the slippery deck boards, started edging toward the railings with each sway of the boat. Guillermo, Luca, Enzo and Mario fought to maintain their grip and prevent the gold from sliding overboard; but by the time the boat stabilized nearly half of the bars had plunged into the depths of the sea.

The resized *Grande Infante* deposited Luca, Enzo, Mario and the captain nearly on top of one another. They filled out most of the remaining deck space and once Piccola and Tony climbed back on board there was barely room for anyone to move. They sat sorrowfully on the remaining gold bars.

"Gold is worth *a lot*, Captain," Luca tried to be optimistic. "It's gold, after all. Maybe we don't need too much to buy the new ship."

"Yeah, how much gold does it take to buy a ship, anyway?" Enzo asked.

"I don't know," Guillermo uttered. "I've never bartered gold bars for a ship before."

The crew floated idly for some time, increasingly anxious. Finally Tony spoke, "I think we're in real trouble. We've barely moved in fifteen minutes. We're just floating here."

"I know," Guillermo concurred. "Our sails look like kites. There's no way they can push all this weight back home."

"And the sun's about to come up," Mario added. He peered down at the cabin door, now just big enough for a cat to squeeze into. "And that means it's going to get hot, and we have nothing to drink."

"Let's try paddling with our hands," Luca offered.

Everyone shifted to get a hand in the water. Each time someone paddled, though, the small craft rocked uneasily and almost tumbled over. It didn't take long to realize that paddling wouldn't work.

"We might have to swim to shore," Tony said.

"He's right," Enzo seconded.

Guillermo considered this. He tried to stand up to better assess the distance but the top weight nearly capsized the boat. "We can't swim home from here. We'll literally all drown. None of us has ever even attempted to swim a tenth that distance."

"Well we're too heavy for the wind to push us," Luca exclaimed. "We only have one choice." With that he jumped into the water as if he'd been swimming his whole life. He grabbed the back of the boat and started kicking.

"Go Luca!" Mario yelled. But the boat was still heavy and Luca's strength was sapped after a few seconds.

"Let's get in there and help him," Tony said as he prepared to dive in.

"No," Guillermo said. He examined the exhausted crew. "Help Luca back onto the boat."

Tony and Mario grabbed him by the underarms and pulled him up.

Guillermo couldn't shake the thought of what had happened to Enzo back in Gibraltar. "As captain, I'm not letting any crew member put themselves in danger again. This ship's too heavy to move. Our sails can't pull all this weight. And the gold bars weigh more than all of us combined. Our only option is to throw over the rest of the gold."

A tear ran down Piccola's cheek. "He's right. None of us can swim that far. Especially not me."

"But we did so much to get that gold. We came so far. And we're so close to home," Tony insisted.

"We want you both to stay in Pizzolungo," Enzo sighed.

Everyone hoped and prayed that somehow the ship would start picking up speed. But the *Grande Infante* ignored everyone's pleas. Soon after, Guillermo reached for the first gold bar. His friends watched aghast as he let it slip out of his hands and into the sea. The gold twirled downwards through the water leaving a trail of disturbed, bubbly sea before vanishing out of sight. Nobody spoke as Guillermo, holding back his own tears, dropped overboard all the bars except for one.

Once lightened, the breeze was sufficient enough to begin nudging the *Grande Infante* toward the shore. The crew held as steady as they could, keeping their heads down to reduce drag. Guillermo wasn't alone in staring down at the last gold bar resting beneath everyone's entangled feet and dreaming of what could have been.

"*Attenzione*! Isn't that Mariner's Fort?" Enzo asked at daybreak.

Luca blocked the eastern sun from his eyes, "I think it is."

"Must be," Guillermo said. "We're getting close."

As the sun rose and the coastline came into view the *Grande Infante* started to shake from side to side again. Everyone tried to hold their balance but the shaking got worse and soon after the boat succumbed to one of its powerful shrinking spells. As it did, the final gold bar slipped toward the side of boat. Guillermo tried to grasp it with one hand and steady himself with the other, but it didn't hold and the last bar plummeted downwards through the water, along with his heart. By the time the boat stopped shaking everyone was in the water and the *Grande Infante* was nearly back to its original size.

The crew floated along with the current thinking about their losses. Guillermo began to imagine what school would be like in far away Siracusa with kids he'd never met before. He wondered if they'd have a tree house in the schoolyard, and if anyone there would even be interested in seafaring. For Mario it began to sink in that were he to win Piccola's heart he'd now have to move to Siracusa and find a kitchen willing to employ him once he finished school. Luca, Tony and Enzo debated how they'd be able to go on playing Captains and Pirates without their captain and his sister.

"It's back to its original size," Piccola observed soon after. "It's just a model ship again."

Eventually the crew floated past Mariner's Fort and the Infante home came into view. As Guillermo approached the shore, he thought back to how the *Grande Infante* was once the biggest ship on the open seas, and how it had towered over da Gama and Columbus's famous vessels. He recalled how Fleury's men had struggled to mount attacks against the enormous craft, and how the kind Tenerife villagers had been frightened by its awesome size. He looked over at the tiny ship bobbing next to him on its side and picked it up out of the water. Everyone watched him with the ship in hand. He carefully placed it back down, right side up.

Finally the crew let the gentle waves push them up onto the sand. Signora Infante strolled out of the house and came down onto the beach. Guillermo looked up at his confused mother just as the *Grande Infante* washed up next to him.

"Where's your dinghy?" she asked.

—Chapter 18—

The Little Treasure

Signora Infante helped Piccola to her feet as the rest of the crew crawled onto the sand and sprawled out on their backs, panting. "Must have been quite a night for you little adventurers out in that shack. I wanted to row out to get you, but your father insisted the storm was pretty far out to sea and you sailors would be just fine."

Guillermo struggled to his feet, "Papa's home?"

Captain Guillermo Infante Sr., dressed in his white and blue captain's suit, made his way out of the house and down to the beach. Piccola immediately jumped into his arms. "*Ciao bella!*" he said as he kissed her forehead. He knelt down next to his son and tussled his hair. "I decided I'd been away from my little ones for too long, so last night I hitched a ride from a friend who was on his way to Sicily."

Guillermo wrapped his arms around his father.

"So, did you defeat the pirates?" the big Captain asked the whole crew with a laugh. "We thought you might miss breakfast and mama's cooking up a good one." He smiled and then noticed the model ship in the sand. He carefully picked up the *Grande Infante*, wiped the water off its hull with a soft cloth, and held it up to the light for inspection. Satisfied that it was in good condition, he gazed at his kids with raised cheeks and a curious grin. Guillermo and Piccola could sense that he had been waiting to collect the ship.

"Where are our parents?" Mario asked, confused. "They must have called the Coast Guard by now."

"Well, it's still early," Signora Infante said. "They're probably assuming you'll eat breakfast here." She patted his tummy. "And lunch."

"Breakfast?" Enzo asked a little more than disturbed. "We've been gone a week!"

Guillermo's parents laughed.

Little Romeo ran over to Mario and began licking his face. "Mario," Captain Infante joked, "it's nice of you to bring over some fresh bacon for the breakfast table but we're fine with what's in the refrigerator."

"That's Romeo, my pet. An old lady sold him to me at the Gibraltar bazaar the other day for a few cents."

"Oh Gibraltar, of course," Signora Infante nodded sarcastically. "Now everyone get upstairs and clean up before we eat. You may have only been gone a night but you look like you haven't showered in a week."

"He really did get Romeo in Gibraltar, right after we outran a fleet of pirates on that ship," Luca exclaimed, pointing at the *Grande Infante* in Captain Infante Sr.'s hands, "and just before we met Juan Cruz, who repaired the hull."

Guillermo's father examined the hull but found nothing wrong with it. He and his wife laughed aloud and ushered the crew toward the house.

"It's true, Papa," Guillermo said with Piccola and everyone else nodding emphatically. "The ship in your hands grew to be enormous and we used it to sail to the Canary Islands... in Spain." He paused to await his parents' reactions, but they offered none. "And the time machine

233

brought us back to 1497 and we were chased by Jean Fleury, the French pirate!"

"Because Tony stole his treasure map," Piccola added.

Tony, still clutching his waterproof iPad case, put both hands in the air, "Guilty as charged."

"Yeah, but then we decided to try and find the treasure before the pirates could," Guillermo continued.

Captain Infante put his arm around his son, "Good decision, little skipper."

"And then Piccola and Enzo went scuba diving and brought up a treasure chest of gold bars from the shipwreck we found using the treasure map."

"That was after Vasco da Gama and Christopher Columbus helped us navigate to the shipwreck," Tony added.

"Naturally," the big Captain laughed, "those men must know a lot about navigation."

Guillermo looked up at his father. "We wanted to use the treasure to help you get a new ship. And because we don't want to move to Siracusa. We want to stay here."

"Yeah," Piccola said tearfully, "we want to stay in Pizzolungo. With our friends." She looked down. "But we lost the treasure when the *Grande Infante* shrunk back to its original size."

"All this is terribly thoughtful of you," the big Captain said lightly, "especially the part about the treasure. But we're not moving anywhere. So you don't have anything to worry about."

Guillermo and Piccola pulled themselves together. "We're not moving?"

"No. We're staying right here, in this house."

All the kids burst into an eruptive cheer as the bemused Infantes held their hands to their ears.

"Now stop fantasizing and go get cleaned up," Captain Infante said. "And Luca and Mario, I have your legionnaire's sword and your breadsticks, with sesame seeds, up at the house. Enzo, Tony, I brought you boys something special as well.

"Thanks, Captain Infante," Mario said, licking his lips. "You. Are. The. Best."

"I see why they're so tired," Signora Infante said to her husband. "They must have been up all night concocting elaborate plots to get you a new ship."

"When they weren't busy being chased around by pirates."

"But it's true!" Piccola protested.

"Come on guys, let's get some breakfast in you," the big Captain said.

Signora Infante had started leading the crew up to the house when she turned back around. "And how many times do I have to tell you kids not to leave your rolling horses in the driveway? Put them in the garage."

"Our *what*?" asked Guillermo.

"Your rolling horses. Don't play the innocent. Move 'em or lose 'em."

All the kids' mouths dropped to the floor in unison as they made their way up to the house.

"How could they not believe us?" Piccola asked as she grabbed a fresh towel off the laundry line.

"Well," Guillermo said, "I guess most people don't believe in growing ships or time travel machines."

"I don't," Mario noted. "I mean, I didn't… before our trip."

Enzo unfurled his portrait in the hallway. "It's a little wet but luckily the paint didn't run much."

"You're actually still carrying that thing around?" Luca asked.

Signora Infante came up the stairs with extra towels and bars of soap. "I know that painting: it's The Portrait of a

235

Young Man." She took a double look. "Funny, the model resembles you, Enzo. I never noticed that before. Where did you get a copy?"

"This is an original. A man painted it for me at the bazaar in Gibraltar. I think his name was Mr. Bowl of Jelly, or something like that. He said he liked my chin and I traded him my broken watch for the painting. But please don't tell my mother about the watch. I'm going to give her the portrait as a gift."

"Bowl of Jelly? That's a strange name for an artist," Signora Infante said. "He must have been a clownish impersonator of Botticelli." She pondered his story and took a second look at the portrait. "But a talented one, for sure. Too bad it's not an original, you'd be rich."

Enzo's eyes lit up and he grabbed the painting, "Mates, I have to go!"

"After you eat," Signora Infante calmed him down.

The crew devoured breakfast and then bid a sleepy farewell to Signore and Signora Infante at the front door. Guillermo and Piccola walked their friends out to the front yard.

"So, um…" Mario was getting up his courage as he turned to face Piccola. "Maybe…?"

"Maybe," she said flirtatiously. Guillermo rolled his eyes. "See you later Six-to-Four," she continued with a loving grin. If Mario hadn't checked, he wouldn't have known his feet were still on the ground.

"OK, this is what I was looking for," Tony said, holding his iPad. "It says here on Wikipedia that one time travel theory suggests that while the traveler may be gone for long periods of time, even years, when he or she returns to his present it may be as if no time has passed at all."

"Right. I've seen *Back to the Future*, I should have known that," Guillermo said.

"So this means we won't get in trouble when we get home?" Mario asked.

"I guess not," Tony said.

Luca put a hand on Guillermo's shoulder, "Until the next adventure?"

"Until the next one."

Luca, Tony and Mario pedaled their 'rolling horses' along the beach promenade toward their homes. Romeo ran alongside Mario. Enzo had already sped ahead and vanished over a hillside, his hand gripping his portrait even tighter than before. The thrill of knowing that their captain and his sister were staying in Pizzolungo provided everyone's legs with just enough adrenaline to get them home.

That night, after a day spent sleeping off their journey and feasting on foods other than pasta, Guillermo and Piccola entered the living room, still almost falling over from exhaustion.

"Papa," Guillermo said, "didn't you see how on the bottom of the ship it says '*Caute: navis crescit en aqua*'? That's Latin for 'Caution: ship grows in water'."

"I did see that," the Captain said. "But it didn't look any bigger when I saw it in the water outside."

"That's because you need to put a special powder around it in the water for it to grow."

Piccola jumped in, "And the boat also came with a golden *inflecto* key, to open the time machine box."

"No doubt, you'll never get a time machine opened without a golden key," the Captain affirmed humorously.

Guillermo stared up at the portrait of his new friend, the Great Lorenzo Infante. "He sure was a brave man," he whispered to Piccola.

"Who are you talking about?" Captain Infante asked.

"Him," Guillermo said, pointing up at the painting.

"Well you're right about that. He was an extremely brave man. Have I told you the story of how he singlehandedly defeated a whole fleet of Venetians?"

"Well, it was more like six Venetians, but nevermind," Piccola said. "Plus, I think he looks better with the beard."

The Captain and his wife exchanged confused glances while looking back up at the portrait of Lorenzo who didn't sport a single stubble on his face.

"So I don't get it. How come we get to stay in Pizzolungo?" Guillermo asked his father.

"Well, there are a few things I'd like to tell you two. And some of this actually relates all the way back to Lorenzo." The Captain sat Guillermo and Piccola down on the couch.

"When I was in Rome arguing with my insurance agent your mother broke some bad news to me. Your great Uncle Ercole passed away. As they say, bad news follows bad news. Ercole was the man who taught my father—your grandfather—how to sail. He was 94-years-old, and I wanted to pay my last respects. So from Rome I traveled down to Anzio."

"I didn't know we had an Uncle Ercole," Piccola said.

"You never met him. He stayed with us when your brother was born," Signora Infante explained, putting her arm around her.

Guillermo and Piccola listened with rapt attention as the Captain resumed the story. "Ercole was the Infante family estate holder, meaning he looked after the family's wealth. Not that there's much to look after anymore but it's a tradition that goes back to Lorenzo's time when the Infante name was synonymous with affluence."

"Lorenzo was wealthy?" Piccola asked, recalling that he'd specifically told them he'd never been a wealthy man.

"Well that's a story unto itself. I once heard that on one of his expeditions a group of generous sailors gave Lorenzo a bar of solid gold to repay him for an act of bravery. Obviously a tale, but somehow it stuck in the family."

"Actually it was two gold bars," Guillermo said under his breath.

"Well, the point of the story is that with the last of those family funds Ercole had bought the cargo ship that he now left for me. A beautiful vessel, even bigger than the *Coraggio*. I'm having it repainted up in Anzio and my crew will be bringing it down the week after next." He thought for a second. "And so as long as I can keep Rumrino away from it we should all be fine and we can stay in Pizzolungo."

"Oh, I wouldn't worry about Rumrino for a while papa—" Guillermo started before Piccola cut him off with a poke.

"So Lorenzo inadvertently kept his word," Piccola whispered to Guillermo. "He promised you he'd return the value of the gold. And he did."

Guillermo leaned back on the couch and thought about the incredible journey the gold must have taken over the preceding five centuries to now land in his father's lap in the form of a new ship.

Signora Infante interrupted Guillermo's thoughts; "You kids must have been eavesdropping the other night when your father called me from Rome."

Guillermo and Piccola flashed embarrassed smiles.

"You know, minding other people's business can land you in a heap of trouble."

"You have no idea," Piccola said, glancing at her brother.

"Papa," Guillermo asked, "Are you going to take me out with you... I mean, take *us* out with you when your new ship arrives?"

"And maybe let us steer?" Piccola added.

"Oh I think you might still be a little small for that, my little friends."

"Well, I was big enough to sail from here to the Canary Islands and back."

"That is impressive."

"And Christopher Columbus himself said he admired my abilities as a captain."

"Anyway, that's great news, Papa… that we can stay in Pizzolungo," Piccola added, interrupting her brother's futile attempts to convince their father of their adventures.

"Well, there's even more news," the Captain continued, "Far bigger news. And this brings us back to Lorenzo." He again glanced up at the portrait. "Lorenzo was a hero where he lived, in Florence. You've heard me speak about his feats before."

"Many times," Guillermo ensured.

"One time he sailed to Spain aboard his ship, the *Infante*. I don't recall exactly where he was but a ruthless pirate sent a cannonball through the side of his starboard and sank him. Lorenzo had to swim ten miles just to get back to shore."

"He didn't swim back to shore," Guillermo interrupted. "He got picked up by… well, I think another ship picked him up." He figured it was better not to complicate his father's story for the time being, since nobody believed him anyway.

"And it happened off of Gibraltar," Piccola said.

"You sure have a lot to say about Gibraltar this morning," Signora Infante pointed out.

The Captain continued, "Lorenzo's closest friend back in Florence was a very special man. Perhaps history's most brilliant inventor, artist and engineer: Leonardo da Vinci."

"Wow, that's so cool!" Piccola exclaimed.

"He never mentioned that," Guillermo said to Piccola.

"As a consolation for the loss of the *Infante*, da Vinci created something extraordinarily unique for Lorenzo: the *Grande Infante*." The Captain opened up the box and took out the model ship.

"*That* was built by Leonardo da Vinci?" Guillermo asked.

"*The* Leonardo da Vinci?" Piccola checked.

The Captain rubbed his hands across the polished frame of the ship. "Da Vinci told Lorenzo that every great inventor builds one thing. One thing into which they infuse all of their life's knowledge and wisdom. For da Vinci, his *one thing* wasn't the Mona Lisa, the Vitruvian Man or even the designs for scuba gear. It was the *Grande Infante*."

"Yeah, because it grows and time travels, like we told you," Guillermo said.

"Just look at its beauty," the Captain said, lost in its magnificence. He held the ship up again and all four Infantes poked their noses up to it. "It's the most extraordinary craftsmanship ever, and inside, though we'll need a magnifying glass to observe this, are miniature versions of the many inventions that da Vinci created, all dozens or hundreds of years ahead of their time."

Guillermo and Piccola exchanged revelatory glances.

"How do you know all this?" Guillermo asked.

"Because Uncle Ercole left *this* for me as well." He unfolded a fragile parchment and showed it to the family. "It's Lorenzo Infante's Last Will & Testament from over 500 years ago. It describes the *Grande Infante* and how it's supposed to be handed down from generation to generation within the Infante family." Captain Infante paused. "What we have here is priceless. So priceless that it would probably be appraised as the most valuable piece of art in the whole world—if anyone ever wanted to sell it. But Lorenzo's will stipulates that it be kept a secret within the Infante family, for fear it could be stolen, misused or damaged."

"Papa, I'm so sorry, I almost destroyed it. I didn't know any of that. I just saw the box with my name on it and—"

"Uh uh, with *my* name on it," the Captain chuckled as he refolded the parchment. "The will says that the ship should always be passed down to the eldest surviving member of the family, and never to anyone under the age of thirty." He eyed Guillermo and Piccola, "Probably because children are liable to do inappropriate things with a da Vinci original."

"Like put it in the water?" Piccola asked.

"Like put it in the water," the Captain repeated.

"We might be the first people to have ever actually… used the ship," Guillermo said to Piccola. He pondered this for a moment. "So the whole time we were sailing on board the greatest treasure ever…"

"Sometimes big treasures come in little boxes," the Captain said. "And it's especially important because Lorenzo died protecting it."

"What do you mean?" Guillermo asked. Piccola looked on in horror as the blood drained from her face.

"Well, legend has it that Lorenzo's sworn enemy, a pirate bent on revenge, found Lorenzo at sea not long after he'd acquired a new vessel using some of the gold he'd been gifted. Sadly, the pirate killed him and his whole crew while they slept. A coward's murder if ever there was one. Only his son survived the attack and was able to salvage the *Grande Infante* and recount the story.

Piccola started to panic, "By a *pirate*?"

"By a French pirate. Toward the very end of the fifteenth century I believe. He died young but lived more than most people twice his age."

"What?!" Guillermo and Piccola sat up erect but felt their stomachs freefall downwards. She clasped his hand.

"Come on my dears, it's time to get some sleep," Signora Infante said as she nudged the kids off the couch and toward the stairs.

Captain Infante gently grabbed their arms, "And don't worry *i miei figli*, we'll sail together one day. There's no rush to grow up, you know. The funny thing about something

242

small is that it almost always grows into something big. But it never happens the other way around."

"You'd be surprised, Papa."

"There's plenty of time little ones," the Captain said as he kissed his children.

Upstairs, Guillermo led Piccola over to their father's chest of seafaring items and raised its lid. He rummaged through its contents until he spotted what he was searching for. "He said he'd treasure it as long as he lived," Guillermo said with a dry throat as he lifted up his father's beloved Admiral's compass. Its shine remained bright and polished and Piccola brought her hand up to it as if she were reaching back out to Lorenzo himself. "To *the One and Only CC Admiral of the Ocean Sea. With best wishes, F&I*," Guillermo read aloud.

"Lorenzo said his son would love it," Piccola recalled. He must have passed it down through the generations."

"Yeah, I remember Papa telling me that he got it from grandpapa." He shook his head, "I wonder if papa knows that CC stands for Christopher Columbus, and that F&I are Ferdinand and Isabella?"

"I wonder if it was Fleury who snuck onto Lorenzo's ship seeking revenge for what happened in Gibraltar," Piccola asked as they both crawled into their beds.

"It had to be," Guillermo said. He stared worriedly out the window, knowing what Piccola was about say.

"If that's true then it means we're the ones responsible for his death. Just because he didn't die that day on the water with us doesn't mean we're not to blame." Piccola gently put her head in her hands. "He never would have crossed paths with Fleury in the first place if he hadn't come to our rescue in Gibraltar."

Guillermo looked up at the ceiling. "He died too young but lived more than most people twice his age." He repeated the words he'd known for years. "He died because of us."

"What should we do?" Piccola asked.

Guillermo and Piccola tossed and turned in bed, their restless minds overcoming their need for rest. After Piccola finally surrendered to her exhaustion Guillermo, a mix of guilt and anger flowing through his veins, got up and gazed out at the sea and the world beyond, all somehow a little smaller to him now.

Later that evening, after Guillermo had fallen asleep, the Captain studied the exquisite model ship with a magnifying glass. He perused the masts, the arsenal, the galley, and the map room with wonder and awe. But something stopped him as he reached one of the many utility rooms down below. He squinted to get a better look and then reached for his tweezers. Deep inside the hull a circular piece of metal stood out from everything else. Its shine had attracted the Captain's eye. Even with the tweezers, though, it was impossible to extricate. Whatever it was, it was too big to slip out of the ship's quarters from where it was trapped. His curiosity growing, the Captain reached for a piece of wire from his workbench. Using the wire he teased the metal object onto its side, allowing him to see that it was a ring—a very familiar-looking ring with a very familiar looking inscription on it that read: "*To Pizzolungo's next great seafarer, Love Papa.*" The Captain stopped what he was doing and rubbed his neck.

"How very odd," Guillermo Sr. said, looking down at the small ring taking up most of the utility room where his son had lost it just the other day, and more than 500 years ago. "How very odd indeed."

The next morning, Guillermo and Piccola ran downstairs and through the kitchen, where their parents were enjoying a leisurely breakfast. The big Captain was reviewing the schematics of his new cargo ship. "Where are you two off to in such a rush?" he asked.

"We're going to Mariner's Fort to try and find the other powder pouch so we can travel back in time to save Lorenzo from the evil pirate Fleury."

"Not until you finish your breakfast, you're not," Signora Infante said sternly.

"Mama…" Guillermo pleaded.

The siblings ate their breakfasts in record speed.

"What's in the bag?" Guillermo's father asked.

"Oh… um, just some captain stuff," Guillermo answered skittishly, using his arm to conceal the top of the *Grande Infante's* mainmast.

As they finished putting their dishes in the sink Guillermo turned back to his father. "Do you want to come with us?"

"No, no, you explorers go and explore." He lifted his pencil from the ship's blueprint. "I'm going to stay here to figure out my new engine requirements. But say hello to Christopher Columbus and the rest of the gang for me."

Guillermo went around the table and pointed to the papers, "If it had sails I'd be able to give you a lot of advice, but I've never captained a cargo ship before. At least, not yet. Anyway, we'll be home tonight."

"Maybe sooner," Piccola added.

They were in the backyard before the door even closed. Just then the front door flung open and Enzo, Tony, Luca, Mario and Romeo rushed in.

"The excitement never ends," Guillermo Sr. said.

Signora Infante motioned toward the backyard. "They're out there."

The crew ran through the kitchen and out into the backyard, with the exception of Mario who palmed two buttered rolls, an apple and some fried potatoes. "Thanks, not sure what food is left on the ship from the last time travel expedition."

Finally, the hurricane subsided and the kitchen fell silent.

"Ah, to be that age again," Guillermo Sr. said as he returned to his schematics. "The age where nothing is bigger than the imagination."

"Let's just enjoy the *little* things, shall we?" Signora Infante said, standing in front of the window. "Like the quiet."

Guillermo Sr. pushed his papers aside, walked over to his wife and took her in his arms, the backyard, the beach and Mariner's Fort framed behind them.

"I was thinking about what the kids said. Maybe I *will* take them out with me next time, once my new ship arrives." He paused for a moment. "On a short voyage, of course."

"I just don't know if they're ready yet, Guillermo. They're still so little."

"Oh, I suppose you're right, *amore mio*."

Unbeknownst to the Infantes, over their shoulders and in the distance, out the window and past Mariner's Fort, the *Grande Infante* unfurled in all its violent, wondrous and mammoth glory, taking out a palm tree as it turned into position, the Time Sailors of Pizzolungo ready to set sail.

"There's plenty of time for that," he said. "Our little ones have all the time in the world."

Behind them, their young son Guillermo Infante Jr. stood at the helm, his little sister Piccola and their friends by his side, commanding the grandest and most extraordinary vessel ever to sail the seven seas.

THE END

Time Sailors of Pizzolungo

Interested in reviewing this book?

We would greatly appreciate it if you would leave us a quick and honest review. Just go to Amazon.com, search for *Time Sailors of Pizzolungo*, and then click the "**Write a customer review**" button near the bottom of the page.

You can also email us with feedback at authors@timesailors.com

We would love to hear from you!

Scott & Adam

Acknowledgements

Woodrow Wilson once quipped "I use all the brains I have and all I can borrow." In producing this book we did the same.

Heather Campbell, a literary coach and old friend from graduate school, provided a thought provoking critique of the original manuscript which helped us radically transform the book. Hala Barbar, a friend and avid reader of children's books, took two spins through with a red pen and left the text in far better shape than she found it. Both Heather and Hala made enormous contributions to the quality of the book's final form.

Niall Doherty offered a bunch of suggestions which we adopted, as did Matt Henderson Ellis.

Wendy Lewison, who has published a number of wonderful children's books herself, offered us a valuable critique and great encouragement.

Mark Webster very generously offered to help organize the book's website. He's a good friend.

Danielle and J.P. Nikota offered a pair of fantastically sharp proofreading eyes.

Jill Ruzicka's generous assistance and artistic vision transformed black and white words on a page into beautiful artwork that recalls the golden era of children's literature.

Zoltan Ecsery's encyclopedic knowledge of history and seafaring has helped ensure it's as realistic as possible (for a fantasy story). Alan and Rochelle Abrams suggested many a scene and word choice to reconsider, which we did, and thank them for it.

In particular, Adam thanks his brother Jesse, for his help not only with the book's artwork, but for his critiques of all of his work, good and bad, and for his partnership in many other writing endeavors. He thanks his mother, Rita, for her advice on the world of authorship and publishing and her constant encouragement.

Most of all he thanks his wife Delia, without whom there would be no reason to write at all. If love, respect, and unwavering support are the nourishment a writer needs to create, then Delia keeps his belly very full.

Scott owes his greatest gratitude to his wife, Annamaria. Some of the most important ideas in this story originated in her mind. She's as good a writer's coach as one could hope for and the book is immeasurably better because of her strategic contribution.

Finally, Scott thanks Dan Macleod for gifting him a special little ship that became the original inspiration for this story.

About the Authors

Scott and Adam are childhood friends from Larchmont, New York. They first collaborated artistically as guitarist and drummer in a 7th grade rock band. Scott soon realized he had no musical talent and moved on, but years later they reunited to draft the script for a feature film which was optioned by a Spanish production company.

Today Adam writes, produces and stars in an assortment of mainstream and independent comedy projects ranging from the Cartoon Network's 'Adult Swim' to 'NBC'. He's also a professional songwriter, producing music for artists, television and film, including The Pussycat Dolls, American Idol, and the Ryan Reynolds/Emma Stone film 'Paper Man'. He even continues to pen the occasional screenplay and science fiction novel when inspiration strikes. He lives with his wife in New York.

Scott is a bit of a globetrotter. He's navigated his way around the world, working, studying and trekking through some 65 diverse countries. Travel is a storyteller's best friend and, to be sure, he's picked up and written about an incredible array of stories along the way. The general idea for this book stemmed from a curious experience he had while vacationing in Sicily, just next to Pizzolungo. He lives in Budapest, Hungary with his wife and young daughter.